Nothing to Lose

A Blackbridge Novel

Claire Boston

BANTILLY
PUBLISHING

First published by Bantilly Publishing in 2019

Nothing to Lose: The Blackbridge Series

EPUB format: 978-1-925696-24-0
Mobi format: 978-1-925696-23-3
Print: 978-1-925696-25-7

Cover design by Lana Pecherczyk
Edited by Ann Harth
Proofread by Teena Raffa-Mulligan

About the Author

Claire Boston is a contemporary romance author who enjoys exploring real life issues on her way to the happily-ever-after. She writes heart-warming stories, with resilient heroines and heroes you'll love. In 2014 she was nominated for an Australian Romance Readers Award for Favourite New Romance Author.

When Claire's not writing she can be found creating her own handmade journals, swinging on a sidecar, or in the garden attempting to grow something other than weeds.

Claire lives in Western Australia with her husband, who loves even her most annoying quirks, and her grubby, but adorable Australian bulldog.

You can connect with Claire through Facebook (https://www.facebook.com/clairebostonauthor) and Twitter (https://www.twitter.com/clairebauthor), or join her reader group (https://www.claireboston.com/reader-group/).

Also by Claire Boston

DEDICATION

To my tech support gurus, Pedro Gonçalves and Evan Wilkinson.
Thanks for all your help.

Chapter 1

Kit van Ross was going to kill him.

No, she'd fire him, *then* she'd kill him. She'd given Paul plenty of chances, even an official warning, and he still hadn't got his act together. She opened the throttle on the dirt bike, needing speed to channel the anger pulsing through her body.

It was hard enough to run a farm with two people let alone when one went AWOL regularly.

Paul should have returned to the yard an hour ago, not be out on the boundary fence doing who knew what. Nothing needed fixing, but the white ute was parked there and Paul was nowhere in sight. Maybe he was taking a nap.

She would definitely kill him.

As the bike bumped over the field, her gaze locked on the ute, waiting for Paul to hear the engine and sit up in the tray and wave.

Nothing.

He had to be there somewhere.

Probably too much of a wimp to face her. He knew how pissed she'd be. She hadn't held back her temper the last time she'd warned him to stop slacking off. And while she'd yelled, he'd stood there with a bored expression and told her to chill.

He used to be her friend once, not just her employee.

She clenched her teeth. She'd given him enough chances. In order for her farm to thrive, he had to go.

She searched the sky for Paul's black drone, which would give her some indication he realised she was there.

Nothing but a few puffy white clouds in the otherwise bright blue sky. She should be enjoying the fine weather while it lasted instead of chasing after an unreliable farmhand.

Kit roared to the ute and cut the engine.

Silence.

The tray was empty.

"Paul! Where the hell are you?" She kicked the stand into position and got off the bike, shading her eyes to scan the nearby bush that marked the boundary between her land and Foley's.

No one.

Stalking around the side of the ute, she saw a foot stretched out on the ground, then a leg.

"Paul, what the hell—" Her footsteps faltered and vomit rose to her throat. She shook her head as if it would change the vision, and her hand came to her mouth. No, no, no.

Her muscles tightened, and she took two steps away, squeezing her eyes closed, wanting to erase the picture.

Get a grip, girl. She needed to see the truth.

Slowly she opened her eyes.

Her gaze found the rifle first. The one she kept locked in the shed, only used if she had an injured animal that couldn't be saved.

Next his boots, the mismatched socks — one blue and one black — and then his outstretched legs, tanned from the summer sun. He leaned back against the vehicle, positioned so much like her father had been. Then she'd been in time, she'd been able to rip the gun away from her dad, convince him life was worth living.

Not so for Paul.

Flies buzzed around the perfect round hole in the centre of his forehead. On the door behind him was a red spray of blood and other matter. No saving Paul.

Her stomach heaved and she spun around, retching, choking on this morning's cereal.

When her stomach was empty and the heaving finally stopped, she wiped her eyes and turned back to Paul.

How long had he been sitting here? He'd been gone all morning, had taken off as soon as he'd entered some data into the computer. He'd snapped at her for coming into the office. She'd snapped back.

That had been the theme of their relationship over the past few months.

She'd known something was wrong, but he wouldn't confide in her and she'd got tired of asking. Some friend she was.

Hands shaking, she dug out her mobile phone, dialled the number she knew by heart.

"Kit, the full moon is bringing out all the crazies, can it wait?" Even the annoyed timbre of Sergeant Lincoln Zanetti's voice brought a measure of comfort.

"Paul's shot himself. He's dead."

Lincoln swore. "Don't touch anything. I'll be right there. Where are you?"

"The back paddock." She hung up and her breath whooshed from her. It would be all right. Lincoln was coming, he'd know what to do.

A fly crawled over Paul's eye and towards the hole in his forehead. She wanted to swat it away, but she couldn't mess with the scene. Even if it was a suicide. She paced away, glad she'd left the dogs back at the shed.

Tears pushed their way into her eyes and she blinked them back. She couldn't cry now. Emotion wouldn't get the better of her. She would be calm, not a hysterical female when Lincoln arrived. Taking a deep breath in, she continued walking, heading away from the vehicle. Her chest tightened and her throat burned. No, she couldn't break down, not here, not now. There would be time later, when she was at home, alone, with no one to see her, where no one would witness her weakness. If she cried now, she wouldn't be able to stop.

Changing direction, Kit headed to the fence line, peered into the bush. A few tall eucalypts interspersed with small prickly shrubs. The road that intersected her property from Foley's farm next door was almost within sight.

Why this spot?

Had Paul felt a sense of belonging here? She'd found him here often enough when he should have been working elsewhere, when he'd added to her workload and risked her livelihood by not doing his tasks. Anger crept its way through her sorrow.

It was just like the selfish bastard he'd become to commit suicide on her land.

The anger soothed the burning in her throat and she clung to it. She couldn't think about the good times they'd had together.

Lately all he'd been was an inconsiderate prick.

And now he hadn't had the decency to kill himself at home. This would cause a shit-tonne more work for her.

Kit strode back towards the ute, her gaze flitting back to Paul and sorrow flooded past the anger as if it was a leaf on a stream. She reached for it but the anguish battered her aside and the tears she'd been holding back flooded in, racking her body with sobs.

Sinking onto the rough, dirt ground she grieved.

The rumble of a car engine perforated her grief and Kit glanced up. The police sedan drove through the gate at the opposite end of the paddock.

Lincoln was here.

Comfort settled over her shoulders even as her stomach tied itself in knots. She stood, dusting off the dirt and wiping her eyes on her singlet. She inhaled a deep shuddery breath. Time to get a hold of herself.

Walking back to the ute, the faint scent of blood reached her nose. Her stomach protested, and she gritted her teeth. She would not vomit again.

Senior Constable Ryan Kilpatrick shut the passenger side door as Lincoln got out of the driver's side, his tall, lean frame unfolding as he stood. His blue police uniform was pristinely pressed, but his chocolate brown hair was dishevelled the way it was when he ran his hands through it too many times. His dark eyes showed their concern, and she longed to throw herself into his arms and weep. She clenched her hands to stop herself from reaching out to him. She couldn't show him how much she still cared for him, couldn't handle another rejection. Tears pricked at her eyes again and she blinked them back, turning her attention to Ryan. She swallowed hard. "He's behind the ute."

"Are you OK?" Lincoln stood only a metre away and the distance might as well have been a mile. They no longer had the easy affection they'd once had, not when they were alone together. If she'd been any of her three best friends, he would have swept her up in a hug, comforted her. But those days were gone, and she only had herself to blame.

Kit nodded.

"Can you tell us what happened?" Ryan asked.

"I came out looking for him when he didn't return at lunch. I found him like this."

"Have you touched anything?" Lincoln asked.

"No. It's clear he's dead." The image flashed into her mind and she blocked it.

"How close did you get?"

They tag-teamed the questions.

"Just around the front of the ute."

"We'll take a look. Do you want to sit in the car?" Lincoln asked.

Kit shook her head, her hand tapping her thigh. She couldn't be still. Stillness allowed stray thoughts into her mind, memories she couldn't confront.

Lincoln sighed and then he and Ryan walked around the vehicle to the body. It was easier to think of it that way — the body, not Paul. Lincoln swore under his breath, a twitch above his eye showing he wasn't as unaffected as he appeared. After a short, murmured conversation between the two cops, Ryan pulled out his phone and Lincoln walked over to Kit. "Whose gun is it?"

"I'm pretty sure it's mine." And if it was, it was one more thing to blame Paul for. It helped to blame him rather than herself.

Lincoln's eyebrows almost disappeared into his hair line.

She shrugged. "It's the same make and model, and Paul has — *had* access to it. It's usually stored in a locked cabinet in the shed."

"I'll need you to confirm that." He hesitated. "Scrap that. Don't touch the cabinet."

"Why not?"

"Please, Kit, for once in your life just do what I ask without questioning it." He ran a hand through his lush hair.

Her anger spiked. She had to take her frustration out on someone. "Why, because I might tamper with the evidence? He committed suicide!"

Lincoln pursed his lips and rocked back on his heels.

Uncertainty filled her. "Didn't he?"

"Forensics will confirm that."

A non-answer if she'd ever heard one, but she expected nothing more from Lincoln. No one wanted Paul dead.

He withdrew his notepad as Ryan came over. "Calls are made."

"We'll take your initial statement now," Lincoln said. "There's not a lot more we can do until the others arrive."

"What do you need to know?"

"Tell us about your day. What have you been doing, where was Paul meant to be? How did he seem?"

It was standard questioning, but Kit didn't like it. She explained her tasks, expanding when they wanted more information.

"You mentioned you were angry, that you were going to fire Paul," Ryan said. "Why?"

She glared at him. "Because he'd become an arsehole. He did none of his work, he disappeared for hours at a time and ignored my attempts to help him." She glanced at them both. "The farm is suffering and I need staff I can rely on."

"And Paul wasn't reliable," Ryan said.

"Not since Christmas. He's been twitchy and secretive since his friend Gordon died a few months ago. He mentioned he had shit happening in his life, but he wouldn't tell me what." She should have pushed him harder for answers. Maybe she could have stopped this. People with problems didn't always open up, didn't always tell the truth.

She'd had first-hand experience.

"Is there anything else?" She wanted to get out of here, away from the body, and the blowflies now swarming around it.

They exchanged glances and Lincoln said, "Not for the moment. We'll be over later to check the gun cabinet and will need to get a full statement from you."

She nodded and got on her bike, her hand shaking as she pressed the ignition button. The engine's loud growl was music to her ears. She needed noise, needed speed, needed to forget everything. She twisted the throttle and quickly changed through the gears, accelerating across the bumpy paddock, fleeing the scene.

Her chest squeezed again as the image of Paul flashed through her mind.

No, she wouldn't think about it now. She had work to do. The bull calves needed to be weighed and prepared for sale. That was why she'd gone looking for Paul. Now she'd have to do it by herself.

The farm was the only constant in her life, always there for her, never leaving. Birth or death, rain or drought, it carried on.

And so did she.

Lincoln passed his hand through his hair as Kit tore off over the paddock. She was one tough cookie, finding Paul like this and not breaking down. No one was as strong as she was.

"This wasn't suicide," Ryan said.

He nodded. "But it's meant to look like it." He examined the body, shutting down his own emotions. He hadn't been close to Paul, but it was hard to see anyone dead. "The gun's in the wrong position and the angle of the shot, there's no way he could have pulled the trigger holding it there."

But who wanted Paul dead?

And why shoot him here, out on Kit's property? Could Kit be in danger?

Lincoln scanned the surroundings. A good place to meet someone. The road the other side of the bush led onto the main highway. And it was close to Foley's shed that had burned down a couple of months ago. That had been drug-related, and they were still tracking down all the players.

Was this connected?

It was possible. Paul had been upset about Gordon's death, and Gordon had been killed as a result of his involvement in the drug ring. Paul could be involved as well. Perhaps he'd been scared he would be next.

If not that, then what else?

No one said anything bad about Paul. He was popular around town, played in the local cricket and football leagues, had worked out here with Kit for the past few years.

Kit was the only person mad at him, but her bark was worse than her bite. "How long until Albany get here?"

Ryan glanced at his watch. "About half an hour. The Perth

guys will be a lot longer."

More than four hours to the capital city and the forensics experts. "I'll tell Sue and Adam what we've got."

He made the call to his other officers and then helped Ryan set up the barricade tape to protect the crime scene.

They weren't going anywhere for a while.

When the Albany detectives arrived, they took over, as Lincoln had expected. Janice Bosch and Navid Khan knew their stuff but tended to think his local team didn't.

And that grated.

He ran the gun's registration and confirmed it was Kit's. Shit. This would get messy.

"Ryan and I can examine the gun cabinet," he suggested to Bosch.

"Where is it?" she asked.

"In the shed."

She raised her eyebrows in question.

"I lived on the farm for a couple of years." Back when Kit was still at high school and had point blank refused to move to Perth with her parents. She'd needed a responsible adult to stay in the house with her, and he'd wanted to move out of his parents' place. It had worked well — until it hadn't.

"You too close to this?" Khan glanced up from his camera.

Lincoln shook his head as a twinge of guilt pinched him. No way was he getting kicked off this case. "I've lived in Blackbridge most of my life," he said. "I have a relationship with many people in the town. If I couldn't segment, I couldn't do my job."

"All right."

Lincoln gestured to Ryan, and they got back into the police car and headed across the paddock.

"You sure you're OK with this?" Ryan asked.

He glanced at his best friend. "Why wouldn't I be?"

"Kit had opportunity, and she was angry at him, Lincoln. She's got to be a suspect and she won't like it."

"She didn't do it."

"That's what I'm talking about. Neither of us believes she's capable of it, but she discovered the body, the gun is hers and Paul had irritated her. If she's not on our suspect list, we're not doing our job."

Damn it, he was right.

And Kit *would* be pissed.

He sighed. "I'll deal with her." He was used to her outbursts, could handle anything she threw at him. He called the station to ensure nothing urgent had cropped up and then directed Ryan to park outside the big silver machinery shed that housed the tractor and other large vehicles.

Kit was working in a nearby yard with the latest herd of year-old calves. She barely glanced at them as they approached. "Give me a second."

Deftly she moved the calf through the gates onto the scales, then sprayed something on its back. She moved with confidence, no concern for the size of the calves, some of which were close to her own height.

Her red plaid shirt was unbuttoned, and she wore a white singlet underneath, damp with sweat. Even working hard, her steel-capped boots covered in dust, her denim jeans clinging to her curves and her hair a mess, she looked sexy.

He couldn't prevent the shock of unwanted lust. Kit was off limits. Experience had taught him anything more *would* ruin what was left of their friendship.

Kit slapped the rump of the calf she was working on and it ambled out of the way. She walked over to them. "What do you need?"

"We need to check your gun cabinet," Ryan said.

She stepped back. "It was my gun." Her voice was flat.

Lincoln nodded.

She closed her eyes briefly, bit her lip, the only sign something was wrong. She was more affected by this than she appeared. But why pretend with him?

Kit climbed over the metal fence and jerked her head towards the dairy. "It's this way."

"When did you last open the cabinet?" Ryan asked.

She hesitated. "About two weeks back. A yearling got through a fence Paul should have repaired and slipped near the river. Broke its leg, and I had to put it down." Her words were clipped, her tone no-nonsense, but her hand trembled a little as she pushed open the shed door.

Maybe still inside her was the seventeen-year-old who had wept in his arms when she'd first put an animal down.

She walked into an office and halted, causing him to crash into her soft warm body. He inhaled, smelling a hint of cinnamon. Focus. He glanced over her head to the gun cabinet in the corner, its door ajar.

"I didn't leave it like this."

Lincoln nudged her aside so Ryan could get past. "When were you last in here?"

"This morning after milking. I wanted to check Paul was entering the latest data. The safe door was closed, and I presumed locked. I don't check it regularly."

"Where's the key kept?"

"There's one on the ute keyring and one in the house."

The ute key was the most likely, but he said, "Can you confirm the house one is still there? But don't touch it if it is."

She nodded. "I'll go now."

"Thanks."

He followed her from the building so he could get their things from the car. Kit didn't acknowledge him, just strode off across the dirt to her motorbike, her blue heelers, Montoya and Roberts at her heels. At her command one jumped on the motorbike tank and the other on the seat behind her and they tore off towards the house. He caught himself staring after her. He needed to be careful. Any sign he was emotionally involved and the detectives would dump him from the case.

His insides twisted. To do things properly, he should declare his conflict of interest now. But his feelings for Kit were unrequited so they didn't count. What was important was helping Kit through this and protecting her if a murderer was on the loose.

He'd already failed to protect her three friends. He wouldn't fail her.

Chapter 2

By the time Kit pulled up in front of her house, the pressure in her chest made it difficult for her to breathe. Her throat ached from unshed tears.

Paul had killed himself using the same gun that had nearly taken her father's life ten years ago. She'd bought the gun safe, and locked the rifle inside. She'd held the keys when her father still lived here. She hadn't been willing to give him a second chance to end his life and he hadn't argued, too ashamed of what he'd been going to do.

After he'd left, she'd grown more lax. It made sense to keep the key with the ute, so that it was easily accessible. But she hadn't thought Paul was at risk.

She stumbled around the side of the house and up the back steps of the verandah. Using the shoe horn shaped like a beetle, she pried off her boots, delaying her entry. Did it make any difference whether the key was there?

Paul was dead.

Her hand shook as she swung open the fly-screen door and headed through the laundry to the pantry. Her keys hung on a board inside: spare house key that had once been Lincoln's, another key to the ute, a key to her document safe… and the gun safe key.

She'd given Paul the means with which to kill himself.

She should have kept the key locked away, shouldn't have

been lazy about fetching it.

Gasping, she slid to the floor, wrapping her arms around Montoya, sliding her fingers along his coarse, dusty hair.

Her chest seized and her stomach heaved, but she clamped her teeth. She couldn't fall apart. She needed to tell Lincoln. Her fingers shook as she drew her phone out of her back pocket and typed him a message.

Then she dropped the phone onto the floor beside her and caved to the fresh wave of tears.

Grief wracked her body, great big sobs wrenched from her lungs. Her body shook with the effort to stop. She didn't want to cry. Farmers had to be tough, otherwise it would be too easy to be overwhelmed.

No one was here but her dogs. She was safe.

Unjudged.

She rocked back and forth, trying to rid herself of the horrid pain ripping her apart. Why did it hurt so much? Paul had been a friend, but not one of her closest.

"Kit, are you here?"

She froze, holding her breath to stop the sobs.

Lincoln was outside on the verandah, only metres away. She mustn't let him see her like this, it would ruin the self-sufficient image she'd portrayed for all these years. She pushed Montoya away and clambered to her feet, wiping her face with her shirt. Taking a deep breath so she could speak, she called, "Yeah, give me a minute." The fly-screen slammed shut and footsteps approached.

Whirling around, she faced the shelf with flour and sugar on it as if it was the most interesting thing in the world. She squeezed her eyes shut and breathed once, twice.

"Kit, are you all right?"

The concern in his voice had tears welling up again. Ruthlessly she blinked, and cleared her throat. "Yeah. Won't be a sec. Why don't you put the kettle on?"

She waited for his footsteps to retreat.

His hand touched her shoulder.

Shit. No. She couldn't deal with this. Not now.

Keeping her head down, she pushed past him and into the kitchen.

Kit stalked out of the pantry, but not before Lincoln glimpsed her tear-stained cheeks. She'd been crying. He'd thought he'd heard sobs, but he hadn't wanted to walk in unannounced. They didn't have that kind of relationship anymore.

Still, he couldn't stand by and let her grieve on her own.

He followed her into the kitchen where she dried her face on a tea towel.

"Cuppa?" She grabbed the kettle from the bench.

"No, thanks." Maybe he should mind his own business. If she wanted to pretend to be fine, shouldn't he respect that?

She filled the kettle, put it on before turning back to him. The water hadn't done a lot to hide her red eyes and flushed face. "What can I do for you then?"

"A couple of things. We'll need access to the farm for the next few days."

"Of course."

"And I'll need you to come down to the station later to answer questions from the detectives."

Kit frowned. "Why?"

"It's standard procedure." He kept his gaze on hers, but she pursed her lips.

"What aren't you telling me?"

Damn. He cleared his throat and repeated, "It's standard procedure." He couldn't tell her they suspected murder, or that she was a potential suspect.

"Why would I need to go to the station for a suicide?"

He could practically see her mind working through the options. He got the tea out of the cupboard, hoping to distract her.

Her eyes widened. "Was it suicide?"

"I can't comment on an active investigation."

Kit gripped the side of the bench as her face paled. "Was he murdered?"

Lincoln gritted his teeth. He hated not being able to tell her, to warn her to be careful.

Her mouth dropped open. "Am I a suspect?"

Hell. What could he say?

"I am, aren't I?" Her eyes were wide, her expression incredulous. "Do you really think I could kill him, Lincoln?" The hurt in her tone almost ripped his heart out of his chest.

"No, I don't. But I need to do things by the book and rule you out." He'd said too much.

"What time?"

"Sorry?"

"What time do I need to be at the station?" She slammed the cupboard door after she got a mug out.

"I'll let you know."

"Fine. I'll see you then." She gave him a pointed look and he took the hint.

Walking outside, he inhaled deeply. He may no longer be on Kit's confidants' list but he knew who was. And he couldn't leave her here, grieving by herself. Dialling the first number, he said, "Hannah Banana, Kit needs you."

After Lincoln left, Kit waited a few minutes to ensure he was gone before heading outside. No time to wallow. The calves wouldn't weigh themselves and with rain forecast for next week she had to sow the new crop. Then the pregnant cows needed to be moved closer to the sheds, the fencing and water troughs had to be checked, and as always the milking had to be done twice a day.

After riding her bike back to the yard, she continued weighing the calves until a white four-wheel drive pulled up. Hannah.

Lincoln must have called her.

Damn him.

Usually she'd be thrilled to see her best friend, but today she wanted solitude, at least until she'd worked things out in her own head. She put down the spray gun and walked over to her. "What are you doing here?"

Hannah frowned, her blonde fringe falling across her face. "I'm not sure. Lincoln said you needed the musketeers, but he wouldn't tell me why. What happened?"

"Are the others on the way?"

"Yeah."

She had twenty minutes max until they arrived and had to get the calves finished today. She needed the data in order to fatten them up before the buyers came in a few weeks.

Yeah, as if that was the most important thing in her life right now.

She glanced at her friend. Hannah's jeans and blue shirt were covered in paint splatters. "Have you been painting?"

"Yeah. The latest cabin is almost finished."

"You shouldn't have stopped. I was going to call you later when I finished work."

"I can help you now I'm here. What are you keeping from me, Kit Kat?"

Kit shook her head. "I can't, not yet. Wait until the others arrive?"

Hannah nodded. "All right. What do you need me to do?"

The other musketeers, Mai and Fleur, arrived together. Kit put them to work. It was one thing she loved about her friends. They got things done without asking unnecessary questions.

As they cleaned up in the dairy, Mai said, "Not that I mind helping, but where's Paul?"

Kit's heart clenched, and her throat closed over. She backed away from them.

"Kit?" Fleur reached out towards her.

She shook her head.

"Did something happen to Paul?" Hannah asked. "Is that why Lincoln called us?"

She nodded.

"What is it?" Mai asked.

Kit took a deep breath in. "He's dead." She had to say it quickly. "I found him in the back paddock, sitting by the ute, my rifle next to him."

The girls gaped at her for a second before moving as one to surround her in a hug. She didn't have to explain. They knew what had happened with her father, they'd been the only ones she'd told.

Hannah stepped back first. "Why didn't Lincoln tell us?"

"Probably because Paul's family needs to be notified first," Mai said. "Any death will be painful, but suicide..."

Kit hesitated. "I thought it was at first, but Lincoln implied it could be murder." She shook her head. "It was almost identical to Dad, the way he sat, the ute, the placement of the gun, only unlike Dad, Paul was dead."

"How horrific." Fleur squeezed her hand. "I think you need a shower and ice cream."

"Booze would be better," Kit replied. Anything to wipe this day from her memory.

"Miss van Ross?" The call came from outside the shed.

It had to be one of the detectives. She walked outside with her friends. Two people in suits — a blonde woman a little shorter than Kit and a man who looked to be of Middle Eastern descent — stood in her yard.

"Can I help you?"

"I'm Detective Bosch, and this is Detective Khan," the woman said. "We'd like you to come to the station so we can ask you some questions."

There was no putting it off. "Sure." She turned to her friends.

"Want us to do the milking?" Fleur asked.

The cows were already gathered outside the building. What would she do without the musketeers? "Yes, please. Do you remember how to do everything?"

Hannah grinned. "It's not like we haven't done it before, Kit. We'll be fine."

They would be. Her dogs were over with the cows, wandering through, making sure they moved forward. Everyone would be OK.

"I'll drive myself," she told the detectives. She climbed into her car and drove on autopilot, her mind running through the day's events.

When she arrived at the station, Bosch asked, "Can I get you something to drink?"

"A coffee would be good." She needed the caffeine.

Khan led her through to an office and indicated for her to sit in a plastic chair.

When Bosch entered with the coffee, Kit asked, "What do you want to know?"

"We'd like to record you," Bosch said.

"Sure."

Khan pressed a button on a recorder. "Can we confirm your full name please?"

Kit winced. "Kitty Jane van Ross." The only thing her biological mother had given her was a shitty name. Who called their kid Kitty like some kind of animal? But then again, her mother had abandoned her, like people did with a pet they got for Christmas. The first of many to leave her.

Bosch's eyebrows raised. "How long had the deceased worked for you?"

The deceased. They didn't have the decency to use his name, he was a classification to them. "Paul started working for me part-time three years ago," she said. "When my other farmhand retired, he became full-time."

"When was that?"

"About a year ago."

"What was he like as a worker?"

She grimaced. "Until about three months ago he was the best. Always arrived on time, got the jobs done, would point out anything I might have missed, and then he changed."

Khan shifted in his seat. "How so?"

"His work became shoddy, he would turn up late, leave early, I'd find him in places on the farm where he shouldn't have been."

"Like where?"

Kit thought about it. "The back paddock I found him in was his favourite, but occasionally I'd find him by the river."

The detectives exchanged a glance.

"Did you speak to him about this?"

She snorted. "I spoke, discussed, shouted and gave him a written warning. It didn't help."

"So he made you angry?" Bosch asked.

No point denying it. "Yeah, he made me angry. I run a two hundred herd dairy farm with only one other person. If he's not pulling his weight, things fall behind."

Khan sipped his water. "Why were you in the back paddock today?"

"I was looking for Paul. He should have been helping me with the calves and he didn't show."

"Did you take the gun with you?" Bosch asked.

The change in subject threw her and she laughed. "No."

"Why do you have it?"

She rolled her eyes. "I only use the gun if an animal gets into trouble and the vet can't save it. I don't even shoot the 'roos like some farmers do."

"Where is it normally kept?"

"I showed Lincoln and Ryan the gun cabinet in the dairy. It's usually locked and there are two keys — one hanging in my pantry and the other on the keyring with the ute keys." They would know all this if they'd spoken with the others or maybe they were trying to catch her in a lie.

"How close are you to Sergeant Zanetti and Senior Constable Kilpatrick?" Bosch asked.

They'd be closer if she hadn't ruined it all at eighteen. "I've known Lincoln all my life. He used to live next door with his parents." She finished her coffee. "Ryan moved to town in December, and he's dating my best friend, so we hang out."

The detective pursed her lips.

Let her think whatever she wanted. "They're both good cops."

"Did Paul ever talk to you about people who might have disliked him?" Khan asked.

"He bitched about my attitude a couple of times and he didn't like being banned from the motocross track."

"Why was that?"

"He and some of his mates took modern bikes out to the track, which isn't allowed because we ride vintage bikes."

"Who decided on the ban?"

"The club voted on it at one of the general meetings, but Fleur had to tell him." She answered the next question before he asked it. "Fleur Lockhart is the club president."

He made a note.

She hesitated, not wanting Fleur to have to deal with these two, but it wasn't her call. "Fleur's back at the farm helping with the milking if you want to chat to her."

"She's a friend of yours?"

"One of my best friends."

His expression turned speculative and she stayed silent. Lincoln had once told her that the more suspects spoke, the more they gave away, or the guiltier they appeared. She glanced at the clock. "Do you have many other questions? I need to get back to the farm."

Khan looked at her. "We'll come with you."

Internally she swore. Just what she needed.
Another delay in her day.
And her friends under suspicion.

19

Chapter 3

Kit sat at her kitchen table eating leftover spaghetti. Aside from the dogs occasionally shifting in their sleep next to her, the house was quiet. And empty.

Last night the musketeers had stayed over to offer her support and comfort, but they had jobs to get to today. She understood. She'd been working hard all day herself, trying to forget about Paul's death. An impossible feat. Not only did she have to do everything herself, but her mind kept circling back to who would want Paul dead. She couldn't think of anyone, which left the possibility some random killer was out there, waiting to strike again.

The verandah outside creaked, and she froze, fork halfway to her mouth. Was someone there?

She listened, waiting for a footstep, another creak.

Nothing.

The house always creaked and groaned as it settled into sleep for the night, the materials contracting in the cool evening air.

No one was out there.

A thud on the roof and then the patter of footsteps.

She huffed. Possums. Just possums using her roof as a highway. But she would drive herself crazy if she stayed here by herself tonight, flinching at every noise.

Maybe Hannah would be free. They could go to the pub, have a couple of drinks, forget about Paul.

She needed to forget — at least for a little while.

She dialled Hannah's number.

"How are you today, Kit Kat?" Hannah asked.

"Restless," Kit answered. "Want to go to the pub?" Silence. Damn. "Have you got plans?"

"Felix has a thing at the Scouts tonight and he asked me to come. You should join us."

Hannah had always been the one friend guaranteed to be available, but she had Ryan and his little boy now.

"Don't worry about it. I'm not fit company. Have fun." She hung up, her heart heavy. Fleur was working and Mai started baking in the middle of the night so she couldn't ask her. The musketeers all had partners and other commitments. She'd been happy being single until her friends had partnered up. Then she'd realised Lincoln was still the only man she really wanted. She couldn't even call Jamie, not in her current mood. He reminded her too much of the man who didn't want her.

Kit headed for her bathroom, pausing outside Lincoln's old bedroom. The darkness inside mocked her. How had she read the situation so wrong? Sure, she'd only been eighteen, but guys had hit on her all the time. She knew when they fancied her. Lincoln's signs had been more subtle, but he'd been six years more mature.

It had been wishful thinking.

Or delusion.

The moment she'd ruined it was etched into her brain — his complete horror when she'd dropped her towel and told him she wanted him.

She cringed and continued to the shower, the hot water easing her aching muscles from a day of farm work. She ran the soap over her firm arms, down her long legs. She needed to hook up, find someone for the night to distract her from everything, make her feel wanted, needed, loved, even if it was only for her body. Sex always empowered her and she needed the boost. It had been a while since she'd been with anyone and if she drove into Albany, she wouldn't have to deal with the disapproval of Blackbridge locals who thought a one-night stand was slutty.

If she was a guy, they'd have no problem.

Another possum leapt on to her roof and she jumped, her heart racing.

She definitely couldn't stay here tonight.

So, the pub it was. She needed to look sexy — her skinny leg jeans showed off her long legs and gave her butt great definition, and her top plunged low.

Though she hated makeup, she took her time to put some on, remembering the lessons Fleur and Mai had taught her about how to make her eyes smoky, and her lips red and glistening. She brushed her long, brown hair, leaving it out so it flowed around her shoulders. She shouldn't have any trouble attracting someone to spend the night with.

Checking the dogs had enough water and leaving them to roam the yard, she got into her ute and headed for Albany.

Lincoln walked out of the station and inhaled the cool, country air. What a day. Albany were keeping their findings about Paul close to their chest and the whole town of Blackbridge had erupted in minor disputes. Gladys had had yet another car park bingle and had blown over the allowed alcohol limit, which meant he'd had to arrest her and put her in the holding cell. Trying to convince a woman over eighty and who no longer had a driver's licence that she couldn't keep driving was a challenge he didn't need. Especially when the cell was tiny. But he'd had to do it.

Then there'd been a domestic dispute out at the Wilson place, followed by a stolen vehicle, a neighbour dispute about a honeysuckle plant and a driver under the influence of meth. He hadn't had a chance to go to Kit's to keep tabs on the investigation.

But at least now his work day was over and he could head home.

He dialed Hannah's number as he opened his front door. "Hannah Banana, how's Kit?"

A loud sigh. "You could call her and ask for yourself."

Never going to happen. Not anymore. "Help me out, Hannah." Kit would have confided in her.

"She's restless. She wanted to go out, but none of us can make it."

So either she was home alone, or she'd gone out alone — he didn't like either option. "Where was she going?"

"If she went out, she'll go to the White Star in Albany."

"Thanks." He hung up and poured himself a glass of water. It was none of his business, not anymore. And no one wanted a police officer hanging around the pub. But if she'd gone to Albany, things were different. It was out of his jurisdiction.

Hannah texted him. *Let me know if you talk to her. She's not answering my call.*

He replied, *Will do.*

Kit was a big girl. She didn't need anyone looking after her.

But she had discovered Paul dead yesterday and had been devastated. Kit made irrational decisions when upset. She'd want to get drunk and then she'd be vulnerable, especially without the musketeers there. And whoever killed Paul could still be around the farm.

She'd be safer with someone.

Maybe Jamie could meet her. His finger paused over the button to call his younger brother. If he called, and Jamie went, they might hook up. And though he had no say over anything Kit did, he didn't want that to happen. Not again. It would be too painful.

An app on his phone caught his attention. He'd installed it when he'd lived with Kit because she always lost her phone, and he used the app to help her find it.

Would he still have access to her details?

He clicked on it. He wasn't spying on her. All he was doing was checking where she was. For her own safety.

The dot hovered over the highway heading to Albany.

He swore.

She shouldn't be going out alone.

And since the musketeers weren't available, he had no other option.

Kit needed to be protected.

It would have to be him.

Lincoln had plenty of time to rethink his decision on the forty-minute drive into Albany. He stopped at Kit's farm in case the app had been wrong, but the ute was gone and the house empty.

He found a parking spot close to The White Star and headed

inside. People crowded around the stage where a live band played rock music. He scanned the bar at the back first. Lots of people were lined up to get their drinks and it took him only a second to spot Kit with three shot glasses full of clear yellow liquid in front of her.

His chest squeezed.

The overhead lights spotlighted her in a halo of light, picking up the lighter strands of blonde in her hair and making them shine. The bright ruby red of her skimpy top was like a siren call to every man in the vicinity, showing them she wasn't afraid to be noticed. It was working. A couple of guys crowded around her, hanging on to her every word — as always.

He didn't want her to go home with some loser she'd just met at the bar.

One of the guys adjusted Kit's strap that had fallen off her shoulder. Lincoln sucked in a breath, controlling the urge to go over and tell him to keep his sleazy hands to himself.

Gritting his teeth, he moved to the other side of the bar and ordered a beer as she licked salt off her hand and then downed the three shots of tequila before sticking a piece of lemon in her glossy red mouth and sucking on it.

The men around her cheered as she swayed a little on those black stiletto heels.

A sober Kit, hell even a drunk Kit, wouldn't have a problem with her balance, wouldn't be using the bar to lean against as if she didn't have the strength to stand straight. Kit would normally have swatted away the short bastard who groped her arse, or stepped back from the other guy who pressed his body against hers.

Lincoln clenched his fist. Kit was a grown woman. She could make her own choices.

But she was alone, without her friends to take care of her, and she was still dealing with Paul's death. She wasn't being rational, and she wouldn't like him storming over and dragging her away. No, if he did that she'd likely double her efforts to flirt with those men just to spite him.

How had they got to this point?

There had been a time when they'd been so close, back when he'd lived on the farm. They'd gelled so well and though he'd never forgotten he was the adult, he'd never had to be. Kit had known what she wanted, from running the farm, to getting good grades at school, and boys hung off her every word. He'd thought it cute until his feelings for Kit had fundamentally shifted.

Kit's throaty laugh cut through his thoughts and he looked over, but she was gone from the bar. He scanned the room and saw her walking outside with one of the men she'd been with.

Hell no.

He followed them out in time to see Kit stumble and the man take the opportunity to cop a feel.

Arsehole.

"Come on, Sweetheart. Let's go back to my place," he said. "I'll take care of you."

Kit's words were too quiet for him to hear.

Over his dead body.

He strode over. "Kit, do you need a hand?"

"Bugger off, mate," the guy said.

Lincoln stared at him. "Kit's a friend."

"She's fine."

"Lincoln?" Kit turned to him, blinking rapidly.

"Kit, how about I take you home?"

She smiled at him, staggered over and wrapped her arms around his neck. She smelled of tequila and beer. "Do you want to take me home, Slinky?" She rubbed herself against him.

His body hardened and he flinched. Damn it. She only wanted him when she was drunk. "Yeah, Kit. Come on." He wrapped an arm around her waist and his fingers brushed the soft skin at the waistband of her jeans.

She moaned.

Bloody hell.

"Hey, wait a second. She's coming with me."

"Sorry, mate, I just got a better offer," Kit said with a smile.

The guy grumbled but backed off. Good. He didn't need a fight.

Now where was her ute? She'd need it in the morning. He'd get Ryan to bring him into Albany tomorrow to fetch his own car.

There it was. "Where are your keys?"

"Pocket."

He yanked them out and then helped her into the passenger seat, making sure she buckled her seatbelt. Her lips brushed his neck and his cheek as she kissed him.

She had no idea what she did to him. But even if she was sober, he wouldn't be her fuck buddy for one night. It would tear his heart out of his chest.

He gritted his teeth and slammed the door with a little more force than necessary. Now he needed to survive the drive back to her farm and get her into bed without any other problems.

He could call Hannah, but she'd be upset about Kit getting herself into such a state. She'd panicked when they were teenagers, and Kit had somehow got hold of alcohol and got absolutely shit faced. Hannah had shaken him awake at two in the morning telling him Kit was violently ill. He'd raced down to the river where they'd been camping to discover Kit was simply suffering from her over indulgence — not nearly dying. He'd driven them back to the house and let them fuss around her for the rest of the night. The next morning she'd been repentant, especially when he'd woken her at six to milk the cows.

But then she'd had the musketeers to take care of her.

Today he wanted to.

How sad was he?

He sent Hannah a text to tell her Kit was fine, then backed out of the car park and headed out of town.

"Lincoln, I knew you wanted me." Kit's hand slipped over his thigh to his crotch, squeezing him.

He tensed, grabbing her hand and holding it over the centre console.

"We have this thing between us." Her words slurred together.

Yeah, they had a *thing* between them but Kit had made it clear that she'd only wanted a hook-up. And if she remembered this conversation in the morning, she would hate him further.

"Why don't you close your eyes, honey? Rest for a minute while I drive." If she fell asleep, he could get her home and into bed without any problems.

"Closing my eyes makes my stomach swirl." She yanked her hand back and placed it over her belly.

He sighed. "OK, then keep them open." The last thing he needed was her vomiting in the car. He wound down her side window.

She groaned.

Damn, he needed to keep her distracted. They were still twenty kilometres from the farm. "Tell me about your day."

"Same as always, except for my farm being a crime scene." Her voice hitched.

In the dim light he saw her eyes squeeze shut for a second. "I'm sorry, Kit."

"I know. You always are."

Lincoln winced at the hit. He'd said the same thing on the day she'd propositioned him, the day it had taken every inch of his willpower to say no, rather than take her into his arms and kiss her senseless. Would he spend his life apologising to her? "Things should settle in a couple of days."

"For the police maybe." Her words were clearer now. Perhaps the subject was sobering her up. "I have to visit Paul's family, and find someone to replace him." Her laugh was bitter. "I'm so heartless. He's dead and I need a replacement quickly."

"You need to run your farm." He was amazed she did it with only two people.

"I do. Elijah is looking for work. I'll call him tomorrow." She fell silent, staring out the side window. At least she didn't look too ill, and she'd stopped touching him.

They drove the rest of the way in silence. He got out of the car and reached her side in time to catch her as she stumbled. "I've got you."

"Thanks," she mumbled.

He led her around the side of the house and in the back door which she hadn't locked. He'd have a word to her about that later. With a murderer around, she had to be more careful.

"Shoes," she said as she reached the kitchen. She bent down to pry them off and fell forward.

"Let me." He lifted her on to the kitchen table and unstrapped the ridiculous high heels that made her legs look amazing.

"I miss you, Lincoln." She sounded almost sober and he glanced up to her face, to the sadness there. Before he could comment, her skin paled.

"I'm going to be sick." She jumped off the table and pushed past him, stumbling for the toilet.

Lincoln cringed as he heard her vomiting. She would regret her binge in the morning. He poured her a glass of water, took a packet of painkillers out of the cupboard and followed the noise down the hallway.

Kit sprawled across the floor of the toilet, holding the seat, her hair draped down across her face. As she retched again, he put the water down and held her hair back. She'd have elastic bands in the bathroom drawer. When she'd finished, he fetched one and tied her hair back for her.

"It was so like Dad, the same gun, the same position."

What was she talking about?

She looked up at him, despair in her eyes. "Why did he have to die?"

Lincoln's heart broke. He wanted to pull her into his arms and tell her everything would be OK, but he would never lie to her. "That's what we're going to find out."

She vomited again and he wet a flannel and brought it to her so she could wipe her face. She took it without a murmur.

When she was done, she'd need to sleep. He checked her bedroom and as he suspected the sheets hung half off the bed, her clothes scattered all over the floor. Some things never changed.

He made the bed and then fetched a bucket from the laundry in case she needed it. He put another glass of water on her bedside table and then went back to the bathroom.

She was drinking the water he'd left for her and the painkiller packet was open.

"Feeling any better?"

"No." She flushed the toilet and then closed her eyes.

"Have you finished throwing up?"

"I think so."

"Let's get you into bed then." He helped her stand and then walked with her down the corridor to her room. She stripped off her shirt, exposing her red bra, and Lincoln's mouth went dry. He hadn't thought this through. He shouldn't be here. He forced himself to step away, turn his back as she finished undressing and climbed under the covers.

"It's OK, Lincoln. You can look now."

He faced her again. "Will you be OK?"

"Sure. You can leave." Some of the surly Kit was returning, which meant she was sobering up.

But he didn't want to leave. He didn't want Kit to be alone. "Sleep tight."

He switched off the lamp and walked down the corridor, turning off the light as he went. His footsteps slowed as he approached the door. She would have the mother of all headaches in the morning. And she'd have to get up early to milk the cows. He couldn't let her go through that alone even if she wouldn't welcome him.

And her tantalising words echoed in his head. What did she mean by she missed him? Did she want to be friends again, more than that?

He had to find out.

He confirmed both dogs were inside, locked the back door and then headed for the bedroom that used to be his.

He'd deal with her anger in the morning.

Chapter 4

A high-pitched squawk woke Kit and she sat bolt upright. Pain ricocheted through her head. She groaned, rubbing her forehead. What the hell had she done?

She slapped the alarm silent and switched on the lamp, wincing at the bright light. A glass of water by the bed caught her eye. At least she'd had enough sense to put it there. Sipping it, and taking two painkillers, she tried to remember her night.

Paul. Wanting to forget.

The musketeers not being available.

Heading into The White Star and having a beer. Some guy buying her tequila shots. How many had she had?

And how had she got home?

She squeezed her eyes shut and willed the painkillers to kick in. Tequila didn't normally hit her so hard.

The guy had been friendly, had wanted to hook up. She'd left the bar with him. And then what?

Lincoln's face floated across her mind. She frowned, trying to catch hold of the memory. Was it wishful thinking?

She focused harder, had a vague recollection of being in her car, groping him.

That had to be a dream.

Please let it be a dream.

She swung her legs off her bed and padded naked down the hallway to the bathroom. She needed a shower and maybe the hot water would wash away some of the fuzziness.

Ten minutes later she was none the wiser. She exited the bathroom and was halfway down the hallway when she stopped, sniffed the air.

Was that bacon and eggs?

Her heart thudded. Lincoln used to cook it for them every weekend.

Was Lincoln here?

She raced back to her room, threw on some clothes and grabbed her phone. Then she crept down the hallway again and peered around the door. Pain stabbed her heart. Lincoln was at her stove cooking, wearing a black dress shirt and jeans. The image took her straight back to being sixteen and the morning after Lincoln had first moved in. He'd made bacon and eggs then to celebrate them both being parent-free.

Why was he here?

Could her memory of groping him be true?

Please no. He could never know she still had a thing for him after all these years. She couldn't bear his pity. She had to get him out of here. Bracing herself, she strode into the room. "What the hell are you doing here?"

"Morning, Kit. How's the head?"

She scowled at him and her head thumped harder. "It's fine."

"You must have got most of the alcohol up last night."

A flash. Her hugging the toilet bowl, Lincoln tying her hair back. She hardened her heart. She would not get sappy. Would not show how touched she was. Better he believe she'd just been scratching an itch when she groped him. "You didn't answer my question."

"I thought you might need a hand this morning, so I stayed in my old room."

Kit stalked over to the fridge and opened it, staring at the contents. This was too familiar, too right, too reminiscent of the happier days when she'd been certain she and Lincoln would end up together forever.

"Can you pass the milk please?" His voice right behind her made her jump.

She grabbed the milk and shoved it at him, pushing past to flick on the kettle. It was already boiling. Even her dogs were happily eating from their bowls. He'd thought of everything.

Damn him.

"Take a seat. It's ready." The warm tones of his voice settled over her like a blanket. No. She couldn't let her guard down.

But the desire to sit was so incredibly strong when she turned to find the warm plate of bacon and eggs and a cup of tea on the table.

She had to eat, even if her stomach was a little tender from her night of excess. She snagged a piece of bacon from the plate and shoved it in her mouth before heading for the bathroom. Sitting down with him would be too domestic. She brushed her hair, wincing at her bloodshot eyes. She looked an absolute mess. Not the image she wanted to project around him. She needed to show him she was capable, that she didn't need him, his rejection had had no lasting effects.

With her hair done, she stopped by the table to pick up her mug of tea and then continued to her office, ignoring the way his eyes tracked her every move. She didn't need to explain herself. She could pretend this was her normal routine, that she didn't sit down to eat. A lot could have changed in the eight years since he'd lived here.

"Everything OK?" he asked on her next pass by the table.

She nodded. "There's a lot to do today." With her already fragile stomach, the additional stress of Lincoln looking fresh and gorgeous, sitting at the table as if he had every right to be there, was too much. "Thanks for breakfast."

She whistled for her dogs and headed for the back door.

"Kit, you need to eat." His footsteps followed her.

Why wouldn't he leave her alone? "I'll eat later, after my stomach has woken up." It grumbled, proving her lie, but she ignored it and shoved her feet into her boots.

He followed her off the verandah to her motorbike. Normally she walked over to the shed, but today she needed a quick getaway. She squinted in the early morning light. Was someone walking around her shed?

Shading her eyes against the first rays of sun, she focused. Yes. Definitely movement of the human kind.

"Who on earth is that?" She swung her leg over the motorbike. It sure as hell wasn't Paul.

Lincoln swore and as the motor roared to life, he jumped on the bike behind her. "You should stay here," he yelled. "It could be anyone."

"Hold on." She kicked the bike into gear and raced towards the shed. The figure ran and leapt on a motorbike. He twisted, pointing at them and dirt kicked up in front of them, a loud bang echoing in the morning air.

Was that a gun shot? As her brain struggled to compute, Lincoln reached around her, yanking the handlebars sideways.

She fought to stop the bike from tipping over and braked as it bumped over the rough ground. The other bike roared away. She twisted and yelled, "What are you doing?"

"He shot at us," Lincoln growled.

Kit's mouth dropped open as her brain finally caught up. An intruder, gun shot, Paul's murder. Holy shit. Her pulse raced as she checked the rider was leaving.

"Go back to the house."

Lincoln's order pierced her consciousness and she shook her head. She wasn't letting Lincoln investigate by himself. It was too dangerous. The intruder had been armed. Her heart still beating heavily in her chest, she turned the bike back towards the shed and ignored Lincoln's protest in her ear.

Pulling up in front of the shed, she switched off the bike and scanned the area for other trespassers.

"Stay here." He dismounted and cold air replaced his warmth and strength.

As if she'd stay there while he entered the shed alone. She kicked the stand down and followed him, the hair on her arms standing on end. No one would be inside. Not if they were smart.

He swore softly.

"My place." Her tone faked confidence. When he didn't move, she slipped past him and slapped on the light. Her office door was wide open and paper was strewn over the floor. "Son of a bitch." At least they were old records. All the new stuff was digital and though she had a computer in here, it was backed up over at the house.

Correction, she'd *had* a computer in here. The monitor now lay smashed on the floor and the terminal had been taken apart, the hard drive removed.

Her shoulders sagged. She didn't need this now, not today —
not ever.

"Don't touch anything, Kit."

She didn't need to be told. He had to do his forensic stuff.
"I'll check the machinery shed."

"Wait for me." He was on the phone to Ryan.

With pleasure. She crossed her arms, unable to shift the sense
of violation seeing her things destroyed. This was her home, her
land, her livelihood. She switched on the equipment in the
milking area and opened the gates for the cows to enter. When
she was done, Lincoln joined her and they walked across the yard
to the machinery shed.

The open doors of the tractor and truck caught her attention
first. Then she walked into the workshop and swore. The bench
was never particularly tidy but now it was clear, the tools scattered
over the ground. In the small shed next to the workshop, the
motocross bikes and sidecar hadn't been touched.

She tugged on her ponytail and her head pounded harder.
What had the guy been looking for?

Did this have something to do with Paul's death?

What had he got himself messed up in? What danger had he
brought to her farm?

She walked out of the bike shed and scanned the area, her
shoulders tight, waiting for something else to go wrong. The cows
milled outside the dairy waiting to be milked, the yards where she
tagged the animals were empty and the hay shed nearby was half
full of bales. She needed to get the seeding started for the next
crop.

Lincoln placed a hand on her shoulder and she flinched.
"How are you?"

"I'll cope." She stepped away from his touch, wanting too
much to close her eyes and lean into him. She had to deal with
the intruder's mess and she'd be damned if she'd let some
arsehole get to her, stop her from doing her job. "I'm going to
milk the cows."

Back in the dairy she got to work, spreading hay in the feeder
and preparing the milking teats.

God, she needed a coffee and an IV of painkillers. She
shouldn't have gone out last night and she certainly shouldn't

have drunk so much.

She groaned.

If she'd known what was going to happen this morning, she would have stayed at Hannah's. She cleaned the first cow's udder and stuck on the teat cups. Turning, she crashed into Lincoln, his hard chest squashing her breasts. She inhaled, orange and spice and all things nice.

He steadied her, holding her in position for a second and she was tempted to stay pressed up against him.

She pushed away. "What are you doing?"

"Helping."

"Don't you have police business?"

"Not until the others get here."

Damn. But she wasn't so far gone as to reject his help. "Take the other side then."

The more distance she kept from him the better. And later today she'd call Elijah and ask if he wanted a job.

Lincoln shook his head. He needed to focus on the intruder and ignore the fact Kit was so close and smelled like cinnamon.

Someone had shot at her and Kit hadn't realised, had driven straight into the line of fire.

If she'd been hit…

It didn't bear thinking about.

It had been too dark to see the shooter's face, but the build was definitely male, short and lean and could ride a motorbike. Didn't narrow down the list of suspects a hell of a lot.

The bike had headed towards the paddock where they'd found Paul yesterday so he'd probably cut a fence to get onto the property. But what was he after? "Did Paul leave any personal items here?"

Kit jumped and swallowed hard, her face still quite pale. "I don't think so. Occasionally he'd leave his hat in the ute, or his lunch in the fridge."

They'd already searched the ute, but he'd check the fridge later. "Tell me if you find anything." It had to be something significant to go to all the effort of taking the computer apart. "Did Paul use the computer much?"

"He was supposed to record any issues with the cows."

"But he didn't?"

"Not lately. I had to remind him constantly and then when he did use it, he'd snap at me if I came too close."

Maybe Paul had saved something important on there. But now the hard drive was gone. He'd have to ask the detectives if they'd found a computer at Paul's place.

The pulsing hush of the milking machine didn't hide the silence between them. When he'd lived here, she'd talk non-stop to him as they milked the cows together, telling him about her day, complaining about the guys in her class, or exclaiming over some new farming method she'd discovered and wanted to try. He'd loved listening to her, feeling her enthusiasm for the farm and her excitement about the future. She'd been so full of optimism.

He hadn't seen that Kit in a long time. Not since the day she'd kicked him out.

Lincoln sighed. And then there was what happened last night. He didn't bother raising the subject with Kit, not after the way she'd reacted this morning. He should have known his attempt to help would be shot down in flames.

It was too bad the image of her walking naked past his bedroom door was branded in his mind and kept replaying over and over. If she'd known he'd seen her…

He was glad she didn't.

He'd always known she had subtle curves. After a shopping trip with the musketeers at seventeen, she'd paraded her new bikini to him.

And he'd almost swallowed his tongue.

At some stage, when Lincoln hadn't been paying attention, Kit had grown up.

As the adult in the house and a rookie cop, he couldn't pursue her. Not if he wanted to keep his reputation, his job and stay out of jail.

Only a year earlier, he'd laughed when Kit's father had warned him about Kit's crush. He hadn't thought it would be an issue.

But after the bikini incident, living with Kit had become an endless exercise in self-control and hiding his true feelings.

He'd very nearly succumbed the night she'd turned eighteen

and she'd thrown herself at him.

He clenched his teeth. Even thinking about it now had him uptight, tense.

He could not go down that memory lane. It had become clear she'd wanted nothing more than a warm body that night. But their relationship had never recovered and they'd settled into this forced politeness whenever they were alone together.

He despised it.

It had taken him months to realise that even though Kit didn't reciprocate his feelings, he still wanted her in his life. And by then, he'd had no idea how to salvage their friendship. Nothing he'd tried had worked. He couldn't crack the stubborn shell she'd built around herself, the shell she only let the musketeers and his brother through.

Though recently she'd let her best friends' partners in too.

By the time Ryan arrived, Lincoln still didn't have a solution to his relationship with Kit. He stepped out of the milking bay and took the bag of clothes Ryan handed him. "Thanks for coming out."

"No problem. Where should we start?"

"The office." He moved into a clean area of the shed and changed into his uniform. Kit could handle the milking on her own.

He had to get to work.

And find the bastard who'd shot at her.

"I'm going to check the fencing." Kit stood at the entrance of the office, both hands on her hips. Defiance oozed from her.

Lincoln frowned. "We'll need to investigate before you can fix it. Why don't you do something else in the meantime?"

She scowled. "If he cut one in the cow paddock, I could have animals all over the place."

Ryan looked up. "Why don't you two check it out? I'll continue here."

"All right." More time alone with Kit. Maybe eventually he'd think of the right thing to say.

"Come on." She stalked outside and straddled her motorbike.

He'd be pressed up against her again. He gritted his teeth and hopped on, hands on her waist. The roar of the bike prevented any conversation. Which was probably a good thing.

Her body radiated heat and he gripped her hips tighter as she rode over bumps. Being this close to Kit, touching her soft hips, was agony.

He had to focus on the task. He scanned the surroundings. A couple of the fields had feed beets in them, there were younger cattle in another. Kit rode through open gate after open gate until they pulled into the paddock where Paul had died. She stopped the bike and pointed. "There."

Sure enough the wire fencing gaped open on the border to the property. "How did you know?" he yelled over the engine.

She turned, her face only inches from his. "None of the other gates were open. He wouldn't have stopped to close them behind himself."

Good point. At least the paddock was empty of livestock.

"Hold on." She headed back to the sheds.

Ryan was at the police car getting something out of the boot and Kit pulled up alongside and switched off the bike.

Lincoln got off, missing the warmth of her body. "The fence doesn't need fixing immediately."

"No," she agreed. She hesitated. "You'll be a couple more hours, won't you?" She looked at Ryan for an answer.

Ryan nodded.

She sighed. "There's not much I can do if I can't access my equipment. If you don't need me for anything, I'll head into town."

What he needed from her was forgiveness, for her to open up so they could go back to being friends. "What for?"

"I have an interview with a new farmhand."

That was good. She'd have the help she needed. "We're fine."

She nodded and roared off to the house.

Lincoln let out a deep breath.

"Why are things so tense between you?" Ryan asked.

He'd never confided in anyone about how he felt for Kit. He wasn't starting now. Stick to the facts. "I saw her in Albany last night. She was drunk and about to go home with a guy."

Ryan's eyebrows raised. "Hannah was worried she'd go out by herself. What were you doing in town?"

What did he say to that? "Looking for her. I thought she might need a friend."

"Sounds like she did." Ryan picked up the forensics kit and they walked over to the machinery shed.

"She doesn't think so." Wow, the bitterness in his voice was clear even to him.

Ryan waited for him to elaborate.

Damn. He should have kept his mouth shut. "She wasn't happy to see me this morning."

"Why were you here?"

Because he hadn't been able to leave. "I figured she'd need help in the morning."

"Lucky. The shooter could have hit Kit."

He frowned. "Yeah. Either he was a bad shot or not trying." His gut told him Paul's murder and the guy trespassing were related to the drug ring they'd been investigating over the past couple of months. They hadn't discovered who was in charge, but he suspected the person was a local. The only guy they'd identified was Harry Smith, dubbed Creepy Guy by Mai, a man for hire.

"Think he was warning you away?"

"Maybe." He hoped that was all it was.

Because if he'd been aiming for Kit, she could be in real danger.

Chapter 5

The ute's engine gave a satisfying throaty roar as Kit put her foot down and accelerated away from the farm. She wasn't running away, she was being productive, doing what she could while her farm was off limits. First she'd meet Elijah for coffee to discuss whether he wanted a job, and then she had to visit Paul's parents in Albany. She needed to tell them how sorry she was and to answer any questions they had.

It would be hideous.

She cranked up her music, letting AC/DC blare through her speakers and shock her out of her dismal mood.

By the time she slowed at Blackbridge town limits, the tension in her shoulders had relaxed. She parked outside the little cafe near the river, but as she got out, her legs trembled. She gave herself a second, gazing at the kids playing on the swings across the road and the couple canoeing down the river. She'd done both with the musketeers. The memory strengthened her, and she sauntered into the cafe. The burst of bright red in a sea of muted colours made it easy to spot Elijah. His brown hair was coiffed with more gel than in a toothpaste tube, and his smile was wide and cheeky. He lifted a hand in a wave. They'd stuck together at the agricultural high school and had been well known — the girl and the gay guy.

She strode over. "Can I buy you a coffee?"

"Already ordered. I got you a cappuccino."

He remembered her preference. "Thanks." She slid into the chair.

"I'm sorry about Paul."

She flinched at the wave of sorrow. She cleared her throat. Focused on why she was here. "I need a new farmhand. Are you interested?"

Elijah squeezed her hand. "I feel guilty for benefiting from Paul's death, but yes I'm interested. Tell me more."

She pulled her hand away. His sympathy would crack her defences. Instead she concentrated on the facts, told him about the tasks she expected of him, the hours he'd have to work and the pay.

"I'm happy with that. When do I start?"

Relief washed through her. Elijah had helped her a couple of times over the past month when Paul had been a no-show and it would be easy working with him. "As soon as you can. Do you have to give notice?"

"I'm casual, so I don't think so," he said.

She hesitated. He needed to know about the incident this morning, but the busy cafe wasn't the place to discuss it. She'd have to ask Lincoln if Elijah would be in danger. "Before you decide, you should come out and I'll show you everything. How about after lunch?" The police should be finished their investigation by then.

"Sounds good."

She dredged up a smile and sipped her coffee. She'd get through this. "So what's new with you?"

A couple of hours later she pulled up in front of Paul's parents' place in Albany. The modest brick and tile house had a freshly mown lawn and colourful flowers blooming in the garden. Fleur could probably tell her what they were.

Kit tapped her fingers on the steering wheel and swallowed hard. She had to do this. It was the decent thing to do. Paul had died while at work, and as his employer, she had a duty to see his next of kin. She wished it wasn't so hard. She walled up her emotions and got out, the slam of the door closing loud in the warm day.

One step in front of the other.

She knocked loudly on the front door. Paul's father answered, dark rings around his eyes. She'd only met him once, when Paul had invited both parents to her New Year's Eve party last year.

Her body tensed. "Mr Maddock, I'm very sorry for your loss."

He nodded. "Thank you, Kit. Come in."

Her legs were heavy as she stepped over the threshold and into the dark house. None of the curtains had been opened to let in the sunshine, and as she followed him through to the kitchen, she found Mrs Maddock sitting at the kitchen table, staring at the cup of tea in front of her. Her heart clenched.

"Kit's here, love," Mr Maddock said.

She glanced up, her eyes red and lacking any life. "Hello, Kit."

"Mrs Maddock," Kit answered. "I'm sorry about Paul." The words were so trite, so meaningless.

"Have a seat, Kit." Mr Maddock indicated a chair.

She didn't want to stay long, but she sat anyway, an intruder on their grief.

"What can you tell us?" Mrs Maddock asked.

Kit straightened. Had the police told them it might be murder and not suicide? "What were you told?"

"Only that he'd been shot and the police were investigating. But Paul would never kill himself. He loved life too much." Her voice broke.

Kit swallowed hard.

Mr Maddock placed a glass of water on the table. "What had his mood been like?"

What words of comfort could she give them? She couldn't say she'd been about to fire him for being slack. It wasn't the last impression she wanted to give them of their son. "He'd been a little distracted lately, but he wouldn't talk to me."

"For how long?"

Three damned months. "Oh, I'm not sure. A little while I guess."

"He kept a lot of things to himself," his mother said.

"Who found him?" Mr Maddock asked.

Her chest tightened. "I did." She could get through this, tell them what happened without breaking down. "He was supposed to meet me at the yards and was late, so I went to find him. Found him in the back paddock…" She squeezed her eyes closed as the image flashed into her mind again, stabbing her.

Mrs Maddock patted her hand. "I'm sorry you had to be the one."

When Kit had the tears under control, she opened her eyes. "Thank you."

"Have the police said anything to you?"

"No. Not yet. I'm sure they'll let you know any news." She wasn't strong enough to deal with them directly again. Not after this. It was too hard.

"Did he leave anything at the farm?" his mother asked. "The police haven't returned his personal possessions and we haven't felt like going to his house yet."

"Not that I've found. I'll tell you if I do."

Mrs Maddock wiped her eyes with a tissue. "They haven't released his body either. How are we supposed to prepare a funeral, say goodbye?"

Kit squeezed her hand, gave what she hoped was a sympathetic smile. "I'm certain Sergeant Zanetti is working as fast as he can." These things took time. Lincoln would ensure everything was done properly and as quickly as possible. She cleared her throat and stood. "I should get back."

"Of course. You must have a lot of work to do." Mr Maddock stood with her.

She nodded, her heart twisting as Paul's mother sniffed. The lump in her throat grew larger. Time to leave. She moved quickly down the corridor and out the front door. "If you have any more questions, please call me," she said to Mr Maddock.

He sighed. "There's nothing more to say, is there?"

"No." She got into her car as he went back inside. Just down the road, out of sight of the house, she pulled over, took a couple of long, deep breaths to calm the grief swirling around inside her. It was done. She'd seen his parents, given them her condolences, hadn't broken down. Only the funeral left.

And the musketeers would be by her side.

She would be fine.

She swallowed and fought back the tears, but some big fat traitors leaked out the sides, threatening to start a deluge. She wiped at them furiously, and let out a shuddery breath, and then another. She couldn't waste her daylight hours grieving, there was plenty of time for that during the long, lonely night.

If she had red eyes when she met with Elijah, he'd ask her to share. Speaking of Elijah… she checked the time and groaned. She needed to get back. She sniffed, wiped her eyes again and cleared her throat. She could do this.

Hopefully the police, and in particular, Lincoln, would be gone. He weakened her defences. She'd always been tough, had to be because farming could destroy weak people.

Like it had almost destroyed her father.

She was stronger than him and couldn't let this, or her feelings for Lincoln get to her.

With a sigh, she put the ute into gear and drove home.

Elijah pulled into Kit's driveway right behind her as she arrived at the farm. Police cars were still parked by the sheds so she stopped outside her house instead.

Elijah frowned as he got out of his car. "Are the police still investigating Paul's death?"

She hesitated. She desperately wanted him to take the job, but she had to be honest. If he passed on it, she'd find someone else — but that could take time. "Someone broke into the sheds this morning," she said. "He shot at me."

His eyebrows rose. "Why?"

"I guess he didn't want to get caught. It looks like he was searching for something."

"What?"

The question of the day. She shrugged. "I don't know."

"That's weird." He bent over to pat Montoya and Roberts who'd run out from the backyard to greet them.

She wanted to tell him Paul's death might not be suicide, but she couldn't betray Lincoln. The news hadn't been made public yet. They were probably waiting for the autopsy report.

"Is he likely to come back?"

Though she needed Elijah's help, she said, "Who knows? Do you want to wait until the police have more information?"

"Will you keep working as normal?"

She nodded.

"Then I'm not leaving you out here alone." He smiled and handed her a red bar. "I bought you a thank you present."

A chocolate Kit Kat. Lincoln used to buy them for her when she'd needed cheering up. She hadn't been able to eat one since he'd left.

"The musketeers call you Kit Kat, right? I figured it was your favourite."

Kit cleared her throat and blinked rapidly to clear the moisture in her eyes. "Right. Thanks." She forced a smile and tucked the chocolate into her back pocket. She had no control over her emotions today. Focus. "You should be safe in the paddock." At least she hoped so. "And if you see anyone unfamiliar, call the police."

"All right." He hugged her. "I will if you will."

She nodded. "Let me give you the extended tour."

They walked over to the sheds, the dogs by their sides.

Lincoln scowled as he spoke to the two Albany detectives, but her heart skipped a beat anyway. Would her heart ever get over him? When she got close enough, she asked, "Have you found any evidence?"

"Miss van Ross, we want to talk to you," Detective Khan said.

Great, another conversation when she needed to get work done. "Fine, but can I fix my fence first?"

Khan bristled.

"Who's this?" Detective Bosch asked, nodding at Elijah.

"My new farmhand, Elijah." The moment she said it, speculation crossed both the detectives' faces. She rolled her eyes and turned to him. "They're going to want to know your whereabouts on the day Paul died."

"I was working at the Vale winery," he told them.

She didn't have time to mess around with their suspicious questions now, but she couldn't hamper the investigation. "Why don't you chat to Elijah while I fix my fence?"

"All right," Bosch said.

"The ute's still impounded, Kit," Lincoln said.

She swore. Of course. She would have to use her personal ute back at the house. Damn it. She stalked back and when she returned with the car, Elijah was still speaking with the detectives. "Call me when you're done." She moved into the workshop to get the fencing equipment and wire, and Ryan and Lincoln were inside talking. "Can I fix the cut fence?"

"Yeah, we're finished here," Ryan said.

Finally. She hefted the wire into the tray of her ute.

"Need a hand?" Lincoln asked.

She scowled. "I've got it." She'd been working mostly on her own for more than eight years. She hadn't had a choice when, one by one, the people she loved had abandoned her. She didn't need some man coming in now thinking she was helpless. Especially Lincoln.

She added the required equipment to the ute, slammed the tray gate closed and climbed into the cab.

When the shed was out of sight, she slowed, releasing the tension in her shoulders as she scanned her property, searching for anything amiss, anything that needed fixing. This was all hers, every blade of grass and grain of soil. She couldn't imagine living anywhere else, doing anything else. It was part of her. She wound down the window and inhaled the earthy scent. The feed beets were ready, so she'd set up the electric fence and move the cows in soon. It would supplement their diet until the next crop of hay was ready.

As she drove into the back paddock, the crime scene tape around where Paul had died fluttered in the breeze. Averting her gaze, she pulled up next to the cut fence. She hauled the equipment out of the ute and then stared into the bush separating her property from Foley's. Had this been a rendezvous point for Paul and whoever had killed him? Could there be some kind of evidence in the bush?

The police would have searched, but that didn't stop her from moving towards the trees. She wanted answers herself to make sure she and Elijah weren't in any danger.

Her feet crunched over the dried leaves on the ground, loud in the otherwise silence. She wouldn't sneak up on anyone, but there was nowhere to hide on this side of the road, the trees too skinny and the shrubs only knee high. Still the hair on her arms stood upright and her gaze flicked back and forth, never focusing on one area for long.

No footprints in the hard ground, no scraps of cloth from a torn bit of clothing, no deep tyre treads. She walked a hundred metres until she came to the road between the two properties. No skid marks, oil stains, or vehicles. Just blue wrens tweeting in the bushes over the road and the occasional squawk of a cockatoo.

She was wasting her time. She had a fence to fix.

As she twisted around, the rumble of a motorbike engine reached her. She froze. Was it someone on Foley's farm, or on the road?

Quickly she closed the distance to the tree line, but there was nowhere to hide. She'd be in plain view of the road.

Her muscles tightened and she hesitated between running back to the ute and wanting to see who it was. Common sense had her hurrying towards her property. The engine grew louder and she turned as a dirt bike pulled off the road and headed towards her. No way she would out run them.

Heart racing, she stepped behind a tree and braced herself. Damn, there wasn't even a decent-sized branch she could use as a weapon.

The rider stopped in front of her and her breath rushed out of her as she recognised his weathered face. "Damn it, Foley, you scared me to death."

He shut off the engine, slid off his helmet and hung it from his handlebar. "Why are you so spooked?"

She didn't want to worry him by telling him about the intruder. "I'm a little edgy. Paul died through there." She pointed.

He winced, ran a hand through his short, dark hair. "It's a messed up business. I was going to drop by this afternoon to check on you."

The wave of grief flowed over her again. Foley had been her mentor after Lincoln had left, had helped her on the farm whenever she needed it. Though he'd never been a shoulder to cry on, he had taught her to shoot and let her take her frustrations out on some unsuspecting beer bottles. He'd always been available at the end of the phone for advice and she admired him. "Thanks. What are you doing out here?"

"Checking the fence line," he said. "After the fire a couple of months back, I've been monitoring the area to make sure whoever left those barrels in my shed hasn't come back."

Wise move, but she couldn't chat to him all afternoon. "I've got to get back to work."

He glanced over. "I'll help you fix the fence." Before she could refuse, the engine roared to life and he rode over to the fence line. She followed him.

"Looks like someone cut it," Foley said, shifting from one foot to another.

"Yeah."

"Was it Paul?"

What could she say? "Might have been the police when they were investigating. I can't imagine them climbing through." She twisted the ends of the wire into loops on one end and Foley did the other.

"Lucky there are no cows in the paddock."

"Yeah." She used the wire stretchers to attach the top wires together.

"It must have been hard finding him." Foley's voice was low, sympathetic.

She nodded as they stretched the second wire together. They'd done this so many times in the past, when she was younger and less experienced. The normality was kind of comforting.

"When's the funeral?"

"I'm not sure. The police haven't released the body yet." With the final wire together, she stood. She didn't want to talk about Paul. "Thanks for your help. I've got to get back. I'm behind on my work."

"How about I send Ian over to help for a couple of days?"

A tempting offer, but Foley's farmhand would have his own work to do and he tended not to think things through. She'd have to constantly monitor him to ensure he didn't do anything stupid. "No need. I've got Elijah Johnson starting." Her phone rang. "That will be him now."

Foley loaded her ute with the equipment while she told Elijah she'd be back shortly.

She shook Foley's hand. "Thanks again."

"Any time, Kit. Just give me a call."

"Will do." She watched him ride away.

He was one man who'd never let her down.

Someone she could rely on.

The day couldn't end soon enough for Lincoln. Kit's cool treatment, followed by being shot at and finally Bosch and Khan's superior attitude, had him ready to pull his hair out. Luckily Ryan had taken point, had dealt with the detectives and reminded him to keep his cool.

He shouldn't have to be reminded. Normally it was his everyday demeanour. People didn't ruffle his feathers.

But Kit wasn't just anyone.

With a sigh, he turned his attention to the paperwork in front of him, but the words didn't capture his attention. How was Kit really coping? Had she called the musketeers, told them about being shot at?

He pushed back his chair, ran a hand through his hair. He had to stop thinking about her. She wouldn't be thinking about him. She'd be in the middle of milking, and Elijah would be with her.

He had no reason to go out and check on her.

Ryan's phone rang in the other room and it sounded like he was talking to Hannah. Which reminded him of something Kit had said last night. He wandered out and motioned to Ryan that he wanted to speak to her.

"Hannah, Lincoln wants a word." He handed over the phone.

"Hi, Hannah Banana. How are things?"

"Hey, Lincoln, what's up?"

He cleared his throat. "Kit said something the other night in passing that I wanted to ask you about."

"Shouldn't you be asking her?"

He'd love to, but that was never going to work. "She said Paul's death was like what happened with her Dad."

A gasp and then instant freeze came through the line. "How odd."

"So it wasn't a drunken thought." What could Kit have meant by it?

Hannah was silent.

"Hannah Banana, help me help her."

"Don't you try to weasel me, Slinky. This is something you should talk to Kit about." Her voice was firm. "I have to go. Tell Ryan I'll see him when he gets home." She hung up.

Lincoln's eyes widened as he handed the phone back to his friend. The musketeers were circling the wagons, which meant whatever it was, it had to be bad.

He almost didn't want to know.

And he desperately needed to know.

"Did you upset Hannah?" Ryan asked.

He nodded. "She said she'd see you when you got home."

"Run me through what Kit said."

It wasn't betraying Kit's confidence if it might have something to do with their case. "She said Paul's death was so like her Dad, the same gun, the same position."

"Did her father try to commit suicide?"

"Not that I know of."

"Could he have been attacked?"

He shook his head. "Mum would have told me about it. She and Kit's step-mum, Monica were close. But maybe something happened while I was in Perth." He'd ask his mother about it tomorrow night when he went for dinner.

If anyone knew, she would.

And he needed to know everything in order to protect Kit.

Chapter 6

On Sunday night, Kit left Elijah to finish the milking and hurried home to shower and change. She hadn't caught up with Mr and Mrs Z in ages, and the invitation to a Sunday roast was a welcome respite from all the craziness of the week. Jamie would be there and she could relax and unwind.

She opened the gate between their properties and drove the remaining distance to the farmhouse.

She loved visiting the Zanettis — the warm welcoming home, the smell of something delicious freshly baking, or the aroma of tomato and garlic if it was close to dinner. This had been more of a home than her own place after her brother had been born. Not that she didn't love Brody — she'd begged for a brother or sister — but she'd always felt second best. He was the boy, the favourite child, her step-mother's *real* child.

And at six years older, she'd always had to know better, to take care of him and to help around the house.

At the Zanettis she could be a child.

The dogs jumped out of the ute as she pulled up and wagged a greeting at the Zanettis' dog. She followed them around the house to the kitchen door, taking her shoes off at the entrance and calling a greeting through the fly screen.

"Come in, Kit," Mrs Z called.

She inhaled the aroma of the lamb roast and was transported back to being a teenager when she and Lincoln had had dinner here every Sunday night. She'd been part of their family and after they'd eaten, they'd played cards or board games. She always preferred when Jamie's girlfriend was over, because it meant Kit could team up with Lincoln. They'd always win, especially when playing Pictionary. They'd understood each other on a different level.

She shook away the memory as Mrs Z turned from setting the long table where there was always room for anyone who might drop by and hugged Kit. "I'm so sorry about Paul."

Kit inhaled her sweet flowery scent, holding on to her softness for a moment longer while the pain swept through her. "Thanks."

"If you need to talk, my door's always open — day and night."

She loved that about Mrs Z, the instant acceptance and comfort. But the knot in her throat prevented her from speaking. She nodded.

"Would you like a drink?"

She wanted a stiff whiskey but if she told Mrs Z that, she'd worry. "Water would be great."

Mrs Z handed her a glass. "The others are in the lounge room. Why don't you join them?"

"Do you need a hand?"

"Of course not."

Kit took her drink into the lounge to find Mr Z and Jamie on the navy blue couches. "Hey."

Mr Z raised his bottle of beer to her and Jamie jumped to his feet and wrapped her in a hug. "Hey, Kit Kat. How's things?"

Damn him. She couldn't deal with his sympathy now, not when Mrs Z had already weakened her defences. She gently pushed him away. "I'm fine. Elijah started work for me so we'll have things back on track in no time."

"I wasn't talking about that."

Someone walked in and she turned, hoping for a good distraction.

Well it was a distraction all right. She inhaled sharply. "Lincoln."

He smiled at her, his eyes dark, and he looked deliciously casual in blue jeans and a white shirt. Why did he have to look so good all the time?

She should have realised he would be here, but he'd been

working the last time she'd had dinner at the Zanettis'.

She still hadn't got to the bottom of why he'd stayed the night at her place after her binge, but now wasn't the time to bring it up. She didn't have the energy to deal with any of the emotions he made her feel now. Her defences were still too low.

"I'll help Mrs Z." She hurried out.

Ten minutes later they sat at the dining table. Kit sat next to Jamie though it meant Lincoln sat across from her. She could mostly ignore him. "What are the new batch of students like at the ag school?"

Jamie laughed. "They'd rather be out on the farm than learning English, but they're pretty good."

She smiled. It had been the same when she'd been there.

"They want to visit a few farms, review different set ups," Jamie continued.

"They can come to mine." She enjoyed teaching the kids, passing on her knowledge.

"That's not a good idea," Lincoln said.

She frowned at him, but it was Mrs Z who asked, "Why not?"

"Kit's place is still a crime scene."

"Are you saying Paul's death wasn't an accident?" Mr Z asked.

Lincoln pursed his lips.

For once it was to her advantage that he never commented on an active investigation. "They always investigate a sudden death." Kit didn't look at him.

"I wasn't referring to that." Lincoln's tone dared her to say something about the shooting.

If Mrs Z knew the truth, she'd worry.

"Kit, what's going on?" Jamie's eyes searched hers and she glanced at her plate. "What happened?" he demanded.

Damn it. He was as tenacious as his brother when he wanted something. "Someone broke into my sheds the other night."

"Was anything taken?" Mr Z asked.

"The computer was trashed."

Lincoln cleared his throat.

For someone who didn't divulge police business he was being remarkably noisy.

"*Kit.*" Jamie persisted.

She stuck a large chunk of roast potato in her mouth.

"Do I need to ask the musketeers?" he asked.

Damn Lincoln and damn Jamie. If she told the musketeers about being shot at, they'd worry too. She glared at Lincoln, but his expression challenged her to tell the truth. "I scared off the trespasser when I went to milk the cows and he shot at me."

"What!" The exclamation came from Jamie and his parents.

"It was nothing, he wanted to scare me so he could get away." At least she hoped that was the reason.

"You shouldn't be out there alone," Mrs Z said. "Jamie you should stay with her for a few nights."

"That's not necessary." The last thing she needed was to put Jamie in any potential danger. "I'm fine. I've got the two dogs inside with me. They'll warn me if anyone comes around."

"And then you'll call Lincoln?" Mrs Z asked, giving her the no-nonsense, don't-you-lie-to-me look.

"Then I'll call the police," Kit agreed. She wasn't putting Lincoln in any danger either.

"Maybe I should stay," Jamie said. "It's basically the same distance from your place to school as it is from here, so it doesn't matter either way."

Lincoln clenched his teeth. What was his problem? "There's no point. I'm sure he won't be back."

Jamie frowned. "What about Lincoln staying?"

"No!" She winced at their surprised looks. Quickly she added, "I don't need a babysitter. I've been living by myself for years without any problems." She had to change the subject. "How are things going with the cheese factory?"

Mr Z gave her a long look before answering, "We've got a new cheese coming out soon."

Relieved they weren't pushing the matter, she continued to eat dinner.

The quicker she finished, the faster she could leave.

She'd had enough of both Zanetti brothers tonight.

Lincoln waited until Kit left, and his parents were in the kitchen before taking his brother aside. He hated to ask Jamie, but there was no one else. "Can you keep an eye on her over the next few days?"

"What aren't you telling us?" Jamie asked. "Why is Kit so mad at you?"

His brother saw too much. Kit had always kept herself slightly apart from him, but usually it wasn't enough for anyone else to notice.

"I can't comment on an active investigation."

"But you can say why Kit is angry. She barely looked at you tonight."

He couldn't say that was her normal reaction to him when they were alone. "I took her home the other night when she was drunk. She didn't appreciate it in the morning."

Jamie frowned. "When?"

"The day after Paul died. She drove to Albany alone, got drunk and almost went home with a guy."

Jamie made a face, but he didn't look as upset as Lincoln expected him to be. "She should have called me."

"So you could take advantage of her instead?" Shit. Why had that come out?

Jamie's mouth dropped open. "What the hell?"

Lincoln clenched his teeth. "She tried Hannah, but she had plans."

"No, no, no, back up a step." Jamie shook his head. "What are you talking about? I would never take advantage of Kit."

"No, you'd just sleep with her?" He couldn't shut himself up. He shouldn't be jealous of the way Kit opened up with Jamie and not him. He had to get out of here. He turned to go and Jamie grabbed his arm.

"What makes you think I've slept with Kit?"

He tried to walk away but Jamie held tight. "New Year's Eve." He spat the words out.

"*Last* New Year's?"

He nodded, jaw tight. He wanted this done.

Jamie laughed, letting go of Lincoln and gasping for breath. "Yeah, we shared a bed, but that's all. Having sex with Kit would be like sleeping with my sister." He grimaced, then his gaze turned speculative. "Why do you even care?"

That was his cue to exit.

He moved towards the kitchen.

"Oh no you don't." Jamie positioned himself in front of the door. "Why do you care who I sleep with?"

The tic above his eye fluttered. "I don't."

Jamie's eyes widened. "But you care who Kit sleeps with." His mouth dropped open. "Do you have a thing for Kit?"

The words were loud, too loud. He dragged his brother away from the door and his parents' ears. "No."

"Liar." Jamie's expression softened. "How long?"

He could not have this conversation. "I'm going."

"Linc, wait a second. Talk to me." He glanced over his shoulder, but no one came to the door. "Kit's one of my best friends and you're my favourite brother. I want you both to be happy."

"I'm your only brother."

"Well I love you, all right? Why haven't you ever made a move?"

Lincoln shook his head. "I value our friendship." When they'd had one.

"Doesn't mean you're going to ruin it by admitting how you feel."

"It was inappropriate. She was my responsibility."

Jamie's eyebrows almost disappeared. "*That* long? Holy shit."

He growled in frustration. He'd said too much again. "Don't say anything."

Jamie ran his hand through his hair. "I won't. But it sounds like you're the one who should be keeping an eye on her, not me."

"She doesn't want me around." And that hurt the most.

"Sure she does. She idolised you when we were kids, it was always Lincoln this and Lincoln that. It used to drive me crazy."

"That was a long time ago." And idolising wasn't the same thing as loving. Reality could never stand up to that kind of fantasy. He needed to change the subject. "I wanted to ask you about something. Hannah clammed up when I mentioned it to her."

Jamie perched on the arm of the couch. "If it's musketeers stuff, I can't guarantee I'll tell you either."

He admired their loyalty to each other when it didn't affect his investigation. "When Kit was drunk the other night, she mentioned Paul's death reminded her of her father."

"Bloody hell," Jamie breathed. "No wonder she went out to get shit-faced."

Lincoln looked down at him. "You know what she's talking about?"

He nodded. "And no, I won't break her confidence, but _you_ really need to hear it from her. Don't let it lie. She's going to need to talk to someone about it, if she hasn't already spoken to the girls."

Damn. It had to be something serious for Jamie not to blow it off. Had her father tried to kill himself?

Jamie checked the time. "You should go now. It's not late and if she's obsessing, it won't be good. Plus if you don't want her to be alone…"

Lincoln hesitated. Going to see Kit while she was alone, possibly already in her pyjamas — no she didn't wear pyjamas, and that wasn't an image he needed burned into his brain right now.

"Linc, go and talk to her. Fix whatever is broken between you two because you used to be good friends."

He wanted that more than he wanted anything. What else did he have to lose? "All right."

He went into the kitchen to say goodbye to his parents. They sat at the table, sipping tea. His mother smiled. "Are you off now?"

"Yeah."

She stood and hugged him, whispering in his ear, "I'm glad you've finally admitted your feelings for Kit." She winked at him.

Damn. They'd heard the whole thing. He groaned.

"See you later, Lincoln. Careful of the 'roos on the way home," his father said.

Lincoln nodded.

Face burning, he left the house and got into his car.

Where to now? The gate separating the property from Kit's was to his left, and the road home was on his right.

With a muttered curse, he turned left.

Chapter 7

Kit had to be civil to Lincoln, otherwise people were going to ask questions. Normally she could pretend everything was fine, but it had been a tough few days. Jamie had given her a couple of confused glances during dinner. He'd probably call as soon as Lincoln left.

This was Lincoln's fault. If he hadn't brought her home the other night… Being alone with him had opened old wounds that had never healed properly. He was the one guy she could never have.

The only man she'd ever wanted.

She'd changed into boxer shorts and a singlet, but going to bed wasn't an option. Instead she paced the living room, unable to settle.

She'd destroyed their friendship by making a move on him when she was younger, more optimistic, too naive. Her face heated. The mortification was still so strong even after all those years. It had been compounded when he'd referred to her as 'practically my sister' only a couple of weeks afterwards at the pub.

She'd wanted to crawl into a hole and die. Instead she'd had a few drinks, danced the night away, and left the pub with a guy whose name she didn't remember. Lincoln would never see her pining after him.

The simple fact was, she didn't inspire dedication, only lust.

Which was why she never dated. Second dates were asking for heartache she didn't need.

She wasn't loveable.

Lincoln had proved that by leaving the second she turned eighteen.

Arsehole.

The name calling didn't make her feel any better because it wasn't true. Lincoln simply didn't love her. It was time she moved on, got over her misery. The Zanettis didn't deserve her moodiness and Mrs Z would call, ask her if she wanted to talk about it.

But Kit couldn't tell the woman that she'd been madly in love with her son for almost a decade.

She kicked the couch and then flinched as pain shot up her foot. That was stupid. She wasn't wearing any boots.

She was stupid. She should go to bed, not pace the house fretting about a man she couldn't have.

Her dogs lay on the rug, Montoya occasionally opening one eye if she got too close. They were used to her moods. And they loved her anyway.

She groaned and then stopped pacing as a sound reached her ears.

Was that an engine?

Goosebumps leapt to her skin when Roberts lifted his head and looked towards the door.

Yes, definitely an engine and it was getting closer. No one should be coming out here at this time of night. She flicked off the lights in the living room and walked in the dark to the front of the house to peer out the window. The lights were coming from the direction of the Zanettis' place.

Was Jamie checking up on her rather than calling?

She stayed where she was as the headlights approached. It wasn't until the vehicle pulled up in front and the lights switched off that she recognised the car.

Her heart leapt.

Lincoln.

What the hell was he doing here?

Immediately she brushed down her singlet and then cursed. He didn't care what she wore. And she couldn't stand here staring at him

She hurried into her kitchen and switched on the kettle. Her ears tuned to the outside as his footsteps trod the wooden floorboards, followed by a long pause at the back door before he knocked, loud and authoritative.

She swallowed.

She should get this over with. See what he wanted and then throw him out again. She strode over to the back door, and pulled it open.

"You should have checked to see who it was," Lincoln grumbled.

Yes, because she was a two-year-old who didn't know the first thing about safety. "I saw you pull up." She stepped back to let him in. "What do you want?"

Tension coiled in the bottom of her stomach as she inhaled his citrus scent. He walked through to the kitchen and she took her time, closing and then locking the back door before following. He poured two cups of tea.

Her heart ached. He looked so at home in her kitchen as if he was meant to be there. She clenched her hands. "Lincoln, it's late. What are you doing here?"

He took his time adding the milk and placing both mugs on the table. She didn't sit. Couldn't.

"Sit down."

She didn't like his kind, cautious tone. "Do you have bad news? Has someone been hurt?" There hadn't been much time between her leaving the Zanettis and now, but maybe he'd received a phone call. She paced away, spun back waiting to hear the worst

"No. Sit down, Kit Kat, I want to ask you about something."

No. He couldn't call her that. He hadn't called her that for a very long time. It was a sure fire way to crack her defences. "What?" she snapped, refusing to approach the table.

He sighed and that made her feel even worse. "The other night, you said something about your father."

Dread lodged heavily in her chest and she stopped pacing. "Did I?" She couldn't ask him what. Didn't want to know.

He nodded and his expression dared her to respond. "You said the way you'd found Paul reminded you of your father."

She tore her gaze away. "That's odd. I was drunk."

"I don't think so. Both Hannah and Jamie refused to tell me what you were referring to."

And of course he'd asked them first and not her. She sealed the crack the nickname had caused. "Maybe because there's nothing to tell."

His tone was gentle, the most gentle it had been since they'd lived together. "What happened with your father, Kit Kat?"

Damn him! She didn't have to answer him, even if part of her longed to confide in him, longed to unburden herself and trust him again. "Go home, Lincoln."

She stalked out of the kitchen. He'd get the hint and leave. He always did. He didn't care enough to stick around.

She slammed her bedroom door behind her, but it didn't have that satisfying bang. She whirled around and Lincoln stood there, one hand on the door, holding it open.

"Don't run from me, Kit."

"Don't follow me, Lincoln." She hated the mimicry in her voice, hated her instant defensiveness but she couldn't break it. It was the only way to protect herself from him.

"How bad was it?"

Damn him. Why wouldn't he get the hint? Why wouldn't he leave? "Not as bad as it could have been if I'd been five minutes later."

His expression was kind, patient, the type of expression she'd seen on his face when speaking with Hannah or Mai or Fleur — but never her.

"Forget about it," she ordered and pushed his hard chest. "Get out."

He didn't budge. "Not until you tell me, Kit."

She swore. He wasn't going to let it go. If she told him now, maybe he'd get the hell out of her house. "Fine." She took a deep breath and released it slowly. No, she couldn't do this here, in her bedroom. She brushed past him, the urge to stay pressed up against the warmth of his body so strong that she had to force herself to continue down the hallway. Back in the living room, she squared her shoulders and faced him.

His silence was unnerving, his gaze didn't leave hers.

How did she start? Where? Context, she needed to give him

some context.

"I'd been on at Dad to teach me how to shoot," she said. "They wouldn't teach us at the ag school, but I'd been reading a bunch of articles about caring for injured animals and I wanted to be prepared in case I ever had to put one down."

He nodded.

Her throat was too dry. She needed a drink. She walked into the kitchen, picked up the tea he'd made and swallowed a couple of mouthfuls. It didn't help.

Lincoln followed her in, still silent.

"One day I got home from school and noticed the rifle was gone." She glanced at him. "It used to be kept in the pantry and the bullets were locked in his office." She'd been so naive. "I figured he had to shoot an animal, so I went looking for him. He couldn't refuse to teach me if he had the gun right there."

His expression changed, a slight awareness in his eyes that told her he'd guessed what was coming next.

She gulped another mouthful of tea and paced away again. "The ute was in one of the back paddocks where we had the crops." No cows or her father in sight. "I pulled up on the motorbike and found him sitting, legs out, leaning against the ute, the gun in his hand." She squeezed her eyes closed and the memory of that day merged with the image of Paul. Her eyes flashed open again. She examined the wall. If she saw any compassion in Lincoln's eyes it would wreck her.

"It took me only a second to realise what he'd been planning to do."

Lincoln swore and took a couple of steps towards her but she backed away, hitting the kitchen bench behind her. "Don't." She put a hand out to stop him, cringing at the hurt in his eyes. "I just can't." Can't let him get too close. She'd break down and she wouldn't be that vulnerable with anyone except the musketeers. To everyone else it would be ammunition.

"What happened?"

She swallowed again. "He was upset, promised to get help, said the farm was destroying him. He begged me not to tell anyone. He was high on something. I don't know if the drugs or the depression had come first."

"So that's when they moved to the city?"

She nodded. That's when they'd abandoned her.

"I'm so sorry, Kit." He frowned. "But why didn't he sell the farm, why leave it to you when it almost killed him?"

He wouldn't like this. She shrugged. "I begged him to. Told him I would tell the town about his addiction if he didn't leave me on the farm." She'd spent her whole life learning how to farm, her sole goal was to one day take it over from her father. All of her worth was wrapped up in this land. Her father hadn't hesitated to leave her behind. "After I turned eighteen, I got a mortgage and paid him back."

Lincoln placed his hands on the back of a chair. "I always wondered why you needed me to stay out here instead of you boarding at the ag school."

She sipped her tea but her mouth was still dry, her insides raw, and she wanted to curl into a ball and cry herself to sleep. The memory of her father in addition to Paul's death was too much. "Now I've answered your question, you should go."

"Kit…"

She waited for him to say something, anything, but he stood there looking at her. She couldn't read his expression. "I'm tired, Lincoln. It's been a shit couple of days." Her voice broke on the last few words. She gritted her teeth and moved past him, but he caught hold of her, turned her towards him and hugged her, her face buried against his chest.

He smelled so damned good and his arms were strong, warm, comforting.

Every inch of her being wanted to hug him back, but if she did that, she would lose herself and she couldn't, wouldn't. She shoved him hard and he stumbled back, his eyes wide, hurt.

Protect yourself. "Don't pretend you care, Lincoln."

"I do."

Not enough. "You left the second I was eighteen."

Disbelief flashed on to his face and anger sparked. "You kicked me out."

Trust him to use that as an excuse. "I gave you an easy out and you took it so fast it made me dizzy." She blinked furiously, refusing to let any tears form. "You were so freaked out, so damn disgusted you couldn't wait to leave me." She swallowed past the lump in her throat and embraced the anger instead. It was her friend. It helped her through all the hard times.

She'd opened her heart to him, had told him how she felt, and he'd squashed her flat.

He gaped like a wall-mounted fish.

"Go back to pretending to care in public, Lincoln. You don't need to fake it when we're alone." She couldn't stand here and wait for him to say something. He was lost for words, didn't have a lie prepared to feed her. She brushed past him and was almost at the hallway when he spoke.

"You were my goddamn ward." The anger in his voice made her flinch and she turned.

He stalked towards her, eyes blazing. She'd never seen him so angry. "I was responsible for your wellbeing. How would it have appeared if I'd given in to my desires?" He didn't wait for a response. "I would have been called a paedophile, both of our reputations would have been ruined and I would have lost my job."

It was her turn to gape. "I was eighteen."

"Just." He bit out. "You'd *literally* just turned eighteen, but that didn't matter. People would have speculated about how long our affair had been going on, how badly I had corrupted you."

"Who cares about what people thought?"

"Me! One of us had to consider the full scenario, had to care about your best interests, because you sure as hell didn't."

How dare he switch this around and make it her fault? "Don't play the knight protector now, Lincoln. You didn't care about me. You told your date I was practically your sister."

He swore. "I lied. I cared too damn much."

Her heart leapt but then he continued.

"But you conned me good. I gave you a couple of days to cool down and when I came to explain, I found you with your tongue down that holiday worker's throat. That showed me how much you really cared." Deep hurt welled in his eyes.

She gasped, the outrage leaving her almost speechless. "You seriously thought I was that fickle?" She wanted to be sick. "That guy kissed *me*. You obviously didn't stick around for long enough to see me push him away, fire his sorry arse and throw him off my property." Hurt and rage fought for dominance. She'd been so damn scared and Lincoln had done nothing to help her.

"You're such an arsehole." The crack in her heart became a canyon. Her throat burned with unshed tears, but she wouldn't give him the satisfaction. "Go to hell, Lincoln."

She strode back down the hallway, and this time she locked her bedroom door behind her.

He'd been wrong about the holiday worker.

The anger and hurt roaring around Lincoln's head let that one realisation filter through to his brain. How could he have got it so wrong?

But he'd been hurting too, trying desperately to figure out how to make it work. He'd been willing to compromise his job for her and then to see her like that...

She'd been right to call him an arsehole.

It hurt to breathe. Had they both been suffering for the past eight years for nothing, but a stupid misunderstanding?

Young, foolish and proud were his only excuses.

But no, he remembered the night at the pub, remembered Kit walking in while he'd faked interest in whatever his date said. Kit had captured his attention so completely that his date had been jealous and he'd had to say something. Afterwards he'd watched Kit dance and grind and then go home with a guy. She hadn't been suffering from a broken heart like him.

But possibly she'd been faking it too.

The slam of her bedroom door jolted him out of his disbelief. His steps drew him closer to her room, his brain trying to catch up.

He tried the door handle, but it didn't twist. Locked.

He knocked. "Kit, let me in. We need to talk."

Silence.

"Please, Kit." He didn't want to tell her his side of the story through a door. He wanted to see her reaction, find out if they possibly had a future.

Nothing.

The lock on the door was simple, more meant for privacy than security. It had never really worked properly. When he'd been living here, he'd learnt how to jiggle it to unlock it on the couple of times Kit had got into a snit and refused to talk to him. After she'd realised he wouldn't let her lock herself away, she'd taken to talking to him — well yelling really — instead of running away. He hoped she'd be as understanding still. He needed to have his say.

A quick jiggle had the lock snicking open. Kit lay face down on her bed, her head buried in her pillow, her body shaking.

He froze. Kit's muffled sobs were audible now he was inside the room. In two steps he was at her bed and placed a hand on her back.

She jolted, lunging away from him off the bed, her eyes wide, tears still pouring down her red face. "The door was locked." He'd never seen her so miserable.

He nodded. "It doesn't work very well, remember?"

She stared at him.

He wasn't doing this right. He stood, moved around the bed and she backed up.

Great. Now she didn't want to be anywhere near him. "Kit Kat, we need to talk."

"Don't call me that." Fire sparked in her eyes.

He preferred the anger to her distress. "I'm so very sorry — for all the misunderstanding, for the hurt, for not believing in you." He stepped forward and her eyes narrowed, but she didn't back away. He needed to tell her everything, not hold back. If there was a chance they could fix this, he had to take it. "I was so happy living with you. We had fun together and you were one of my best friends."

She flinched.

"But then I realised I thought of you as more than a friend. I wanted to go to the movies with you without the other musketeers tagging along, I wanted to hold you and kiss you." He ran a hand through his hair. "It was torture."

"Glad the idea was so repulsive to you," she snapped, wiping the tears from her face.

His eyes widened. Why hadn't he realised her temper was a finely tuned defence mechanism? "At the time we had a guy out on parole who'd moved to the area, and we needed to monitor him," he continued. "He'd been jailed for three years for sex with a minor. At the time, he'd been twenty and she wasn't quite sixteen."

Awareness dawned on her face.

"Others at the station thought he was the worst scum, taking advantage of the girl when he'd clearly been much older than her. The court had agreed and he was jailed and put on the sex offenders' register for life." He'd been horrified when he'd heard the story, had waited for weeks until he'd had a chance to talk to the man alone. "The guy had been dating the girl for six months. He was in love with her, had been planning to marry her when she was old enough and she'd loved him too. It was her parents who charged him. They didn't approve."

"I was eighteen, Lincoln."

He nodded. "But people would have questioned whether anything had happened earlier and your parents might have accused me. Your father warned me not to take advantage of you. The jail time if the assault happened while under the care of the accused is up to fifteen years."

Her mouth dropped open.

"I couldn't risk my career or jail time, but I'd come up with a solution. I was going to move out, ask you to wait six months, perhaps a year, and then start dating. I figured we'd still see each other often enough around town and no one would care then." It might have been slightly optimistic to think there wouldn't be any rumours, but he'd wanted her so badly, had loved her. "When I saw you with the holiday worker, it devastated me. I'd been willing to risk my career and my freedom for you."

She bit her lip, took half a step forward. "All I saw was another rejection."

He had to put it all out there, time to risk it all. "Never." He closed the distance between them, pulled her into his arms. "It's only ever been you, Kit."

Chapter 8

Kit's heart stopped.

Every muscle, every atom in her body froze, and Lincoln's words echoed in her ears. With his arms around her waist, her breasts pressed up against his chest, breathing wasn't possible.

Had she fallen asleep? Was this a dream? She didn't want to speak in case it was. She had no words anyway.

"Kit?" Worry crossed his face and he pulled back.

No. She wasn't letting him go.

She flung her arms around his neck and yanked him closer. Her lips met his.

Finally.

His lips were soft, warm and he tasted like… Lincoln. She needed more, wanted more, she'd waited long enough. Her tongue teased him and he opened for her with a groan.

Lust shot straight to her core.

His hands roamed her body, igniting every nerve ending.

She needed this more than she needed air. She'd deal with the consequences in the morning.

Lincoln was here, he wanted her, she couldn't let him think, couldn't give him the chance to change his mind. Running her hands under his shirt, she longed to lick every warm inch of his skin. But she needed to expose it first. She shoved the fabric up and he obliged her, yanking the shirt off.

The light reflected off his tanned skin, defining the contours of his muscles.

God, he was beautiful.

More. She had to have more.

Pushing him back until his legs hit her bed, she gave another shove to send him down onto the mattress. She stripped off her tank top and then straddled him.

"Kit." The breathless way he said her name was a bow to her heart strings.

Kissing him again, she slid lower, tasting and sucking, loving the way he moaned. She unbuckled his belt, making swift work of his jeans button and fly.

He was hard and hot.

Before she could lower his pants, he grabbed her, hauling her up against his chest and then rolling her underneath him. "Not so fast. I've waited far too many years to rush now." No one had ever looked at her with such passion, such desire, such need. It was terrifying.

She closed her eyes and his lips were on hers, taking his own sweet time to taste, lick, nip and suck. She ached and arched up, rubbing herself against him.

"All in good time, my Kit." He nibbled her neck and she willed her heart to be strong, to not give in to the sensual way he was loving her body.

His kisses followed their own path to her breasts, and he sucked gently on one nipple.

Kit threw her head back as sensations shot through her like lightning.

"Your breasts are so perfect. The size, the shape, the taste." He dipped his head to taste again as his thumb teased the other nipple.

Holy sexballs. She was going to come with him simply touching her breasts. What was he doing to her? Heat pooled between her legs and she groaned. "Lincoln, hurry up already." She reached between them, trying to touch him, but he brushed her hand away, catching it in his and pinning it up above her head.

"No." His chuckle wove its way around her heart and she tried to stop it from knotting.

She was at his mercy, both hands now held in place above her head with one of his, while the other explored her body, stroking up and down, dipping close to her crotch, but never close enough.

It was sensuous torture. She wanted it to stop and she never wanted it to end.

"Please, Lincoln." She pressed her lips together.

His gaze met hers, dark and intense, and something flickered in it. "As you wish."

In a flash, he dragged her boxer shorts down her legs and his lips and tongue met her core. She bucked, unable to stop herself and he held her in place while he again took his time tasting her, teasing her. She was definitely going to come. "Lincoln, stop."

He glanced at her, a small smile on his lips. "Come for me, Kit." His eyes still on hers, his tongue flicked over her clitoris and she was done. She yelled as the orgasm overpowered her, flooding her with pleasure, her body shaking.

On and on it went as he tasted her, drawing every bit of pleasure from her until she was limp and sated.

Slowly reality returned to her. She lay on her bed, satisfied and *Lincoln* knelt above her still half clothed. She pinched herself. "Ow."

He chuckled. "It's not a dream."

She wasn't so sure. This had always been her dream. She shifted up on to her elbow. "Lincoln, I..." What the hell was she supposed to say?

His grin sent her pulse racing. "You're a goddess when you come." His eyes intense, he ran his tongue over his top lip. "I want to be inside you the next time it happens." He stripped off his jeans and stood before her, a perfect specimen of man. Her groin throbbed. She still wanted him.

He lowered himself on to the bed, kissing her again, long, slow, drugging kisses.

What was he doing to her? Was he trying to melt all her resistance?

Her hands slid along his back, pulling him closer. She needed hot, fast sex. She opened her legs, encircling his waist and tempting him further.

Lincoln groaned. "Please tell me you have a condom."

Right. Condoms. It hadn't occurred to her, and she *always* made certain she was protected. He short-circuited her brain cells. "Bathroom."

He swore and rolled out of bed, disappearing briefly before returning with the box. He joined her on the bed and his hands shook as he unwrapped the foil packet.

Concern leapt to her. "Are you OK?"

He let out a shaky laugh. "Absolutely. I've waited so long for this. I don't want to mess it up."

His confession blasted away all of her barriers. She would do anything to make him hers for eternity.

As he slid the condom on, and then covered her body again, he kissed her sweetly. "Ready?"

She lifted her hips in answer and he slid into her, his eyes locked on hers. She couldn't prevent the tears from welling as they joined. Everything in this moment was right.

Together they moved and the sensation was exquisite, the way he kissed her and caressed her and whispered in her ear. And this time when she came, he did too.

An arm snaked around Kit's waist, pulling her closer and out of her slumber. Her eyes flashed open. Who the hell was in bed with her? She inhaled deeply and her fear receded.

Lincoln.

She raised her head to check the time on the luminous clock next to her bed. Five minutes until she had to get up. She should switch the alarm off before it woke Lincoln, leave so things weren't awkward. After the passion last night, she had no clue what to say to him and she couldn't bear to see regret on his face this morning.

But it was so warm, so comforting lying in his arms.

She should rebuild the walls he'd decimated, she might need protection from the emotional onslaught to come. She always paid a heavy price when her dreams came true.

"I can hear you thinking." Lincoln's breath brushed her ear and then he kissed her neck.

Damn. So much for sneaking out before he woke. "I was running over what I need to do today."

He reached over her and flicked on the bedside lamp.

She squinted at the glare, didn't meet his gaze.

"You were thinking of running."

Defence. Always defence. "Not everything revolves around what we did last night."

His half-smile was amused. "I don't know why I didn't see it before."

"What?" She shifted away from him.

"The way you attack before anyone has a chance to attack you."

No. He wasn't supposed to see the truth. She flung back the sheets and stood, quickly dressing for the day.

"I'm not going to attack you, Kit Kat. I don't regret last night." He was right behind her, naked, and as she slipped on her jeans, he stepped forward, hugging her from behind.

She closed her eyes. Could she really trust this was true, that there would be no horrible unexpected outcome because of their relationship?

"Open your eyes, Kit."

She did and her gaze caught his in the mirror. Damn it.

"I meant what I said last night. I'm not going to let you go."

She had no words. She could barely breathe.

Uncertainty flickered in his eyes. "Unless you want me to."

This was her chance to end it, to stop it going so far. But she couldn't. It was already too late. Her heart was his. She swallowed hard. "Don't let me go," she whispered.

Gently he turned her around and his mouth was on hers, soft, soothing, loving. "I won't."

She stared at him for a long moment until her alarm squawked loud and harsh. She jumped and Lincoln swore.

A timely reprieve.

"I can't believe you still use that awful alarm." He pulled on his shirt as she switched it off.

"It gets me up in the morning." Now he wasn't touching her, she could assess what was happening.

"I can think of nicer ways to wake up."

So could she. At the top of the list was waking up the way she had this morning, in Lincoln's arms. "You don't need to get up yet."

"I do if I want to spend time with you before work." He buttoned his jeans and held out his hand. "Breakfast?"

Why did he have to be so damn perfect? It made it so difficult to be careful. She forced a smile. "As long as you're cooking."

"Of course."

It was easy to fall into the trap of domesticity with him. He cooked bacon and eggs while she fed the dogs and made the coffee, just as they'd done many a morning back when they'd lived together. Though this time when he placed her plate on the table, it came with a deep, mind-numbing kiss.

She could get used to this. "What have you got on today?"

He hesitated. "We should get the autopsy report."

Reality shoved its head into the kitchen and shattered the bliss. "It will confirm whether it was murder or suicide?"

He nodded. "Are you going to the funeral tomorrow?"

"Yes, with the musketeers."

"Good. I'm not sure I'll make it, but I'll try. I want to be there for you."

Her heart twinged. She wasn't used to having a man to rely on. Not even Jamie had stuck around. "I'd like that."

He sipped his coffee. "Have you finished weighing the calves?"

"Yeah and Elijah officially starts today. He said he's a bit rusty on some stuff but he'll catch up quickly, and he's going to do the evening milking from now on." Which meant she might actually get some of her life back.

"That's great."

She checked the time. "I'd better get going."

"Not so fast." Lincoln stood and kissed her. His lips were addictive. One kiss wasn't enough. Neither were a hundred.

"Can I come over tonight?" he asked.

Things were moving fast, a little out of control. She wanted to press pause, have time to assess, but she yearned to see him. She nodded.

"I'll call if I'm going to be later than six."

"All right." She whistled to her dogs and left the house.

Could her heart handle Lincoln Zanetti?

Or would she lose everything again?

The back door closed behind Kit and Lincoln sighed. It broke his heart to see Kit so uncertain. Had all her toughness been an act?

Maybe this was her true self.

He had to prove to her that he wouldn't leave her. Show her that now he had her, he wasn't letting her go.

Last night had been beyond his wildest dreams. His perfect fantasy — Kit in his arms, kissing her, loving her, exploring her body and then having her curled up next to him as he slept.

How had he read the situation so wrong when he was younger? He'd left her with the holiday worker, rather than protecting her against his unwanted advances.

She'd been right to be furious with him.

He was a fool.

It was lucky Kit could protect herself.

Lincoln washed the dishes and then made the bed and moved her dirty clothes to the laundry. Kit had taught him to be tidy. One of them had to be, because he'd discovered soon after moving in with her that he hated to live in a dirty, messy house. So he'd kept it tidy and once a week, the pair of them had cleaned, music blasting from the speakers.

She'd danced around the house, always finding the fun. He smiled.

On his way out of the house, he snagged the spare key from the pantry. Kit might not have a problem leaving the house unlocked during the day, but he did. Someone was still searching for something. And he wasn't leaving Kit unprotected anymore.

The autopsy report arrived in his inbox mid-morning. The cause of death was the bullet as suspected and it matched Kit's gun, but the shot was not self-inflicted. Paul *had* been murdered. Lincoln sat back, blew out a breath. It wasn't a surprise, but he still hadn't figured out a motive and didn't know whether Kit was in danger.

He had to do a better job protecting her than he had the other musketeers.

Sue stuck her head into the office. "Just got a call from Paul's parents. They went around to his house and it's been broken into. Should I advise Albany?"

If she did, they'd be instructed to leave it for the investigative team. "We'll call them after we've checked it out." The police had been to Paul's place after he'd been killed, so the break-in must have happened over the weekend.

She grinned. "Sounds good."

Paul's parents were waiting outside the miller-style cottage when Lincoln and Sue arrived, Paul's mother in tears. Lincoln braced himself as he walked over to them. "Can you tell me what happened?"

"We came over to get a few things for the funeral and the place was a mess," Mr Maddock said. "At first I thought Paul hadn't cleaned in a while, but then I noticed the drawers were all empty and stuff had been dumped everywhere."

Someone had searched the place. "How did you get in?"

"We have a front door key."

"Did you touch anything?" Sue asked.

"The door, and Margaret picked up a few things before we realised it wasn't his mess."

Margaret sniffed. "Just a couple of DVDs."

He made a note. "When were you last here?"

"He had us over for dinner a couple of weeks ago. We've been putting off coming since he died." Her eyes filled with tears.

Lincoln gave a sympathetic smile. "I understand. Sue and I will take a look inside."

"Can we get the things we came for?" Mr Maddock asked.

He shook his head. "We need to investigate first. Why don't you write me a list of what you want?"

He walked in and gave a low whistle. In the living room DVDs had been thrown off the shelves, drawers had been emptied and the television had been smashed.

"Someone was searching for something," Sue said.

"And getting frustrated." As he scanned the room, he noted a drone on the coffee table and two more of different sizes, broken on the floor. Paul had loved his drones and Lincoln had had to stop him a few times from using them in public areas.

He walked through the house. No room had been untouched. Cupboards had been emptied and mattresses had been ripped off the beds.

"They were thorough."

"The question is, did they find what they were looking for?" Lincoln doubted Paul's parents would have any clue if anything was missing but he'd ask. It was going to take some time to process the whole place. "I'll give Albany a call."

Elijah was a saint.

Kit wanted to nominate him and make his sainthood official. He'd arrived on time, and ready to work. She'd shared with him her plan for the week and he'd suggested a couple of good adjustments. And since Paul's funeral was early the next morning, he'd offered to do both milking sessions.

He'd taken next to no time fixing the irrigation in the pasture and was seeding as she worked on her schedule for artificially inseminating the cows.

She'd brought her laptop over from the house to work in her office in the dairy. Most of the paperwork had been refiled, but traces of fingerprint dust were still visible, and the gun cabinet right behind her reminded her of what had happened. She didn't want her gun back.

Ugh.

A spider crawled up the office wall and she blinked, bringing her attention back to her screen. She was the one slacking off today.

Waking up this morning wrapped in Lincoln's arms had been a dream come true.

The more she thought about it, the more certain she was something would go wrong. It always did. Not knowing what made her edgy.

She didn't know how to do relationships. The sudden change was way too quick, way too confusing. She was likely to stuff it up. Maybe she should call one of her friends. They'd know what to do. Her phone rang and relieved with the interruption, she answered.

"Hey, Kit Kat. I wanted to confirm you're still interested in showing the kids a different dairy set up."

She smiled at Jamie's voice. "Why are you calling? An English teacher shouldn't be organising it."

"I told them I had a contact," he replied. "Plus I wanted to ask how it went with Lincoln last night."

Her whole body froze. "What do you mean?"

"Lincoln asked me about your dad and I told him to go and ask you. Did he pike out?" Jamie growled.

She cleared her throat. "No, he came over. I told him about it."

"Finding Paul must have been awful."

"I'm coping." The quicker she got him off the phone, the better. "When do you want to do the field trip?"

"Next month."

Things should have settled down by then. "All right. Tell whoever's organising the visit to call me. I'm gearing up to inseminate the cows, and it will be calving season. Elijah will probably have finished the seeding by then."

"Elijah Johnson?"

Was that interest in his tone? "Yeah. I mentioned him last night."

"I didn't get a chance to confirm."

"And?" There was more to the story.

"He's cute."

Wow. That was big news. Jamie had never been totally comfortable coming out as bi-sexual before he'd left for university. He'd had boyfriends and girlfriends in the city though. "Will you ask him out?"

"I'm not sure yet."

"I can mention you to Elijah if you want, gauge his reaction."

Jamie groaned. "Don't you dare. We're not in fifth grade anymore. I'll sort it out in my own time." He paused. "Speaking of which, what happened between you and Linc? Things were kind of tense last night."

Shit. What could she say? "You know how protective he gets. It annoyed me."

"Someone shot at you, Kit. I think he has a right."

"We worked it out." Sort of. Maybe.

"Good. I don't like it when my two favourite people are fighting."

How would he feel about his two favourite people sleeping together? She wasn't entirely certain. "I've got to go."

"All right. Want me to give you a lift to Hannah's tomorrow?"

They were going to the funeral together. "That would be great. I'll see you then."

How would Jamie and the musketeers react seeing her and Lincoln together? If he made it to the funeral, it would be their first outing as a couple.

Part of her wanted to stake her claim, show people he was hers now, but the other part cringed away from making it public knowledge. If no one knew, then maybe there'd be no price to pay.

She rolled her shoulders to dislodge the tension.

Maybe this time things would be different.

Chapter 9

Kit walked into her kitchen that evening and stopped short. No dishes in the sink, no crumbs on the table, everything immaculate.

Lincoln must have cleaned before he left, as he did when they'd lived together.

In one way it felt so familiar, and yet in another it was so incredibly jarring. This wasn't what her kitchen was normally like. She wouldn't call herself a slob, but at five-thirty in the morning, the last thing she cared about was the state of her kitchen. She wandered through the house, scanning for other changes.

Her bed was neatly made, the floor clear of any clothing. She frowned. Maybe the cost of the relationship would be a tidy house. She could handle that.

Roberts bumped her leg as he rubbed against her. She ran her hand through his wiry fur, and calm settled over her. She shouldn't expect something bad to happen.

Montoya barked from down the corridor, his head turned towards her to see if she was following. They wanted their dinner.

She filled the dog bowls. Lincoln was due at any minute — at least he hadn't called to say he'd be late, or wasn't coming. He hadn't mentioned dinner either. Should she prepare something? What if he brought something with him?

The kitchen was too small a space to pace in. She headed into the living room, every muscle in her body tense. This was so stupid. Just because she'd never had men over to her place didn't mean she had to stress about it. This was Lincoln. Yet too much was unknown, she had no control, there were too many ways she could get it wrong.

All of which was too scary.

What if when he arrived they were back to the awkwardness of days gone by? What if she said the wrong thing and Lincoln walked out?

And how pathetic was she that she let a man tie her up in so many knots?

She huffed. No point second-guessing. She'd prepare dinner. If Lincoln arrived and was hungry, she'd share, if he brought something, he could eat it himself.

Pleased with the decision, she returned to the kitchen to throw together a simple pasta. After watching Mrs Z cook for so many years, pasta was always her go-to meal for something quick and easy.

She switched on the stereo so she wouldn't strain her ears listening for Lincoln's car on the drive and sang along to her favourite rock songs. When he did arrive, he'd find her calm, in control, not panicked at all.

She was an expert at faking it around him.

Kit almost didn't hear the tap on her back door, but as she lowered the volume, Lincoln called, "Can I come in?"

Nerves flooded her body like a cattle stampede. She fought them back and yelled, "Yeah." She stirred the pan one last time, and turned to find Lincoln leaning against the kitchen doorframe.

Her heart raced.

He'd changed out of his police uniform and the low-slung jeans hugged his hips, while the burgundy T-shirt clung to his muscled chest. Afraid she would drool, she flashed him a smile. "Hi."

She brushed back the loose hair falling from her ponytail and glanced at the dirt on her navy blue tank top. She should have showered before he arrived.

He brought a hand out from behind his back and stepped forward, waving something red in his hand. "I bought you a treat."

Her breath caught in her throat. A Kit Kat. She hadn't been able to eat the one Elijah had given her the other day.

"Thank you." Her feet were rooted to the spot; she was too scared to step forward, unable to step away.

He slid the chocolate onto the table and walked over to her. "Is everything all right?"

She hoped so. She nodded, running her hands up his chest until they clasped behind his neck, and inhaled his masculine scent. The heat from his chest warmed her, and his strong hands tugged her closer. "How was your day?" She could get lost in his eyes, the colour of rich, dark roast coffee.

"Better now I'm here." Slowly, he dipped his head and his lips met hers. The gentle, sweet kiss set her pulse throbbing a slow, aching beat. He pulled away. "How was yours?"

It took a second for her mind to surface. "Fine." She needed to do better than that. She couldn't let him beguile her, had to keep her wits about her. She stepped back and switched the stove off. "Elijah's been really great." Draining the pasta, she asked, "Are you hungry?"

"Yeah."

When she turned around, he was getting bowls out of the cupboard.

She could easily get used to him being here.

Quickly she dished up the pasta and sauce while he poured two glasses of red wine.

Emotional quicksand had her in its grips, but the more she struggled, the deeper she'd sink. She needed to keep things light, friendly, take it one step at a time. "Elijah fixed the broken reticulation, and he's been seeding. I left him milking the cows, but he should be finished by now."

"That's great. He was a nice kid."

She raised her eyebrows. "You remember him?"

"There weren't many people you brought out to the farm, so yes, I remember him. If you hadn't told me he was gay, I might have been jealous."

She'd had no idea. "He's a much happier person than he was back then. Getting out of Blackbridge was good for him." She placed both bowls on the table and sat.

"So why did he come back?"

"He was ready to come home." And she was glad he had. Elijah had always held a special spot in her heart. But she didn't want to talk about him, she wanted to hear about Lincoln's day. It wasn't something he'd shared with her when they'd been younger. "You got the autopsy report?"

He frowned. "It's hardly dinner conversation."

She put down her fork. "Don't be daft."

His smile was quick, almost unwilling. "It confirmed Paul was murdered." He paused, debating with himself.

"What else?"

"Nothing."

She leaned back in her chair. He wasn't telling her something. Weren't couples supposed to share?

Lincoln sipped his wine. "Paul never told you what was bothering him, did he?"

She shook her head. "He barely made small talk in the last couple of months. He'd come in, get his tasks for the day and leave."

"That's odd for him."

"I know. He was so gutted by Gordon's death. His cousin died from an overdose about six months earlier, and then Gordon died because he'd been drugged. I thought I'd give him some time to process."

"Could he have been involved in the drug ring?"

She hesitated. "He wasn't a choir boy, but I don't think so. He was outspoken against drugs after his cousin died." Her appetite left her as Paul's face flashed into her mind. She pushed her bowl away and took a long gulp of her wine, the fruity alcohol doing nothing to wash away the bad taste in her mouth.

"I told you it wasn't dinner conversation." Lincoln gathered both their bowls and took them to the sink. He put the kettle on and scraped the remains of their dinner into the compost bucket.

"You're right, but I want to hear about your day."

"How about next time we talk about it after we eat?" he suggested. "Over a cuppa."

"All right." She cleared the rest of the table and filled the sink with soapy water.

When the dishes were done, they took their tea and the Kit Kat into the living room. Kit split the four chocolate-wafer bars apart and handed him two.

"I bought it for you."

"We always share."

He looked at her for a long moment before he said, "I wasn't sure you'd remember."

Was he kidding? "I remember everything about you living here."

"Really? What about the day you went shopping with the musketeers and brought home a tiny bikini that you had to show me?"

She smiled and sipped her tea. "I bought it to make you notice me."

He raised his eyebrow. "It worked. I almost swallowed my tongue. I couldn't pretend you were Jamie's little friend anymore."

She hadn't had a clue. All he'd said was, "Nice" and then continued watching television. It had been a kick to the ego. "Remind me not to play poker with you."

He laughed.

While they were talking about their past, she wanted to know more. "I thought I was a burden to you."

"Some days you were."

Her mouth dropped open and he quickly added, "Not in a bad way, just an… uncomfortable way. I genuinely enjoyed living with you, Kit. It was easy. At times I forgot I was supposed to be the responsible adult." He drank his tea. "But when you went from Jamie's friend to a girl I wanted to date, it made life hard. I second-guessed everything we did together to ensure it couldn't be considered inappropriate."

That decency again. She couldn't be angry about his rejection. She bit into the Kit Kat's chocolate wafer goodness. She'd missed this, just like she'd missed Lincoln.

Could this be their future — lovers and friends, not people with an uncomfortable history? "I'm sorry I made it difficult for you."

"I'm sorry I didn't protect you from the holiday worker."

She put her mug on the coffee table and then placed his there too. No more regret. She wanted to move on, move forward. For however long this lasted, she would make the most of it. Shuffling across, she straddled Lincoln and he grabbed her butt, pulling her closer. "There's one way you can make it up to me."

His grin was instant. "Anything."

Then his mouth met hers and Kit forgot about everything but the now.

Detective Khan called on Tuesday morning as Lincoln was about to leave the station.

"We want two of your team at the funeral," he said.

Lincoln frowned. "Why?" The Albany station was closer to the crematorium.

"We want to show the town the police are working on the case. You're to identify anyone you don't recognise or who shouldn't be there."

Lincoln rolled his eyes. "You want me to wear my uniform?"

"Of course."

They would be clearly visible. He hung up and called out, "Adam, you're coming to Paul's funeral with me." Ryan and Sue were tied up with another matter.

Adam glanced up from his desk. "Sure. Why?"

"Albany want us to watch the mourners, see if we see anything suspicious."

They walked out to the police car.

"Won't that be kind of obvious?"

"Yeah. Officially we're there to pay our condolences to the family."

When he parked at the Albany crematorium, he noticed Detectives Bosch and Khan among the people dressed in black milling about.

Didn't they trust him to do his job?

Lincoln caught Detective Bosch's eye and she shook her head slightly. Right, so he wasn't to acknowledge them. This was stupid.

"What are we looking for?" Adam asked.

"Take a note of everyone you recognise. Anyone seem out of place?"

They needed a suspect because right now they had no one. All they had was a boot print at the scene. Everyone they'd interviewed had been upset about Paul's death, had said how likeable he was. The only person who'd had anything negative to say was Kit. And while the detectives hadn't taken her off the list, he had.

Shit. If the detectives saw him kiss Kit, he'd be in trouble. He had to warn her. He scanned the mourners and Hannah's voice behind him said, "Hi, Lincoln."

He turned to find the musketeers.

Kit wore a black pant suit, her hair plaited, but the uncertainty on her face caught his attention.

Hadn't she told the musketeers about them?

Hannah hugged him, followed by Mai. As Fleur came in for her hug, he glanced over her shoulder to where the detectives watched him, speculation on their faces.

Damn.

He drew Kit in for a hug, keeping his touch gentle and PG-rated. She tilted her head to kiss his mouth and he turned his cheek at the last moment, hating to do so. "Not here," he murmured.

Hurt flashed in her eyes and then she spun around and walked away, her back stiff.

Damn it. He took two steps after her, but the hearse arrived and people moved into his way. The other musketeers hurried after her and Jamie said, "What have you done now?"

He shook his head and his brother followed his friends.

He'd messed up. A deep dread lodged in his stomach. He should have texted or called her to explain the situation. Now she thought he was embarrassed about their relationship.

Kit was fragile enough already. What was this going to do?

"What's going on?" Adam asked.

He wasn't putting Adam in the awkward position of having to report him for a conflict of interest. "Don't worry about it." He nodded to the procession. "We'll stay at the back."

By the time they got into the small chapel it was standing room only. Kit sat with her friends in one of the last rows of pews on the opposite side of the room. Her gaze focused on the front and she dabbed at her eyes. Crap. Had he made her cry? His chest squeezed, but he couldn't approach her. People were seated and the celebrant approached the lectern.

"Are they Paul's parents up front?" Adam murmured.

"Yeah." He scanned the crowd. Paul's friends sat behind the

family. Lincoln recognised a few guys he played basketball with and Foley and his farmhand, Ian. Gladys sat next to her grandson, who hopefully had driven today, Mr Corson was without his dog for a change, and Shirley Jameson sat with Hannah's grandparents. Also in the crowd was Mai's brother, Kim, and a few of his friends. No one out of the ordinary.

At the front, a slideshow played photos of Paul, and his brother gave the eulogy. Some drone footage showed the beautiful southern coastline.

Lincoln straightened. The memory cards had been missing from the drones at Paul's place and Paul's laptop had been stolen. Where had the footage come from?

He made a note to ask Paul's parents later.

As people filed out of the chapel, Lincoln hung back with Adam, unwilling to push through people to get to Kit. She wouldn't thank him for making a scene.

"This is the man who arrested me." Gladys's voice was loud and shrill. A few people turned back, frowning.

Lincoln smothered a groan and faced the older woman. "How are you today, Gladys?"

"Upset. Why haven't you caught the person who did this? You should be investigating real crimes rather than arresting old ladies who want to buy milk."

"We're doing everything we can to catch the culprit." Lincoln glanced at Gladys's grandson who he'd gone to school with. "Did you drive today?"

He nodded, an apologetic expression on his face.

"It's been almost a week. You should have him locked up by now."

Gladys's grandson took her arm. "They're working on it, Granny. Let's give our condolences to the family."

She nodded and let herself be led away.

The room was nearly empty, but outside people gathered in a small courtyard. Kit hugged Hannah, but when he caught her eye, she turned away.

He needed to fix this fast, but he couldn't be seen talking with her for longer than anyone else. The detectives would be able to read Kit's body language.

"Did you notice anything?" Adam asked as they walked

outside.

He couldn't talk to Kit with Adam by his side. Guilt lodged in Lincoln's stomach. He was obliged to divulge any relationship he had with suspects, should remove himself from the investigation. By keeping his relationship with Kit a secret, he wasn't treading a fine line, he'd scribbled it out. But the alternative was not being involved, not being able to protect Kit to his full ability. And that wasn't an option. He needed to prove Kit was innocent as soon as possible. "I want to know where they got the drone footage from." Paul's parents were surrounded by people and now wasn't the best time to ask.

"Why?"

"The drones we found at Paul's place were missing their memory cards. If the footage was Paul's they might have access to more."

Adam winced. "Right. I missed that."

Lincoln turned his attention to his constable. "You haven't been involved in the case."

"Yeah, but I knew about the drones."

"Don't sweat it."

Kit was speaking to Paul's parents, the musketeers by her side. His phone rang, loud and intrusive and people looked his way.

He fumbled to get it out of his pocket. Ryan. Something was wrong. "What is it?"

"Elijah's been shot," Ryan said. "An ambulance is on its way and we're en route. Sounds like he caught someone searching Kit's house."

Lincoln's gut clenched. "How bad is it?"

"He managed to call for help and he's lucid."

Good. "Where do you need me?"

"We've got it covered. Can you tell Kit? They'll take him to Albany hospital."

"Yeah." The detectives were already heading for their car. "Keep me up to date."

"Will do."

Lincoln hung up. Kit was now over talking with Foley and Ian. Foley hugged her awkwardly. He wasn't a man in touch with his emotions.

"This way," Lincoln said to Adam. He strode over, his body

tense. Someone was desperate to find whatever Paul had hidden.

"Kit, can I have a word?"

She didn't look at him. "Not now, Lincoln."

He gritted his teeth. He couldn't say anything in front of Foley. The news would be all over Blackbridge by the time he got back. "It's about the farm."

"Can it wait?"

"No, it's urgent."

Fleur stepped over. "What's wrong, Lincoln?"

That made Kit turn around.

"Excuse us for a minute, Foley." He drew her away from her neighbour.

She snatched her arm back. "What is it?"

She was good and mad. He had to explain as soon as possible. He kept his voice low. "Elijah's been shot. He'll be taken to Albany hospital."

"What?" Kit's face drained of blood and she swayed.

Fleur wrapped her arm around Kit's waist.

"He caught someone at your house. I don't have all the details — there's an ambulance on the way. I'll take you to the hospital if you want."

"I need to call Will," Fleur said.

Of course. Fleur's partner would want to know his roommate had been injured.

"Get Hannah." Kit was already heading towards the car park.

"My car's faster."

She swore and changed direction, heading for the police car.

"We'll meet you there," Fleur called.

It was a tense and silent ride to the hospital. He pulled into the emergency department and Kit jumped out before he'd switched off the engine. "Park the car," he said to Adam and hurried after her.

"Elijah Johnson, gunshot wound," Kit told the woman at the desk.

The woman glanced at Lincoln in his uniform. "Still en route."

Kit paced away and then swore. "I should call his parents."

"I'll see to it," Lincoln said.

"No, he's my employee, my friend." She dragged her phone out of her pocket and tapped the screen.

"Kit, about earlier—"

"Not now, Lincoln." She put her phone to her ear and paced away. "Mrs Johnson, this is Kit van Ross."

She shouldn't have to do that. He stepped closer as Adam hurried into the emergency room.

"Car's parked outside."

Damn. He'd missed his opportunity and the sirens were coming closer.

Kit hung up as the ambulance pulled in and doctors and nurses rushed to greet it. She stayed back, tugging on her ponytail.

He stepped closer to put his arm around her shoulders, but she shrugged him off.

He winced.

The stretcher was pulled out of the ambulance and Elijah was lying down, bandages on his arm, his eyes closed.

"Elijah!" Kit called, moving closer.

He opened his eyes, grinned at her. "Hey. Did you know that getting shot hurts like a mother-f'er?"

Relief swept through Lincoln. Elijah would be all right.

Kit sagged against him. "No, I didn't."

"I don't recommend it," Elijah continued.

"We'll keep you updated on his progress," the doctor said.

Lincoln gently pulled Kit out of the way as they rolled Elijah through a different set of external doors.

"He's going to be all right, isn't he?" Kit asked one of the nurses, a waver in her voice as she stepped away from him.

His heart jolted. He had to comfort her.

"Looks like he'll be fine," the nurse replied. "It's a flesh wound."

"I should call his parents back." She walked away from him as he reached for her.

"Do we need to stick around and interview him?" Adam asked.

Lincoln dropped his hand. The detectives would do it, but he didn't want to leave Kit here by herself. "I'll find out." He switched his radio back on.

At that moment, the musketeers and Jamie ran into the emergency room.

"How is he?" Jamie asked.

Lincoln frowned. Jamie sounded really worried. "He was smiling and talking when he arrived. He's been taken out the back to be examined."

Jamie sighed. "That's good, right?" He looked to Lincoln for reassurance.

"Yeah." He stepped away and radioed for information.

"Albany's taken over the investigation," the dispatcher said. "The van Ross place has been broken into and searched. We need you back in Blackbridge."

He scowled. He wanted to stay with Kit, explain the situation, make sure she was all right. But he had an obligation, he couldn't leave his team in the lurch. "All right."

After the musketeers finished hugging Kit, he pulled her aside. Adam was still within earshot. He had to be careful what he said. "I have to go. The person who shot Elijah also broke into your house. Officers are there investigating. Can you hang out with one of the musketeers in the meantime?"

She nodded.

"We'll talk tonight. I'll explain everything." He squeezed her arm, but she snatched it away. Ouch.

"I'll see you later." She moved back to her friends.

He sighed. He'd really made a mess of this. He had to fix this tonight.

Chapter 10

Kit's heart squeezed painfully in her chest as she returned to the musketeers. She'd known it was too good to be true.

Last night Lincoln had assured her he wanted to be there for her. Today he couldn't even bear for her to kiss him.

His rejection had completely blindsided her. What possible reason could he have?

"What did Lincoln do this time?" Jamie asked.

She couldn't tell him, hadn't told the musketeers anything about her and Lincoln, hadn't wanted to jinx it. Just as well. "Nothing."

An older couple hurried into the emergency room. They hadn't changed much since the last time she'd seen them at her high school graduation. "Elijah Johnson was brought here. We're his parents." They must have broken several speed limits to arrive so quickly.

The nurse nodded. "He's being seen by the doctors at the moment."

Kit braced herself and walked over. "Mr and Mrs Johnson? I'm Kit van Ross."

"What happened?" Mr Johnson asked.

"I'm not entirely sure. I was told he was shot by someone trespassing on the farm." She'd said he wouldn't be in any danger, had told him to call the police if he saw someone hanging around. What had gone wrong?

"What did the police say?" his father asked.

"They're investigating." She sounded like Lincoln now. "How long until we can see him?" she asked the nurse. She wasn't leaving the hospital until she was certain Elijah was all right.

"Depends on what damage has been done," she said.

"How about we get a coffee?" Fleur suggested, coming up behind Kit.

"I'd prefer to wait here," his mother said.

Kit didn't want to stay here with them. She wanted to keep busy, start thinking about what these bastards were after and avoid obsessing about Lincoln. "I'll be back later."

She followed the musketeers into the hospital cafe and ordered a coffee. When they were all sitting, Hannah asked, "Why was Elijah shot?"

"Do you think the trespasser who shot at you came back?" Jamie asked.

"What trespasser?" Hannah asked.

"You were shot at?" Mai stared at her.

Kit made a face. "Last week I surprised someone over at the sheds. He shot at me and took off."

"Why didn't you tell us?" Fleur asked.

She shrugged. "It wasn't a big deal. Lincoln believes Paul might have left something on the farm that the murderer is looking for."

"That *is* a big deal," Fleur said. "What could it be?"

"I've got no idea. He was barely at the sheds over the last few months."

"Let's begin with that." Mai got a notebook out of her bag. "When did he start getting unreliable?"

"When Gordon died."

"Gordon was killed because he'd been involved with the drug ring," Mai said. "Could Paul have known something about it? Could he have evidence on them?"

"Maybe." It made sense. "Perhaps Gordon gave him something before he died? Some kind of insurance policy?"

"Or maybe Paul took Gordon's place supplying drugs," Jamie suggested

Kit shook her head. "He was vocally against drugs — his cousin died remember?"

Fleur tapped her fingers on the table. "So it could be some evidence — photos or video or something?"

"Didn't Gordon and Paul both have drones?" Hannah asked.

Paul and his stupid drones. She'd had to confiscate the damn things on more than one occasion when he'd been slacking off. But she had to admit, it was cool seeing her land from the air.

"Maybe they filmed something they shouldn't have," Hannah said.

Kit sipped her coffee, excitement pooling in her stomach. "He loaded some footage onto my computer. I'll take a look at it." And tell the police to check Paul's house. She wanted this case solved, she wanted people to stop shooting up her property, she wanted to feel safe again.

She wanted to put this whole nightmare behind her.

Including Lincoln.

It was another hour before Kit saw Elijah. She waited until his parents had seen him and he was moved onto a ward before she went into his room with the musketeers.

He sat in bed, his face a little paler than normal, his arm wrapped in a bandage. He smiled when he saw her and guilt slapped her.

"I'm so sorry, Elijah."

"It's not your fault, Kit. You told me to call the police."

That didn't matter. Her farm was dangerous. "What did the doctors say?"

"It's not too bad, a clean shot, straight through." He grimaced. "I can't do any heavy lifting until the stitches come out, but it's really only a flesh wound."

Her shoulders relaxed. "Good. What happened?"

"I left my water bottle at the shed, so I drove back and saw a motorbike outside your house. I thought someone might be looking for you, so I went over and surprised a short weedy-looking guy coming out with a full backpack. I tried to stop him, he shot me and then took off."

"Did you recognise him?"

Elijah shook his head. "He was kind of creepy."

Her skin crawled and she got out her phone, swiping through

some photos. "Did he look like this?" She showed him the police sketch of the guy who'd threatened Mai a couple of months ago.

His eyes widened. "Yeah, that's him."

"Mai, can you call Lincoln and let him know Creepy Guy is still in town?" The idea of talking to Lincoln made her lungs constrict.

Mai nodded and got out her phone.

Kit swallowed back the pain and asked, "How long will you be in here?"

"Just overnight. I should be right to keep seeding."

He couldn't possibly want to go back to the farm. "Don't you want to quit?"

He laughed. "Hell no. Working with you is like my dream job."

Her heart twisted. And the cost of his dream job was being shot. She couldn't risk anything else happening to him. "Take the next week off. I don't want to see you."

"Kit, it's not your fault something weird is going on."

She ignored him. "You'll get sick pay." He hadn't earned any leave but she didn't care. She had to keep him safe.

"Don't be ridiculous." Elijah scowled at her.

The two detectives walked in and for once she was happy to see them. "Call me if you need anything and I'll see you next week."

Elijah glanced at Fleur. "Can you tell Will what happened?"

"Already have. He said he'd drop by this afternoon."

As Kit left the room, Detective Bosch pulled her aside. "We'll need to talk to you as well."

Kit nodded. "I'll be out at my farm." Finding out what Creepy Guy had stolen.

Hannah looped her arm around Kit's as she walked down the corridor. "How are you holding up?"

"I'm fine. I want to get home and track down the drone footage." She scowled. "Then I'm going to find the son-of-a-bitch and see him behind bars."

"Kit, things have escalated if he's shooting at innocent bystanders," Fleur said.

"Yeah." She didn't want to end up dead. They all piled into Hannah's four-wheel drive and her phone rang. Lincoln. She stared at the screen.

"Aren't you going to answer?" Jamie asked.

She hit the end call button. "I don't have the energy."

"Did you two have a fight?"

Kit stared out the window. "No." It wasn't a fight if he was too embarrassed to be seen with her.

"Are you sure?"

She glared at him. "Drop it, JJ."

"Yes, ma'am."

Hannah glanced at her in the rear-view mirror. "Do you need help on the farm?"

"Depends if the police are still there." If they were, she'd get the musketeers to help, but if they weren't, she'd send them home. She wasn't risking their lives as well.

"You might need a hand cleaning up the house at least," Mai said.

Right. "That would be great." Chances were good Creepy Guy had got whatever he came for.

Several police cars were parked outside the farmhouse as Hannah pulled up. "They must have called in Albany."

The officers weren't people Kit recognised, which meant Lincoln probably wasn't here. She sighed in relief.

One of the men blocked the front gate as Kit walked up to it. "Can I help you?"

She smiled. "I'm Kit van Ross. This is my house."

"Sergeant Dargatz." He shook her hand.

Kit glanced around. "Where are my dogs?" They always met the car. Her heart raced. Had they been shot?

"Sergeant Zanetti put them in the dairy. They were getting in the way."

She huffed out a sigh. "OK." They would be fine in there for now. "Can I see the damage?"

"We're still investigating. It's best if you don't go in yet."

Kit gritted her teeth. It wasn't his fault people were being shot on her land. "Fine. I'll be over at the sheds when you're done. Come and see me."

She turned to the musketeers. They all still wore their funeral clothes. Her shoulders slumped and she asked the cop, "Can I get a change of clothes?"

He shook his head. "'Fraid not."

Jamie squeezed her shoulder. "I've got clothes you can borrow, and Mum will have something to fit Mai."

She nodded. "Let's go. I've got a lot to do."

No matter what, the farm always carried on.

Kit wasn't answering his calls.

Lincoln shouldn't be surprised or hurt but he was both. Particularly since her house had been broken into and he might have been calling with news.

OK, so he'd been calling to see how Elijah was, and to explain, but he couldn't get through.

"Lincoln we've had a report of a break-in at Foley's farm," Sue called. "Thought you might like to respond."

Foley lived right next door to Kit's.

Had Harry Smith been after supplies? Elijah had said he'd been carrying a backpack, and if Harry was camping somewhere, he'd need to replenish his food.

Two break-ins on the same day was too much of a coincidence, even if people knew much of the town would be at Paul's funeral.

"Adam, let's go," Lincoln called.

Foley waited for them outside the brick and tile farmhouse. It had none of the charm of Kit's place, lacking any wrap-around verandah, and sweet-smelling honeysuckle. Foley's house looked much like any other house built in the nineties. He shook Lincoln's hand. "Thanks for coming out so quickly."

Lincoln nodded. "Tell us what happened."

"I got back from Paul's funeral and discovered the front door wide open. I went in, saw the office had been trashed and called you."

"Was there anyone on the farm this morning?"

"No. Ian came to the funeral with me. Paul was a good mate." He frowned. "Any closer to finding out who killed him?"

"We're working on it."

Adam shifted by his side. "What time did you arrive back?"

"About half an hour ago. We went to the wake, wanted to give our condolences to his family and see how Kit was. I didn't see her again after you spoke to her."

He'd forgotten Foley and Kit were close. "She had to leave."

"Her farmhand was shot," Adam added.

"Who — Elijah?"

Lincoln winced. No keeping it a secret now. "Yes. He's in hospital, but he's fine."

"Who shot him?"

"We're investigating," Lincoln said. "How about you show us inside?"

"Right. OK." He shook his head as if bringing himself back to the present and led them up the front path to the house. "I've always thought Blackbridge was a safe town, but lately it's all gone to hell."

Lincoln didn't comment.

The white-tiled hallway was cold with no pictures lining the walls, no personality whatsoever. Stepping into the lounge room, Lincoln blinked at the mismatched furniture — couches in two different fabrics and styles, a wooden crate for a coffee table, and a brand new big screen TV on the wall which was completely at odds with the rest. Foley obviously had certain priorities when it came to replacing the furniture his ex had taken during the divorce last year.

"Through here."

The office had a single wide wooden desk with a computer monitor on top. Papers had been strewn over the floor and the filing cabinet had been emptied. Lincoln pressed his lips together. He'd stopped by Kit's place on the way back to Blackbridge and this didn't have the same manic destruction as Kit's house had. "Is it only this room?"

Foley nodded.

Kit's whole house had been turned upside-down. "Have you touched anything?"

"No. Thought I'd better call you."

"Has anything been taken?" Adam asked.

"Not that I can see."

"What about in the rest of the house?"

"I don't think so."

Lincoln frowned. "What information do you keep in here?"

"Just the accounts and farm-related records. It's no use to anyone but me."

Something wasn't quite right. "Have you had any arguments with other farmers lately, any of your neighbours?"

"No. We're a pretty tight community. Farming's bloody hard work, so we help each other when we can."

But someone was looking for something. "We'll see if we can get some prints. Do you have some work you need to get to?"

"Always."

"I'll call you when we're finished."

"Thanks, mate." Foley left and Lincoln and Adam returned to the car to get their things.

Adam screwed up his face. "Sorry about telling him about Elijah."

Lincoln couldn't be too hard on him. During his rookie days he'd been just as eager to please. "People often reveal more when we don't tell them everything," Lincoln said. "They feel they have to fill the silence and sometimes they give themselves away."

"But Foley's a victim, not a suspect." Adam took the kit out of the car.

"Maybe." He glanced over as Foley walked to his shed. That's what bugged him. Foley hadn't seemed upset.

"You think he trashed his own office?"

He wasn't sure what to think. "Compare the two break-ins," he said. "How are they different?"

"Kit's whole house was trashed, whereas it was only Foley's office."

Which break-in had occurred first? Lincoln shut the boot of the car. "And in the office?" He said it aloud as much for himself as for Adam.

Lincoln walked back into the house with Adam right behind him. They stood at the doorway of the office.

"The computer's on the desk, in one piece," Adam said.

Lincoln nodded. "What else?"

"The files are dumped in piles," Adam continued. "The paper in Kit's office had been flicked through at least."

Yeah. This mess looked like it would be easy to clean up.

"The two break-ins might not be related," Adam said.

"True, but it's a hell of a coincidence."

"Everyone knew they'd be at the funeral."

But why hadn't the burglar taken anything? The big screen TV was enticing and they'd had time to take it off the wall. "Yeah. Just keep it in mind." His gut told him they were connected.

But what was the link?

Chapter 11

Kit couldn't erase the unease of her friends working on the farm that afternoon. Her ears strained for the sound of gunshots, though rationally she knew Creepy Guy wouldn't be back with all the cops around. Mai was out in the paddock seeding, her experience driving the fire tanker making her the perfect person to drive the heavy machinery while Hannah and Jamie worked on the irrigation in the pastures in the middle of the property, away from any boundary fences. Fleur helped her review the paddock where the cows would go to dry off, ready to be inseminated again. The water trough was blocked and a couple of the fence posts needed fixing.

She'd asked Paul to fix them a month ago.

By the time they were finished, they had to milk the cows. As she opened the gates of the dairy for the first wave of cows, her phone rang.

"It's Foley. I heard about Elijah. Is he all right?"

News travelled fast. "Yeah, he'll be home tomorrow."

"That's good. Do you want me to send Ian over? You must be getting behind."

It was sweet of him to offer. "No, thanks. I've had the musketeers working hard for me all day. We're about caught up." Sort of.

"Are you sure? I don't want you struggling."

"Yeah." She wasn't putting Ian at risk. "I'll give you a call if I need help."

"Good."

She hung up.

"Who was that?" Fleur asked.

"Foley." She explained his offer.

"That's nice of him. And you know we're always around to help."

"I'll be fine." She'd been carrying most of the workload for the past few months anyway. She placed the milking cups on the cows. "How are things going with you and Will?" She liked Fleur's partner. He'd helped her in the dairy last month when Paul had flaked on her and once he'd got past his shyness he'd shown he had a good sense of humour.

"Really great. His parents are coming down next month to visit."

"Are you moving in together anytime soon?"

She shrugged. "Will doesn't want to leave Elijah in the lurch with the rent, so he'll stay until he finds someone to take over the lease. I'm working a lot of afternoon and night shifts over the next few weeks, so it makes no sense for him to hang around my place by himself."

"Good point." Nights were always the loneliest.

"So, what's going on with you and Lincoln?"

Crap. "Nothing."

"Don't lie to me, Kit Kat. You gave him next level freeze at the funeral."

She shrugged and busied herself checking the readings on the gauges.

"Kit, talk to me."

She hesitated, but she wanted to talk to someone about it. "We slept together." The words were barely a whisper from her mouth.

"What?"

She spun around. "We had sex." That's all it was, a physical action, not a declaration of love. "He promised he'd be there for me, made it seem like he cared, and then he wouldn't kiss me in public." Her throat burned with unshed pain.

Fleur's eyes widened. "Bloody hell." She wrapped her arms around Kit. "Kit Kat, I know what he means to you. There has to be a reason."

Yeah, it was because she didn't inspire people to stick around. "He got what he wanted. I shouldn't be surprised."

"Lincoln's not like that."

Except his actions proved otherwise. "Forget about it. I was stupid to sleep with him."

"Talk to him. It has to be a misunderstanding."

Kit wished she had as much faith as Fleur, but why would Lincoln be any different from everyone else? "They always leave."

By the time the milking was finished, the other musketeers had returned to the shed. "Thanks for your help today," Kit said.

"Want us to help tidy the house?" Jamie asked.

Damn, she'd forgotten about it. She hadn't heard from the police so they were probably still over there. "You don't need to."

"No, but we want to," Hannah said. "We've had a lot of practice cleaning up mess in the last few months."

"If you've got some eggs, I can whip us up a quiche for dinner," Mai said.

Kit hadn't checked the chooks in a few days. It had been Paul's job and he used to take most of the eggs home with him to make into protein shakes or something equally disgusting. "We'll stop at the chook pen on our way to the house. I just need to add some figures to my records." She walked into her office. No computer.

Shit. She hadn't replaced the one that had been trashed. She'd have to use her laptop in the house — if it was still there.

Fleur wrapped her arm around Kit's waist. "We'll get a new one. Have you called the insurers yet?"

"Yeah. I'll have to call them back when I assess today's damage." She whistled for her dogs and the group of them walked back to the house as the light faded. Some cockatoos screeched in the dusk, the chooks clucked and cows mooed — the sounds of home. She inhaled deeply and let the peace settle over her. They stopped at the hen house and Kit shook her head at the ridiculous structure. Her step-mother had insisted it look like a mini-farmhouse, refusing to let it be an eyesore on the farm. Brick pillars formed the corners with a small brick wall joining them.

The chicken wire made up the walls of the 'garden' section and the whole pen had a tiled roof with a fake chimney sticking out the top. Inside, the actual house had multiple perches for the chickens to sit in comfort and after the first fox attack, more reinforced wire had been added to the fence line to keep them out. At least they hadn't had a problem since then.

The musketeers gathered the eggs while Kit checked their food and water. It would need cleaning and topping up tomorrow.

One police car was still outside the house, and Sergeant Dargatz met her at the back door.

"Ms van Ross, could I have a few minutes of your time?"

She nodded. "Can I start cleaning up?"

He hesitated. "I'd ask your friends to stay outside until you've looked around."

"All right."

Jamie stepped up. "I can go with you."

He was a sweetheart, but she didn't want him to see her reaction to the mess. She smiled. "I'll be fine. It shouldn't take long."

Once inside the sergeant said, "If you could go through each room and tell me if there's anything missing."

Cereal flakes crunched under her feet as she looked into the pantry. Her heart lurched. Jars smashed on the ground, ants everywhere and next to nothing left on the shelves. Swallowing the lump in her throat, she said, "This might take some time." She stepped in, her gaze stopping on the board where all her keys hung. "Not all of my keys are there."

"What's missing?"

"The house, document safe and gun safe keys." She rubbed at the goosebumps on her skin. She'd need to change the locks. The idea of someone sneaking inside while she slept was creepy. "Unless they're under the mess on the floor.

"I'll need you to confirm."

She nodded. At least the food would be easy to replace. She moved into the kitchen and swore. The bastard had done a thorough job. All the cupboards were open, shards of broken crockery on the ground. She'd worked so hard to prove she could make it without her parents, and someone had trashed it in an instant.

She gritted her teeth. This was simply another bump in the road. She'd deal with this, like she dealt with all the other shit thrown her way over the years.

In the living room the cushions had been thrown off the sofas, and all her books were on the floor. Her stomach clenched. Keep going. She moved from room to room, but each one had been violated, cupboard doors opened, items torn out.

She braced herself before stepping inside her bedroom. Bed sheets ripped, clothes tossed out of her wardrobe and on the floor lay the packet of condoms and her vibrator.

She shuddered. No way she was using it again. The bastard had succeeded in making her uncomfortable in her own home, her one sanctuary.

Son of a bitch.

Finally she went into her office. Papers all over the floor, the drawers open and her laptop wasn't on the desk. She scanned the floor, noticed her fire-proof safe open and empty. Shit.

"My laptop's missing." She dug through the papers on the floor. Her contracts, passport, and birth certificate were all there but, "My backup drive is missing."

"It was in the safe?"

"Yeah. I updated it on Saturday after the shed was broken into."

"What information do you keep on it?"

"Everything. All my business and personal information."

Dargatz grimaced. "So you've lost the lot."

"No." Thank God for Mai. "A copy of everything gets backed up to the cloud on a weekly basis."

He frowned. "That's organised."

"My friend Mai is a volunteer fire-fighter. She's seen families lose everything, so she made me set up regular backups."

"We're going to need a copy of the information."

"Why?"

"Because it appears this person is searching for something digital. Both your computers and the backup have been taken. If we can figure out what that is, we might be able to catch them."

Maybe it was the drone footage. "I'll need a computer and a location to copy it to." She ran a hand through her hair. She'd had enough for today. She wanted to crawl into a ball and forget about the outside world for a while. "Do you have any other questions for me?"

"Do you know what they could be looking for?"

She wasn't willing to discuss her theories with him in case they confiscated her data before she had a chance to go through her records herself. "Not yet."

"Will you tell me if you think of anything?" He handed her his card.

"Sure. If there's nothing else, I need to clean this place up."

"All right."

She walked him out. The light had faded to almost night and the musketeers sat on the verandah. After Dargatz drove off, she turned to them. "Ready for some more work?"

They nodded.

She checked her phone. No missed calls despite the fact Lincoln had said they'd talk tonight. She wouldn't hold her breath.

She straightened her shoulders. "Let's get to it then."

Taking the fingerprints into Albany station himself had been a bad idea. Lincoln had been stuck there for the past couple of hours while he'd reviewed the case with the detectives. And while he appreciated them including him in the investigation, he hadn't had a chance to call Kit again.

He couldn't break his promise to her.

As he stepped outside the station, he checked the time. He'd been planning on making Kit dinner tonight, but she'd probably already prepared something.

Should he call her now, or was it better if he just showed up?

As he stood in front of the car park, Sergeant Dargatz pulled up. He'd been investigating Kit's break-in. Lincoln strode over. "How did it go at the van Ross place?"

The man crossed his arms. "It wasn't pretty, but Ms van Ross is a cool customer. Didn't even flinch at all the mess."

He could imagine. "Anything stolen?"

"Laptop and backup drive." He opened his notebook. "Maybe her house and gun safe keys."

He hadn't told her he'd taken her spare key. He couldn't tell Dargatz without being asked why he had it. "Have you come from there?"

"Yeah. She and her friends are cleaning up."

"Thanks." The musketeers were there. That was good for Kit, not so great if he wanted to talk to her privately, but he'd manage. He headed for his car.

The drive to the farm didn't take long and Montoya and Roberts pranced around him as he got out of the car. He ruffled their fur, the coarse hair dusty, and then whistled for them to follow him inside.

The aroma of quiche wafted out the back door and he tapped on the door frame before walking in. Mai peered down the corridor. "Hey, Slinky. You're in time for dinner. Kit's either in her room or the office."

He smiled. "Thanks." At least one person didn't mind him being there. Had Kit not told them about the misunderstanding?

The food from the pantry had been swept up, and the lounge where his brother and the other musketeers sat was tidy, all the books back on their shelves. No evidence the house had been broken into. "You've done a great job."

Fleur frowned at him, but Hannah said, "Kit's finishing her bedroom."

This was his chance to talk to her alone.

"Make it right, Slinky," Fleur said.

Jamie and Hannah glanced at her when he nodded. As he walked down the corridor Jamie asked, "Do you know what they're fighting about?"

He didn't wait for Fleur's answer. In the bedroom, Kit stood on tiptoes on a chair, reaching into her wardrobe, her clothes all over the floor.

"What are you doing?"

She shrieked and twisted, the chair wobbling and her arms flailing. Lincoln jumped forward, wrapping his arms around her waist to stop her from falling. She smelled like hay and cinnamon. His Kit.

Kit pushed him away and stepped off the chair, away from him. "Checking for cameras."

He blinked. "Cameras?"

She didn't spare him a glance as she picked her clothes off the floor. "The guy who broke into Hannah's place left a camera behind. I want to make sure Creepy Guy didn't as well."

His heart twisted. Smith better not have. "I can help you."

"I'm sure you've got better things to do."

She was distancing him again, but that was his fault. He moved forward. "I'm sorry about today."

"Which part? The bit where you were too embarrassed to kiss me, or when you lied about being there for me?"

He flinched. "I wasn't embarrassed."

Kit didn't pause as she folded her clothes. "No? You just don't want anyone to know?"

He placed a hand on her arm, stopping her. "I want *everyone* to know," he said. "But the detectives were there."

"So it was unprofessional?" She scowled, wrenching her arm free of his grasp.

"No. If they find out we're involved, they'll take me off the case."

"Yeah, right."

He gritted his teeth. She didn't understand. "It's a conflict of interest."

"That's stupid. You would never let your personal feelings cloud your judgement."

Her faith in him gave him hope. "I'm still human, Kit." He took her hand, tugged her closer. "I could get into real trouble if they find out I didn't declare my relationship with you."

She stepped back. "How much trouble?"

He cleared his throat. "It depends. After the shooting today, you're no longer a suspect, so it might just be a talking to."

She crossed her arms, her eyes narrowed. "What's the worst case scenario?"

He grimaced. "Suspension and an investigation."

Her eyes widened. "Could you lose your job?"

He wouldn't lie to her. "It's a possibility."

She backed away from him. "That can't happen, Lincoln. I won't be responsible for ruining your career."

"It's unlikely, Kit." Though the same concern hovered like a cloud. Would he always be required to choose between his career and Kit?

She squeezed her eyes closed, let out a breath. "Then we can't see each other."

Panic swept through him. He couldn't let her push him away. "Yes, we can." As long as no one found out about them, the risk of him losing his job was low, and if he solved the case, it would be even lower.

She shook her head. "No. The cost is too high." She opened her mouth to say more but Mai called, "Dinner's ready!"

She hurried out of the room.

Lincoln ran his hand through his hair. The irony wasn't lost on him. She was rejecting him to save his career like he'd done to her all those years ago. With a sigh, he followed her down the hall.

Kit sat at the opposite end of the table from him and chatted to the musketeers as if nothing was wrong — an expert at hiding how she felt.

He wouldn't lose Kit again, but he had to come up with a decent justification for the department.

The detectives had been surprised that Kit's place had been searched again. They'd spoken about setting up surveillance.

Perhaps that was the answer.

If the detectives questioned him, he could say he was watching the place and staying for her protection.

The detectives didn't need to know he loved her and didn't want to be apart from her.

Still the idea of fudging the truth made him nauseous. He'd always done things by the book, the law was there for a reason.

Kit laughed at something Fleur said, her laugh loud and raucous and her eyes sparkling. It hit him right in the gut, smothered all his concerns. This woman brought light into his life. He couldn't let anything happen to her.

As they finished eating, Jamie asked, "Want to come over and use my computer tonight, Kit?"

She glanced at Lincoln. "Maybe. It can probably wait until I buy a new computer tomorrow."

He frowned. "What do you need?"

"We were discussing what Creepy Guy could be after," Hannah said, "and Kit thought it might be drone footage. Maybe

Paul or Gordon recorded something they shouldn't have."

Lincoln's skin tingled. It fit. "Did he give you footage?"

She nodded. "Some."

He swore. "But your computers were stolen."

"She's got online backups," Mai said.

He grinned. "That's fantastic. We definitely need to check it out." Finally a break. "You could stay the night with me, use my computer."

Silence, with various expressions of surprise on the musketeers' faces.

Oh, right. Maybe they didn't know everything.

Kit's face flushed and Hannah got up, started clearing the plates. Fleur helped her. "Jamie, why don't you put the kettle on?"

Mai stood too. "I'll get the dessert."

In seconds they had the dining room to themselves. Subtle.

"It makes sense," he said. "I'm worried about you being here alone and I want to spend more time with you."

She hesitated and then shook her head. "I'm always alone on the farm and if someone notices I've stayed at your place, it will be all over town by the end of the day."

Since when had Kit cared about what people thought? "Then we borrow Jamie's computer and I'll stay here. I'll need to review the footage anyway."

She arched an eyebrow. "And if Albany come back to do more investigation?"

"They won't come that early." He covered her hand with his. "I don't want work to come between us again."

Her expression was concerned as she pulled her hand back. "I'll ask Jamie to get his laptop." She headed for the kitchen.

It didn't mean she'd agreed to him staying. But she hadn't asked him to leave either.

He'd take it as a win, for now.

Chapter 12

Kit's skin prickled as she logged into her cloud drive from Jamie's laptop an hour later. The musketeers sat around the table with her and Lincoln stood behind, watching over her shoulder, his presence impossible to ignore. She'd deal with him later, but she wasn't sure how. She couldn't put her own desires before his happiness, couldn't let him lose his job.

He'd resent her, and their relationship would be doomed.

And that was the likely result. One of them had to pay the price.

Her finger tapped the table as the folder loaded.

Waiting for the case to be solved meant a delay in their relationship. It gave her time to get used to the change, figure out how to make it work.

She sucked at being patient.

Kit scrolled through her data until she found the relevant folder and hit download. Would an answer to Paul's murder be on there?

"Can you give me a copy of everything?" Lincoln asked.

"Tell me where you want it."

Would it hurt if he stayed tonight? The idea of someone coming back to finish searching — with her house key — creeped her out. Maybe he could sleep in his old room and then he wouldn't need to lie if he was asked.

She hated being scared in her own home.

She clicked on the first video file and it played, a silent view of her peering over Paul's shoulder as he showed her what the drone could do. He'd bought the new drone and had been keen to show it off, bragging about how silent it was. It had been just before the problems with him had begun and she'd been excited too. It was amazing to see her farm, all her land, from a different perspective. She clicked it closed. "It's not that one."

She opened each file and though there was close to an hour of footage, none had anything more interesting than Paul riding a motorbike across a paddock.

She closed the last file, her shoulders slumping. "That's it." They had nothing to point to Paul's murderer.

Lincoln swore. "There aren't any more videos?"

"I don't think so."

"The police will do a thorough search." Lincoln stepped away to make a phone call.

Hannah put her hand on Kit's. "Maybe he hid it in a different folder."

He had been secretive around the computer over the last few weeks, shutting down windows if she'd come close. "Maybe." She should do a file search.

Lincoln came back. "Albany station is going to email you a link. Can you set up a file transfer to it?"

"Sure." It would likely take all night with her internet speed. She'd do the search in the morning. "Can I return your laptop tomorrow?" she asked Jamie.

"Keep it as long as you need. I've got my work one I can use."

She wouldn't keep it long. She had to replace her own computers and it would be a pain. All the damned software she had to install. She eyed Mai. "Could you help me when I get the new machines?"

Mai smiled. "Of course. Call me when you get them." She got to her feet. "I need to go. I have to be up again in a few hours."

Guilt hit her. "Sorry." She should have told Mai to go home hours ago. She hugged her friend. "Thanks for all your help."

"Any time."

Fleur stood. "I didn't notice the time. I've got an early shift at the hospital tomorrow."

Lincoln hung back as her friends got their things together and headed for the back door. She really should tell him to go.

Jamie glanced at his brother and then at Kit. "You all right with him staying?"

She didn't know what she wanted. "I think Creepy Guy stole my spare key. I don't really want to be alone until I change the locks."

Lincoln looked up. "I have the spare. I took it on Monday so I could lock up after myself." He winced. "Sorry I didn't tell you."

"That's a relief." But now the vision of Creepy Guy sneaking into her house while she slept had taken hold, it was hard to shake.

She walked her friends out and waved to them as the light from the car faded away. The darkness beyond the reach of the verandah light deepened. Shadows loomed — the bottlebrush by the gate, the grevillea near the clothesline, the dark lump next to the eucalypt. She frowned, squinting. What was that? She sniffed. Was that cigarette smoke?

Was Creepy Guy out there, watching her?

She rubbed the goosebumps on her arm and hurried up the steps, whistling for her dogs. She wanted to be inside, surrounded by walls.

She sighed as the deadbolt thunked into place. It was strong, weighty, much better than the lock on her bedroom door. She stood there for a second to get her heart rate under control and then went to find Lincoln. He still sat in the dining room, going through the files on the laptop. She longed to climb onto his lap, have him tell her everything would be all right, draw comfort from his arms around her.

But she couldn't put him in a compromising position. She gritted her teeth. "I'm going to bed. You can sleep in the spare room."

He pushed back his chair. "Kit, wait."

She crossed her arms. "What, Lincoln?"

He stopped less than a metre away. "Please don't shut me out."

Her heart squeezed. It was difficult to say no to him. "Your job is important to you, Lincoln. We've waited years to be together, we can wait a little longer." She couldn't believe she was being the sensible one.

"My job isn't as important to me as you."

A warmth spread through her, but she couldn't be lulled by it. She needed to be firm. "You say that now, but if you lost it, you'd soon blame me."

He frowned. "Don't you trust me?"

"It's not that…" She bit her lip. How could she convince him? "Life has taught me there's always a price for getting what I want."

He stepped closer, ran a hand along her arm. "I don't want to wait."

She yearned to step forward into his arms. She was weak with him. He was her kryptonite. She gripped her resolve and looked him in the eyes. "It won't be long. Good night, Lincoln." She walked away and he let her go.

Kit woke before her alarm went off the next morning, her bed cold and empty. How had she got used to Lincoln being with her so quickly?

She yawned and rubbed a hand over her face. If only she could turn over and go back to sleep. She'd stared at the wall of her bedroom for way too many hours last night, her thoughts a tangled mess about Lincoln, his job, the case, and what Paul could have hidden on the farm. She wasn't convinced she should have let Lincoln stay the night. What if Albany found out? What if he did lose his job?

Her chest squeezed.

Her alarm blared and she slapped it off before it could wake Lincoln down the hall. She dressed quickly, the light dim. She'd leave immediately, before Lincoln woke. If she had another cosy breakfast with him, she'd forget about her good intentions. She'd grab an apple on her way out of the door and make a cup of coffee over at the kitchenette in the dairy.

"Need a hand with the milking?"

She flinched and turned.

Lincoln stood there, his dark hair sticking up at all sorts of angles, and his police uniform crinkled and untidy, but he still could have won the award for the sexiest man on the planet. Damn him.

Quickly she filled the dogs' bowls with food. "Never needed it before." Inwardly she winced at the snark. She didn't have to be nasty to keep him at arm's length.

He sighed. "What are you doing, Kit?" His voice was low.

"I'm going to work." She snatched her hat off the bench.

"Kit." He raised his eyebrows, daring her to confront the situation.

She swallowed hard. "I can't get involved with you until after the case is solved." Her voice shook. "And if I have breakfast with you, I'll forget my resolve."

"I'm fine with that." He winked.

She glared at him. "I'm not. I won't have you lose your job over me."

She whistled to her dogs and walked out.

The slam of the back door echoed through the house as Kit left. Lincoln swore. Making light of the situation hadn't worked, but he'd never thought Kit would be so worried about his job.

He'd underestimated her again.

He should be the one protecting her, not the other way around — which meant he needed to go to the sheds with her in case Smith came back.

With that in mind, he pulled on his shoes and headed outside as the roar of her motorbike pierced the quiet. He ran for the front of the house, but she was already halfway to the shed.

Damn it.

He jogged after her, scanning for movement as Kit arrived at the dairy.

No random motorbikes.

The sun had made it over the horizon, but had yet to warm up the day. He rubbed his arms to warm them, his breath clouding in the air.

His gaze caught on the first class chicken coop a good fifty metres away.

He squinted. Something was on the roof next to the chimney, a black lump too big to be nuts from the overhanging eucalyptus. He moved closer, shielding his eyes but the sun behind the chimney made it difficult to see.

He glanced over at the dairy. The cows had already started entering which meant Kit hadn't run into anyone inside.

Changing direction, he headed for the coop and the lump took a more definitive shape, almost like it had legs. But the angles were too sharp for it to be an animal, it was more robotic.

His mouth dropped open. Could it be a drone?

He jogged closer, examined the structure. He should be able to hoist himself onto the roof.

The chickens clucked and squawked, fluttering away from him as he stepped up onto the half wall which provided the base walls of their pen. He reached up and pressed his hands onto the tiled roof, his heart beating faster.

Would the roof hold his weight, or was it mostly there for show?

He wasn't certain.

He tested, putting a bit of his weight on the edge and lifting himself up. It groaned in protest, but he'd seen what he'd needed to. It was definitely a drone, just out of his reach.

It had to be Paul's.

A bunch of small branches lay underneath the gum tree. Lincoln chose the longest, sturdiest of them. If this didn't work, he'd get a ladder from the shed, but he'd rather Kit wasn't involved. If she didn't see the footage, she couldn't be a target.

The stick scraped against the ceramic tiles, inching closer and he managed to hook the object under one of its rotor arms. With a flick, it moved a tiny bit closer.

Another flick and the drone was within arm's reach. He dumped the stick on the ground took his shirt off, hissing at the cold air, and used the cloth to pick up the drone.

He grinned.

Now to see what information it contained.

Back at the house, he placed the drone on the kitchen table and booted up Jamie's laptop. The file transfer had completed successfully last night.

He hesitated.

The quicker he got the drone off Kit's property the better.

He checked his watch. Fifteen minutes since Kit had left. She'd be well into the milking and Elijah would be here soon. This evidence had to be processed. The footage might lead to an arrest that would wrap up this case. And then he could be with Kit.

Cautious not to touch the drone with his bare hands, he carried it out to his car, placed it carefully in the boot. Quickly he changed into his spare uniform and then scanned the farm again. Nothing seemed out of place. Cows were already moving away from the dairy and the dogs wandered among them, undisturbed. Kit was fine and reviewing the memory card had to be the priority. It could keep her safe.

He hoped.

When Lincoln arrived at the station, Ryan and Sue were already there. "I've found a drone." He went straight into his office and they joined him.

"Where?" Ryan asked.

"On top of Kit's hen house." He placed it on the desk. "It was next to the chimney, so it was hard to spot. Can you get me the card reader?"

Ryan went to fetch it and Sue said, "Have you dusted it for prints yet?"

"No." He booted up his computer and slapped on some rubber gloves, his chest tight. This had to be what Harry was looking for. He logged on and then Sue handed him the finger print dust. Carefully he applied it and found a couple of partial prints.

"I'll run them into Albany this morning," she said.

"Thanks." He found the memory card slot and pressed it. Bingo.

His hands steady, he inserted the card and connected it to his computer. A brief pause and then a folder popped up on the desktop with a couple of files in it.

Yes!

His skin tingled as he clicked on the first one dated the day before Paul died. Brown bricks and then the drone rose into the air above the hen house and Paul stood next to it, a controller in his hand. Paul moved away and the drone followed him over to the shed. He glanced up, pressed a button and the drone flew back to the hen house, landing where it had started.

"Test run?" Ryan asked.

"Maybe." But climbing up to put the drone on the hen house meant Paul hadn't wanted anyone to find it, at least not immediately. Had he known he was in danger?

Tension stirred in his stomach as Lincoln clicked on the second movie, the one dated the day of Paul's death. As in the first one, the drone lifted from the hen house roof, but this time it followed the ute as Paul drove through the farm to the location where he had died.

Shit.

Were they really going to get his murder on film?

Paul stayed in the car and the drone circled around, hovering above the tree line so it faced the ute. Paul glanced out the window and then bent and tucked something, presumably the controller, under the seat.

"Who searched the car?" Lincoln asked.

"I'll check with Albany," Ryan said.

Paul got out and then reached through the open window and dragged something closer.

Kit's rifle.

Lincoln swore.

Paul leaned up against the side and lit a cigarette, his stance casual. The footage was crystal clear as a person walked into view a minute later.

Harry Smith.

Paul greeted him, held out a hand, but Harry didn't take it. Instead the tightness of his muscles, and his hands gripped into fists showed he wasn't happy.

If only this thing had audio.

Paul said something else and then Harry reached into his jacket and pulled out a plastic bag full of white crystals.

Meth.

Sue whistled. "There's a small fortune in that bag."

The street value would be close to fifty grand. So Paul *was* involved in the drug ring.

Paul took the bag, threw it on the front seat and then reached in and dragged out the gun, pointing it at Harry.

What the hell was he doing?

Smith backed off, and Paul smiled.

Lincoln's muscles tensed. The kid had no idea. Harry wasn't a man to mess with.

Harry turned, and before Lincoln could blink, he spun around and grabbed the gun out of Paul's hand so fast there wasn't even a struggle.

Damn it. What the hell had Paul been thinking?

Now Paul backed away, hands up. Lincoln knew the ending.

Harry gestured to the ground and Paul yelled at him. Then Paul's eyes widened and he looked behind Harry, at something out of camera range.

Lincoln itched to be able to control the footage, to pivot the drone to see exactly what Paul had spotted.

Paul frowned and then his face screwed up in rage and he shouted.

It had to be a person. "He knows whoever it is," Lincoln said.

"Yeah. Let's hope he comes closer," Ryan replied.

Harry gestured to the ground again and Paul yelled. Harry stepped forward, put the rifle tip on Paul's forehead and Paul dropped to the ground. They couldn't see his face from where Harry stood, but his hands shook.

Lincoln swore.

Harry glanced over his shoulder, said something to the person still out of shot and then nodded. Without flinching, he pulled the trigger and then wiped down the gun, positioning Paul the way they'd found him, the gun next to him.

Lincoln noted the video time. Twelve minutes. That's all it took for Paul to stuff up his foolhardy plan and be killed for it.

Harry tensed, looked around as if searching for something. He said something to the person off camera and then peered into the car. At that moment the drone shot straight up in the air, had to be sixty metres or more, and as it pivoted towards the sheds, the figure in the bush behind Harry came into view.

"There!" Lincoln pointed. The image was too small to see the face.

"Maybe forensics can get a zoom on it," Ryan suggested.

The drone flew over the paddocks, past the sheds and Lincoln spotted Kit getting on her motorbike. His gut clenched. Was this when she went to find Paul? Had she been that close to witnessing the whole thing?

The drone hovered above the hen house again before slowly descending and landing where it had taken off from.

"How the hell did it do that?" Lincoln asked.

"My husband's got a similar drone," Sue said. "It has a return to home function when the battery gets low. It's a fail-safe so you don't lose it. It beeps first and I'll bet that's what Harry heard before the drone took off."

Which is why they'd been searching for it.

Hell. He copied the file onto his computer and then picked up the phone. "I'll get forensics right on this. We have to identify the mystery person. This should warrant a more thorough search for Harry."

Harry had to be camping nearby. He couldn't be staying in any accommodation because they'd sent notification to everyone within a fifty kilometre radius, so that left him bunking with whoever was working with him, or camping, probably in the national park. It was easy to get lost in there.

If they caught Harry, it would wrap up Paul's case and Harry could tell them who the drug ring leader was.

Then they could close it down.

And Kit would be safe.

Chapter 13

Kit slapped on the overhead lights in the dairy and went to let the cows in, scanning for anything out of place as she flicked switches on. Nothing was different from yesterday.

She let out a breath and turned her attention to her other concern — Lincoln.

How could he be so cavalier about his job? He loved being a cop, was so damned good at it. She couldn't let him throw it away.

For once she was doing the right thing.

She scowled.

A hopeful little voice in her head said maybe this time would be different, maybe there would be no price to pay, but the heavy pressure of experience weighed her down.

Life sucked.

Finally she had everything she wanted, and she was too scared to take it She loved him too much to ruin his life.

Had to keep him at a distance until the case was solved.

Only she'd feel so much safer having him around.

Not even the heavy rock tunes could shake her out of her mood today and she had the volume so loud it was a wonder the whole damn dairy wasn't shaking.

Someone touched her shoulder and she whirled around, fist swinging, almost hitting Elijah as he leaped back. Her breath rushed out of her as she pulled her punch. "Holy shit, Elijah. You scared me to death."

"I called twice," he yelled. His arm was still bandaged underneath the bright red of his shirt.

She turned the music off, her ears ringing.

"Is there some new research which proves deaf cows provide more milk?" Elijah asked.

She rolled her eyes. "Very funny. What are you doing here?"

"I work here," he said. "They're forecasting rain later in the week, and the more we get done now, the better."

She shook her head. "I gave you the week off. You should still be in hospital."

"They discharged me yesterday. Said I was fine for light duties."

Her insides twisted. "It's not safe and you're injured."

"I can still drive the tractor, and I promise not to investigate any more strangers."

"No, Elijah."

He shrugged. "You're not stopping me, Kit. I just dropped in to tell you where I'll be."

"I could have you arrested for trespassing."

"But you wouldn't." He winked at her. "I should be finished seeding by the end of the week."

She didn't like it, but the rational part of her brain said Creepy Guy had already searched the vehicles. Elijah should be fine. She hugged him. "I appreciate it, but you have to be careful."

"I will be. I don't want a repeat of yesterday." He held up his phone. "The first sign of a stranger and I'll call the police."

Good.

She mentally revised her plans for the day. If he was going to deal with the crop, she should go into Albany. She needed her data to work out which cows to dry off. "I have to buy a new computer, so I'll be away from the farm for a couple of hours."

"No problem. I'll be fine." He waved and walked away.

She was glad Elijah was back in Blackbridge, pleased she could give him a job.

She just hoped she could keep him safe.

After she'd cleaned the dairy, she headed to the house to call her insurance company. Lincoln's car wasn't out the front, not that she expected it to be. It was far better he was gone, though her heart pinched at his absence. It would be a while before she saw him again.

She walked into her office. Aside from her laptop and backup drive, she had to replace everything Creepy Guy had broken and her gun.

An hour later she hung up and growled, only just resisting slamming the phone down on the desk.

How many hoops did she have to jump through to get the money that was owed to her? Too many. And she couldn't wait for the money to go into her account. She needed at least one new computer now. The rest could wait. She would also have to use her nice ute for the farm work as the other one would be tied up by the police for the foreseeable future. Because Paul hadn't been decent enough to use his own damn car to get shot in front of.

She huffed out a breath.

The anger wasn't helping.

Focus. A new gun meant a new gun safe, or she had to change the locks. Was that even possible? She headed to the kitchen and booted up Jamie's laptop. She called a couple of locksmiths, organised for one to come out in the morning, and then drove into town.

When Kit arrived in Albany, she went straight to the electronics shop armed with the specifications to run her dairy software. The shop assistant did his best to convince her she needed more than she did, but she cut him off. "Do you want the sale or not?"

He scowled, packaged the laptop and told her the computer she'd ordered for the dairy would be ready for collection next week. Satisfied, she headed back to her ute. Next stop, the firearm shop. Though she hated using a gun, it was far better than waiting with an injured animal for the vet to come out.

She drove down the street and parked a couple of bays from the door. She might need to apply for an additional gun on her licence, but that shouldn't be a problem. She hated going into the shop and seeing all the weapons lining the walls. So many ways to kill, but at least when she did it, it was a mercy killing.

As she sat there psyching herself up, a short skinny guy came out, his dark hair combed flat, but something about him seemed kind of familiar. He walked over to a white four-wheel drive with wide tyres, a heavy 'roo bar and roof racks on top. He wasn't someone from the motocross club, and couldn't be a farmhand, not with the lack of muscles on him. Why were the hairs on her arms standing on end?

He glanced around and she got a good look at his face. Kit swore. It was Creepy Guy.

Her hands turned to ice and she slid down in her seat as he got into his car. She had to call the police.

By the time she got her phone out of her pocket, Creepy Guy was at the exit. She couldn't let him get away. She started her car as someone answered. "Do you need police, fire or ambulance?"

"Police. In Albany, Western Australia." She drove after him, keeping her distance as he drove along Albany Highway. Her pulse raced. He'd be caught and they'd discover why he'd been searching her place. "I'm following Harry Smith, a wanted felon. He's heading north on Albany Highway." They were in the middle of town, but Kit didn't want to get too close, not if he was armed.

She answered the dispatcher's questions as she came to the big roundabout. Traffic was heavy and she stopped directly behind Creepy Guy's car. She clenched her teeth as she stared out her side window, every nerve in her body humming. She couldn't make eye contact with him. He might not realise she'd seen him. If he got out she was screwed. Another four-wheel drive was right behind her.

The traffic inched forward as cars waited for their turn to enter the roundabout. Finally Creepy Guy took the South West Highway exit heading towards Blackbridge.

Kit accelerated after him and the blast of a horn had her slamming on the brakes. A red mustang swerved, narrowly missing her. The driver gave her the finger. Her heart thumped. She hadn't even checked, too focused on Creepy Guy.

"Where are you now?" the dispatcher asked.

Kit told him and this time navigated the roundabout without any issues, accelerating to catch up with Creepy Guy. Damn, there were too many white four-wheel drives on the road. Where the hell was he?

The roof racks on a car about a hundred metres ahead caught

her attention. Hopefully that was him. She pushed the speed limit as she drove out of town, farmland on either side of the road. Creepy Guy passed a huge truck going about ten kilometres under the speed limit and she lost sight of him.

Kit sped right up behind the truck and inched out. Three cars were approaching in the opposite lane. She swerved back, slamming her hand on the steering wheel. She was going to lose him.

She dropped back, moving to the left side, mindful of the loose gravel on the edge. The four-wheel drive turned off the highway and onto a smaller side street. Tourist signs pointed to a sandalwood factory and she fed the information through to the dispatcher.

"The police car's only a couple of kilometres behind you," the dispatcher told her.

Thank God. She turned down the street.

The road was empty.

No. She couldn't lose him now. She accelerated, willing him to appear on the road ahead. Trees and fields surrounded her. The only side roads out here were access into farms.

Was he going to one of them?

A flash of movement came from the left in her peripheral vision and she barely had time to register it before an almighty crash and her car was shoved off the road.

Glass shattered and her engine whined as the car hit something on the other side of the road. Her head hit the side airbag and her vision blurred at the impact.

What the hell?

Ears ringing and chest throbbing from the seatbelt restraint, she blinked as she registered the 'roo bar of the white four-wheel drive below the airbag of her passenger side window.

Creepy Guy had hit her.

Fear flooded her. She had to get out of here. He was armed. She pressed the accelerator. Nothing. Hands shaking, she turned the key. The motor coughed, spluttered and died.

Frantically she pressed the seatbelt button until it released, grabbed her door handle and pushed. It didn't budge. She fumbled with the airbag, lifting it until she saw a tree trunk right outside, blocking the door. No getting out that way.

The dispatcher's voice pierced her confusion.

"He crashed into me. I'm trapped." The slam of a car door. "He's getting out." She glanced in her rear-view mirror, trying to spot him.

With both doors blocked, the windscreen was her only option.

She drew her knees to her chest and then froze as she glanced out the window. Creepy Guy stood in front of the car, grinning, holding a gun.

Her insides turned to water. "He has a gun."

"Stay calm. The police are almost there," the dispatcher said.

Kit laughed. Easy for him to say. He wasn't staring at an armed psycho. She had to distract Creepy Guy, had to stop him shooting her somehow.

"Where's the drone?" Creepy Guy growled.

She blinked. "Drone?"

"Tell me where the damn thing is and I'll let you live."

Stall. She had to stall until the police arrived. She breathed deeply, trying to calm her racing heart. "I've got no idea what you're talking about."

"Don't play dumb with me."

"Are you talking about Paul's drones? I told him constantly not to fly the damned things."

"He should have listened to you."

"Yeah, he never did. I was about to fire him." Maybe by pretending she didn't like Paul, he wouldn't shoot her.

He laughed. "Then I did you a favour. Now do me one."

Favour? Did he mean he'd killed Paul?

He raised his weapon, pointing it at her. "I won't ask again. Where is Paul's drone?"

Would he kill her if she didn't know?

Lincoln's face flashed into her mind. Was this the price she'd have to pay for two happy nights with Lincoln? No, that wasn't acceptable. She wasn't going to die. She opened her mouth to lie when the wail of a police siren pierced the air.

Relief washed through her. The cavalry had arrived.

"Where's the drone?" Creepy Guy yelled as he lifted his gaze behind her. He swore and ran for his car.

Kit slumped down in her seat as his car roared to life and he backed away, the creak of broken metal making her flinch. The four-wheel drive sped down the road, away from the sirens. Moments later a police car pulled up and officers jumped out, guns ready.

The first officer reached her. "Are you all right?"

"I'm fine. You need to go after him." She pointed.

"I can't. You might be injured."

Frustration swept through her. "He has to be caught," she yelled. "He killed Paul."

The other officer looked down the road after the four-wheel drive. "There are more cars en route."

"Then they can help me. Go after him."

The officer shook his head.

She swore. It was too late. Creepy Guy was long gone. All of this for nothing. She shifted, wincing as she did so. She wanted to get out of this cage. "Can you break the windscreen?"

"Ambulance and fire and emergency services are on the way," he told her.

She wanted out now. A well-aimed kick on the windscreen is all it would take to break it because it was already cracked. How hard could it be?

"Ma'am, please don't move. You might be injured."

She glared at him. "My name's Kit van Ross. You need to contact detectives Khan and Bosch. The guy who crashed into me is wanted for a number of offences."

The second officer spoke quietly into his radio.

"Miss van Ross, please stay where you are until the ambulance arrives."

She didn't want to. The cab was crumpled, the sides much closer together than they should be. Her car was toast, a complete write-off.

But Fleur would be ticked if she discovered Kit had tried getting out on her own. Kit could already hear her lecture about potential internal injuries. With a sigh, she settled back in her seat. This was just another thing to add to her shit week.

More sirens reached her ears.

She closed her eyes and waited.

In the end, they'd needed the jaws of life to extract Kit from her car. She'd been taken to the hospital for scans and after the doctors had given her the all clear, she sat in the police station being questioned by detectives Khan and Bosch. Her face and arms stung from all the little cuts, and her side was bruised from the impact. She ached all over and repeating her story to them didn't help her mood. She pushed back her chair. "I have to get back to the farm."

"It might not be safe for you."

She frowned. "Will Harry come after me?"

Bosch hesitated. "We don't know. He's obviously still after the drone Sergeant Zanetti found this morning."

Kit's stomach lurched. "Lincoln found the drone? Where?"

"On your farm," Khan replied.

What? She narrowed her eyes. The bastard. He must have found it after she'd gone over to the sheds and he hadn't said a word. She'd shared her information with him, and he'd refused to do the same. Didn't he trust her?

"I thought you knew," Bosch said. "Sergeant Zanetti had your permission to be out there this morning, didn't he?"

Crap, what had Lincoln told them? "Of course. I gave him full access to take what he needed." Or she would have if he'd asked. "He must have found it while I milked the cows." She picked up her laptop box, which had survived the crash. "What did the footage show?"

Bosch pursed her lips. "We can't tell you."

Of course not. She'd ask Lincoln. She walked out of the interview room and to the front desk. "I need to apply for a new gun licence."

"Why?" Bosch asked, following her out.

"Because you have my other one." Kit didn't bother looking at her. "And I might need it on the farm."

"Your gun safe isn't secure if the keys are missing."

"Which is why I'm getting the locks changed tomorrow." She told the constable behind the desk what she wanted.

"Good," Khan said. "But you're not to confront Smith."

She wouldn't go after him, but she would protect herself. She nodded.

"Have a good day, Ms van Ross," Bosch said.

Kit snorted. Like that was going to happen. She had to hope

it wouldn't get any worse at least. She finished her application and walked outside, inhaling the salty air from the nearby harbour.

All she wanted was to curl up in bed next to Lincoln and forget today ever happened.

But she wasn't a quitter.

She pursed her lips. Plus there was the little issue that he hadn't told her about the drone. He'd better have a good excuse.

She sighed. First things first. The police had arranged for her ute to be towed, so she needed a new one. She called the closest hire place and arranged to pick up a work ute. Then she walked down the street to catch a taxi.

Afterwards, she drove to the gun shop, ordered a replacement gun, and then headed home. On the way, she called Elijah.

"Are you back now?" he asked over the rumble of the tractor in the background.

"Almost. I ran into a bit of trouble. Just wanted to tell you there'll be a hire ute at the sheds. It's mine and not something to worry about."

"What happened to your car?"

She hesitated.

"Kit, what aren't you telling me?"

She sighed. It would get back to him eventually. "I saw Creepy Guy in Albany. He rammed my car."

"What?!"

"I'm fine, but the car is a write-off."

"Holy shit, this is ridiculous. Do you want me to come in, stick around the sheds with you?"

"No. You're safer out there." He wouldn't be a target. He barely knew Paul.

"But you won't be."

She sighed. "I need you working more than I need a protector right now, Elijah. Please. If the farm work is being done, it's one less thing for me to worry about."

He was silent for a moment. "All right."

She hung up and glanced at the laptop box next to her. She grimaced. In order for everything to get back to normal, she needed to set up the computer. Even though it would worry the musketeers, she needed Mai's help, and if they heard about her being rammed from Elijah, they'd be upset.

The added advantage was if they came around, she and Lincoln wouldn't be alone.

And Creepy Guy would stay away if more people were there. She hoped.

"Lincoln, Mr Maddock gave us access to Paul's drone footage file." Adam walked into Lincoln's office. "He said Paul shared the cloud folder with them months ago."

Lincoln looked up. He'd forgotten he'd asked Adam to follow it up. "Anything interesting in it?"

Adam frowned. "A couple of things. I heard rumours Paul had been banned from the vintage motocross club for riding modern bikes."

"That's right."

"Well that's the thing. There's footage of the motocross track, and Paul talking to some guys on farm bikes, but they're not riding on the track."

Lincoln got to his feet. "Show me." Maybe this would give them a clue who the mystery guy was. He followed Adam to his computer.

The video showed Paul on a red and white farm bike that looked suspiciously like Kit's, and next to him was Gordon. The other two guys had helmets on, but from the build of one, he'd swear it was Harry Smith. Which left the final man. The bike he rode was identical to Paul's.

"Ryan, Sue, come take a look at this." He waited until they were there and pointed to the screen. "That's Gordon and Paul, and that looks like Harry. Any idea who the fourth guy is?"

"With a bike like that, he's a farmer." Sue frowned. "Could be Foley's farmhand, Ian. He was friends with Paul, wasn't he?"

"We should get Kit to have a look," Ryan said. "She might be able to tell us."

Though Lincoln didn't want to involve Kit more than necessary, Ryan was right. "Send a copy to Albany," he told Adam. "Forensics should be able to zoom in."

"There's this as well." Adam clicked on a document. It had dates, times, coordinates and phone numbers on it.

"Collection times?" Ryan asked.

"Maybe. Can you run those coordinates, Adam?"

Adam nodded.

"Anything else in there?"

"No Just a lot of boring footage of the national park and different farms."

Lincoln frowned. "Show me."

Adam brought up the footage and Lincoln watched a couple of the videos. Adam was right, it was boring, but the footage over the national park was different, the drone going back and forth above the tree line, almost like it was searching for something. "Do these things capture coordinates?" he asked Sue.

"Yeah. I'd have to ask my husband how to get them."

"Adam, I want you to extract the coordinates and then map the locations. I want to see where Paul was searching."

"Sure."

Perhaps Paul had more information in a separate cloud folder. He'd have to get a warrant. He returned to his office. It was almost five and still he hadn't heard anything from Albany.

He dialled Bosch's direct number. "It's Sergeant Zanetti," he said when she answered. "Any update from forensics?"

"Not yet." She paused. "Why didn't Ms van Ross know you'd found the drone?"

Lincoln's skin prickled. "When did you speak to Kit?"

"When she was involved in an incident this morning."

His heart stopped. "What happened?"

"She saw Harry Smith in Albany and followed him. He rammed her off the road and pulled a gun on her."

His blood pressure skyrocketed as fear slithered down his spine. "Is she all right?"

"She's fine, a few cuts and bruises."

"Start at the beginning." His grip on the handset got tighter and tighter as Bosch relayed what had happened. "Why am I only just hearing about this?"

"It's in the daily report you'll be sent shortly," Bosch said.

He ground his teeth. Kit should have called him, should have told him. Except if Bosch knew he hadn't told Kit about the drone it meant Kit knew about it. He cringed. She'd be mad.

"Are you going to answer my original question?" Bosch asked.

"Kit was milking," he said. "I thought it more prudent to get the information to forensics as soon as possible, rather than tell her."

"And why were you there so early?"

He swore to himself. What had Kit told them? "She felt uneasy after the break-in," he said. "She was happy for me to stay the night, so that I would be on site if the burglar returned."

"That's highly inappropriate."

"She has a spare room, and we've known each other for years. My mother would have skinned me alive if I'd left her by herself."

Silence. "I'll talk to Khan about this."

He bit his tongue to stop protesting. The more he did, the more it would seem like he'd lost his ability to be unbiased. "Fine. Constable Marshall is sending you more drone footage. We've identified Paul and Gordon, who were involved with the drug ring, and we believe one of the men is Harry Smith. We're trying to get a firm ID on the fourth man. There's also a document which may contain details of drop locations."

"Thanks. I'll look over it."

Lincoln hung up and his hand hovered over the buttons on the phone. Would Kit answer if he called? It was milking time, so probably not.

Yeah, like that was the reason she wouldn't answer. If Kit hadn't called him after the incident it meant she was serious about keeping away from him until after Smith had been caught.

"Any news?" Ryan walked into his office and placed both hands on the back of the visitor's chair.

"Harry Smith rammed Kit off the road," Lincoln growled.

Ryan straightened and swore. "What?"

Lincoln explained what had happened.

"And Kit?"

"She was cut up, and they needed the jaws of life to get her out." His blood was ice.

"She didn't call you?"

He shook his head. Maybe she was simply mad about the drone.

"Why not?"

Lincoln looked at his best friend. Telling him about Kit would put him in an awkward position with the Albany detectives. He wouldn't do that to Ryan.

He shrugged. "She probably called the musketeers."

In any case, he had to see her. Had to confirm with his own eyes that she was fine.

Had to explain about the drone.

132

Chapter 14

Lincoln drove to the farm armed with Kit's favourite movie and the ingredients to make his mother's special pasta sauce. Pampering her with two of her favourite things couldn't hurt, especially if she was mad about the drone. At the entrance, the gate was closed. Kit never shut the gate. There was no need. The dogs didn't wander that far and guests were always welcome.

Unless she was being cautious about Smith.

Or shutting him out.

Unease settled over his skin as he drove through and shut the gates behind him. Cows meandered away from the milking shed so she had to be almost finished for the day. Hopefully it would give him enough time to prepare the meal before she got home.

His frown deepened as he spotted cars parked outside her house. The musketeers — including Jamie — were there.

Maybe he wouldn't be welcome.

He picked up the groceries and movie and headed around the side of the house. Loud music and voices were coming from the kitchen. He toed off his shoes and called, "Can I come in?"

He didn't wait for an answer. His brother and Mai were in the kitchen preparing dinner. Damn. He was too late. Jamie raised his eyebrows, but Lincoln ignored him, dropping the groceries on the bench and continuing to the lounge where Fleur and Hannah chatted with Kit. His breath caught in his throat at the dozen micro cuts all over Kit's face and forearms. He moved towards her, swept her up in his arms and held her close, her soft breasts pressed to his chest. She clung to him and in that moment he realised how fragile she was, how close he'd come to losing her. He wanted to destroy Harry Smith.

She trembled against him and then pushed him away. "You can't be here." Her voice was firm.

He swallowed. She couldn't push him away now. "I wanted to make sure you were all right."

"I'm fine." She brushed her hair out of her face, stepped back.

He moved closer. "What happened?"

She raised an eyebrow and her back stiffened, the fragility vanishing. "Didn't the detectives fill you in?"

"Not in detail."

"It sucks when people don't tell you things, doesn't it?" Her tone was light, almost pleasant, but her displeasure showed in her eyes.

He winced. She'd moved past scared into annoyed. "I'm sorry I didn't tell you about the drone."

"Was it Paul's drone?" Hannah asked.

"Where did you find it?" Fleur added.

Mai and Jamie hurried in. "Are we talking about the case?" Mai asked.

Kit tapped her hand on her thigh, her eyes narrowed.

Damn. He had to tell her something. "As I was going to the dairy this morning, I noticed something on the hen house. It was Paul's missing drone."

Kit's jaw clenched. "You didn't think to fetch me?"

She wouldn't like this. "I thought about it and decided it was safer for you not to know."

Her jaw dropped.

He hurried to explain. "I didn't know what was on there, and the information could have put you in danger. Plus I wanted to get it to forensics immediately."

He couldn't read her expression.

"Did you get any useful information?" Mai asked.

He nodded.

"Don't leave us in suspense, Lincoln," Fleur complained. "What was it?"

Kit bit her lip. She only did that when she was upset. "He's not going to tell us." She folded her arms. "It's police business."

"You're right." He was already breaking the rules by not divulging his relationship with Kit. Telling them confidential information about the case would really get him into trouble. His chest tightened. "I can tell you the information is essential to the case and we hope to have an arrest soon."

"That's bullshit, Lincoln," Kit hissed. "You found the drone on my land. I've been shot at, rammed and Elijah's been shot. I have a right to know."

He ran a hand through his hair. "It's confidential."

Fire sparked in her eyes. "If I hadn't let you stay the night, you wouldn't have found it."

He clenched his teeth, all his training told him he couldn't tell her, but he wanted to, desperately.

"You don't trust me." She stepped back as she said it, her eyes wide. "If you did, you would have called me back, would have shown me the footage. Am I still a suspect?" The hurt in her voice killed him.

"No, of course not."

Her expression hardened. "Get out."

Panic filled him. "Kit, it's not like that—"

She shook her head, closing her eyes. "I don't want to hear your excuses. You need to leave."

Hannah placed a hand on his arm, her expression sympathetic. "This *is* a musketeer meeting, so no guys allowed."

The others said nothing, but it was clear they weren't going to stand up for him. Not now at least. Damn it. He glanced at his brother. "Are you leaving?"

Jamie smirked. "I'm the exception. I'll walk you out."

Kit turned away, murmuring something to Fleur.

He huffed out a breath. He had to regroup.

As they walked out onto the verandah, Jamie said, "Linc, you've got to get your shit together."

Lincoln scowled. "Why don't you mind your own business?"

"Kit is my business. You said you cared for her."

"I do."

"Then why didn't you tell her about the drone?"

His own heart squeezed. "It's police business."

They walked down the darkened path to Lincoln's car.

"You weren't here on police business at the time," Jamie said. He pursed his lips. "She was milking."

"That's no excuse. You could have told her."

"It's for her own protection." His excuses sounded weak.

Jamie shook his head. "Ignorance is never a way to protect." His brother was right.

Jamie clapped his hand on Lincoln's shoulder. "Don't shut her out of the investigation. She was pretty upset when I arrived and not just about the crash."

He hated he hadn't been there for her. "So what do I do?"

"You tell her everything you can about the case. She doesn't like being left out. She's not as tough as she pretends." He stopped at Lincoln's car. "Trust is really important to her. Do you remember the vow you made when the musketeers made you their knight protector?"

It was over fifteen years ago. "Something about protecting them always."

Jamie nodded. "To protect the musketeers always and never abandon them." He glanced towards the house. "Guess who added the phrase about abandonment."

"Kit?"

"Yeah. She had issues even then about her biological mother leaving her. She didn't trust people to stick around. She already knew Monica loved Brody more than she loved Kit and then her fear was realised when her family left her behind when they went to Perth."

"She wanted to stay." She'd been adamant about it.

"Yeah, and she wanted them to stay with her. You not trusting her with the drone is just the first sign of rejection for her."

Lincoln sucked in his breath. Why hadn't he recognised she had abandonment issues? His rejection when she was eighteen would have been another hit. "I'll do what I can." He couldn't mess this up. He sighed. "When did you get so smart?"

"Learned everything from my big brother. He's normally really intelligent."

He shoved Jamie lightly. "Yeah, well not about Kit it seems."

"Don't stuff this up, Linc."

He wouldn't. He'd already done that once.

He wouldn't lose her again.

Kit woke the next morning hugging the pillow Lincoln had used a couple of nights ago. It still smelled like him and gave her a measure of comfort, but was a poor substitute for the real thing.

But maybe she was fooling herself. Without trust, they had no relationship. She pushed the pillow away.

It would be easy to ignore the fact he'd kept the drone from her. Yesterday's run in with Creepy Guy had made her realise life wasn't guaranteed. She wanted to be with Lincoln for as much time as she had left.

But if he didn't trust her enough to share such a vital part of the case, then did they even have a relationship?

She tossed back the sheets and dressed. She would understand if he'd found the drone while investigating the break-in. Then it would be part of the investigation and he couldn't share it with her.

But his conscious decision to keep her in the dark was a real kick to the gut.

She headed for the kitchen, moving quietly past the spare room where Jamie slept after he'd insisted on staying the night. She was pretty sure Lincoln had put him up to it.

She'd had a flood of elation when Lincoln had walked in last night, had felt so secure in his arms.

She'd been weak, but she wasn't normally a helpless female. Damsels in distress had never done it for her. She preferred a kick-ass heroine who saved herself.

If Lincoln couldn't handle that, if he didn't trust her, then he wasn't the one for her.

Her heart hurt as she walked out to the dairy.

After she'd finished milking her phone rang. Her stomach fluttered. Lincoln. She was pathetic. She shouldn't answer, should make him aware she wouldn't drop everything when he called. The ringing stopped and a text message vibrated in her pocket shortly after. Her fingers itched to see what it said.

She was hopeless.

Dragging out her phone, she read it.

Can you come into the station to view the drone footage today?

Well, damn. Had he got permission to show her? As much as she wanted to see it, she didn't want to get him in further trouble.

What time?

The response was immediate.

The detectives will be at the station at 11.

That answered her concern. The locksmith was due any minute but he should be done by then.

I'll be there.

She walked into her office and called the panel beaters who confirmed her car was a write-off. Did her insurance cover being rammed by a wanted felon?

That would be a fun phone call.

Elijah arrived as she stepped out of the dairy, and he looked refreshed and ready to go. The man always looked gorgeous in a casual, offhand way, even though he was about to work on a tractor for the next eight hours. She walked over to him. "How's the shoulder?"

"A little sore today."

"You should go home and rest."

He smiled at her. "I'm fine. I've got a new audiobook to listen to while I work." He tapped his phone in his pocket and then frowned "Who's that?"

A white van drove up the drive.

Her shoulders tensed. "Probably the locksmith. He's redoing the locks on the gun safe." The logo on the side became clear and she relaxed. "You should get started."

"In a minute." Elijah waited until the locksmith had parked and introduced himself. Then he turned to Kit. "Call me if you need anything."

"Will do." Her heart warmed that he was watching out for her. Then she gestured to the locksmith. "It's this way."

As Kit drove into Blackbridge later that morning, tension prickled her skin. Would the detectives realise her relationship with Lincoln had changed? She tapped the steering wheel. There was nothing to worry about. She didn't know where their relationship was at herself, so they couldn't possibly know. Besides, she'd had years of hiding her attraction, this was no different.

Spotting the police station up ahead, she turned left, driving past Mai's bakery site to see the progress. Last night Mai had mentioned they were almost at lock up and it was strange to see a modern concrete building where once an old, slightly run down nineteen-twenties structure had stood. The new, bigger building did have touches of the past in its facade, calling back to the old building. It would be a great place to have coffee with her friends.

She waved at the builders and continued driving.

Time to stop procrastinating.

She parked outside the police station and entered, finding Adam behind the desk.

"Hi, Kit. Lincoln mentioned you'd be by. Come through."

She walked through the interview room and out the back of the station, greeting Sue and Ryan who were at their desks. Ryan stood. "We've got the footage set up in Lincoln's office."

Her chest squeezed as she walked in. Lincoln sat behind his desk, looking gorgeous as ever and across from him sat the two detectives. He stood, his smile cautious. "Thanks for coming in, Kit."

"How can I help?"

"We need you to identify someone if you can," Bosch said, turning to her.

Lincoln indicated his chair. "Take a seat."

She brushed past him, inhaled his citrus scent and sat on his chair still warm from his body, hugging her.

"This may be difficult," he said.

"What you're about to see is confidential," Bosch said.

Kit nodded. The video was paused on the monitor, the drone more than fifty metres from the ground. She squinted. Two figures were next to a white ute. Her stomach lurched. "Is this after Paul has been shot?"

"What makes you say that?" Khan asked, his expression intense.

"I assumed the drone had to have captured something fairly significant," she told him. "That looks like my white ute and Paul's body next to it."

Bosch nodded. "Yes. You don't need to see what happened."

Holy crap. They'd caught the murder on film which meant they knew who killed Paul.

"Is it Harry with Paul?"

"We can't confirm or deny that," Khan said.

Of course not.

Lincoln reached past her and clicked the mouse. The footage played, the drone turning away from the ute, and there was a flash of red in the trees beneath it. Even through the branches it was clear it was a person, but their features were indistinguishable. Then the drone sped back towards the shed and she saw herself getting onto her motorbike.

Chills ran along her arms. She'd been going to search for Paul and the murderer was still there.

"Anything?" Lincoln asked.

She folded her arms. "Can I see it again, slowly this time?" She reached for the mouse, brushed his hand away from it and warmth tingled along her fingers. She ignored it, instead focusing on the screen, rewinding the video. She set the playback to a slower speed. No, it really was too small to make out any distinguishing features.

She watched it again, this time focusing on the rest of the scene. There had to be a vehicle somewhere.

A speck of white and red next to a tree. She paused and pointed to it. "Is that a motorbike?"

Lincoln leaned closer. "Looks like it. We'll ask forensics to clean up the image."

"It looks like a farm bike," Kit said. "It's a popular model. I've got one, Foley's got a couple as do half the farmers in the area." She replayed it. "And that could be a car." The trees covered it but there was definite white underneath the leaves.

"Good work, Ms van Ross," Bosch said. "Do you recognise the other guy?"

She watched it for a final time, staring at the figure, willing recognition to hit her. "No, sorry."

Lincoln's smile was gentle. "Thanks for trying."

She shifted her gaze. She wouldn't lose herself in his eyes. "Do you need anything else from me?"

"There's another video you should see," Khan said.

"Paul's parents gave us access to more of his drone footage," Lincoln said. "We need to identify the people in it." Lincoln brought up the video and pressed play.

The motocross track, but the riders were on modern bikes.

She pointed to the screen. "That's Paul and Gordon."

"What about the other two guys?" Ryan asked.

"He looks like Creepy Guy." If this video had been taken when Paul had been banned from the track, it was long before all the drug stuff started happening — that they'd known about.

"And the last guy?" Lincoln asked.

Something in his tone had her glancing up. They wanted her to identify that person. He wore a black dirt bike helmet with a skull design on it. She knew someone with a helmet like that. She visualised a motocross meet, running through all the people. No, it wouldn't come to her. "I've seen the helmet somewhere, probably the motocross."

"Thanks, Kit," Lincoln said.

Disappointment swept over her. She'd been no help whatsoever. Part of her had hoped she would see something that would solve the case. She'd read too many Nancy Drew books as a child. Standing, she said, "I'll see you later."

"Let me walk you out." Lincoln followed her.

Kit wanted to refuse, but she couldn't make a scene in front of the detectives. Her shoulder blades itched as they walked out. "What are you doing, Lincoln?"

"I need to talk to you and you didn't answer my call."

She sighed. "I need time and we agreed not to see each other until after the case was solved."

"I didn't agree to that." They reached her car and he touched her arm to stop her climbing inside. "I'm sorry about yesterday. I didn't tell you about the drone because I wanted to protect you."

Could she believe him? "At least I could be honest when I told Creepy Guy I had no idea what he was talking about."

"I know. I'm sorry. Can I cook you dinner tonight? We can talk."

Her heart leapt. Damn the weak, traitorous thing. "That's not a good idea, Lincoln."

"Please, Kit. I don't want you to be alone. I want to be there for you."

She should walk away before she cost him his job and she had her heart broken, but the words out of her mouth were, "I finish milking about six."

"Great. I'll be there."

She got into her car and glanced towards the station. Detective Bosch stood at the window of Lincoln's office, frowning.

Crap. She should have said no.

Kit was still berating herself as she drove down the tree-lined drive of her farm. She let out a deep breath. Stop stressing. Lincoln could handle himself. He was a good cop and the detectives had to recognise that.

Focus on the farm. It was the one thing she could control. She might have to fight with Mother Nature, but she always knew where she stood.

She pulled up outside the machinery shed and greeted her dogs who ran out to meet her. As she straightened, she caught sight of two red and white motorbikes inside the shed.

She only had one.

Slowly she scanned the surroundings. If it was a friend, they would have come out when they heard her arrive.

Every hair on her skin stood on end. She swallowed hard.

Was the person watching her now, waiting to see what she did? Would she be shot before she took the phone out of her pocket?

Make a decision.

The crunch of footsteps had her whirling around.

"Hey, Kit. I didn't hear you arrive." Ian pulled the earbuds from his ears as he walked over.

She exhaled noisily. "You scared the shit out of me, Ian. What are you doing here?"

He frowned. "Why are you so jumpy?"

"Side effect of discovering your farmhand was murdered, I guess." Her sarcasm was thick.

He blanched. "Sorry. I forgot about that."

As if she ever would. "What do you want?"

"Foley's fencing clamps broke and we need to fix a fence fast. He sent me over to borrow yours."

She walked towards the workshop. "I'll need them back as soon as possible."

"Sure." He fell into step beside her. "Got a new ute?"

"It's hired. Mine's in the shop," she said. "And the police still have the other one."

"Right. Shit, I'm sorry. I should have thought. Foley's got a spare vehicle he'd lend you."

"I've got this one now." She'd relied enough on Foley when she was younger. She wasn't going to burden him now. In the shed she found the clamps and handed them to Ian.

"Thanks, Kit. I'll get it back to you." He walked back to his bike and then glanced between the bike and the heavy clamps. "Shit. I didn't think about how to carry it."

Trust him not to consider the practicalities. "I'll strap it to the back mudguard." She grabbed an occy strap from her bench. "Call me when you've finished with them and I'll pick them up." She didn't want him turning up unannounced again.

"Sure thing." He got onto the motorbike and roared down the drive.

Kit tugged on her ponytail. She was too jumpy. The yard was too quiet, with too many places a person could hide, too many ways they could sneak up on her. Normally she liked to have music playing — it blocked out the memory of her father whistling while he worked — but not today. She had to be alert.

And she despised being scared on her own property.

The calves mooed in the paddock nearby. She needed to check them. Get the males ready for sale, which meant she could spend time away from the sheds. She'd see anyone coming.

Though she hoped Smith had lost interest in her.

Chapter 15

Lincoln waited for Kit to drive away before heading back into the station. He'd made it over the first hurdle — she was talking to him again. Next he needed to find Smith so he could focus on building his relationship with Kit.

Both detectives were still in his office when he walked in.

Bosch cleared her throat. "Sergeant Zanetti, what is your relationship with Ms van Ross?"

Dread lodged in his stomach. It was one thing to neglect to mention something and another to lie when asked a direct question. "I've known Kit since she was a child."

"She's like a sister to you?" Khan asked.

"I wouldn't say that."

"What would you say?" Bosch probed.

He hesitated. "It's complicated."

"In what way?" Bosch asked.

He closed his eyes. He couldn't lie. He wouldn't pretend he felt something less for Kit than he did. He'd deal with the consequences. "Over the past couple of days, it's moved away from being platonic."

"How far away?" Khan asked.

"We've slept together."

Bosch's eyebrows raised. "In that case, it's best if we remove you from the case."

His stomach clenched. "It's not necessary. I can still do my job."

"You know the rules, Zanetti," Khan said. "We have to protect the integrity of the case."

Any hint of a conflict of interest would give a defence lawyer a field day. He gritted his teeth. "What about my team?"

"They'll be updated as required."

Lincoln shook his head. "That's ridiculous. I have to protect my town," he said. "I need to protect Kit, and Smith's after her."

"We'll make sure she's protected." Bosch stood. "Lincoln, I have to report this." She looked like she was sorry.

He briefly closed his eyes and then nodded and walked them out of the station. Nausea stirred in his stomach. He'd deal with his supervisor. He had a good reputation. It would be fine.

He sighed and went back into his office.

Ryan joined him and closed the door. "Why didn't you tell me about Kit?"

"You would have had to report me."

Ryan shook his head. "I told you about Hannah." Ryan had met Hannah while investigating her stalker.

"That was different. I'm your supervisor. I deemed there wasn't a conflict."

His friend snorted. "I could have taken lead on this." He held up a hand before Lincoln could protest. "You know I would have kept you in the loop."

Lincoln sat down. "I have to protect her."

"You will. We all will. I know what you're going through, mate. You should have trusted me."

Ryan was right. "Sorry." Lincoln placed his head in his hands. "What am I going to do now? Kit's going to freak out. She thinks I'll lose my job."

"You won't. You're a good cop. You'll probably have to do a course on ethics or something."

Lincoln cringed. Hopefully Ryan was right. "What about the case? Smith's getting desperate and we're still no closer to finding him."

"Isn't there a motocross meeting this weekend?"

Lincoln frowned. "Yeah." He'd forgotten about it.

"Think our mystery guy might be there?"

Lincoln sat up straight. Genius. "Maybe." He'd be there as a particpant, but he could do his own surveillance work.

And now he didn't have to hide his relationship with Kit, he could be by her side, ensure Smith didn't get to her.

Now to figure out how to tell her he'd been taken off the case.

And hope she wasn't too mad.

Nerves hummed along Lincoln's skin as he drove out to Kit's farm that night. He'd called in a favour from Ryan to ensure he left work on time for once.

He'd briefly considered not telling her, but if she found out from someone else, she'd never trust him again.

He'd break it to her gently, after he'd made her a nice dinner, run her a bath and pampered her. No, he couldn't imagine Kit actually relaxing in a bath. That wasn't her thing.

But he'd do something else to show her he loved her.

Cows gathered around the dairy as he drove up to the house. He'd take the groceries inside, then go over and see if Kit needed a hand. The pasta dish wouldn't take more than ten minutes to throw together.

She'd left the back door unlocked, with only the fly screen between him and the house. Damn it. She should be more careful.

He left the groceries by the door as he went inside and checked room by room for intruders.

All clear.

After putting the food in the fridge, he locked up and walked to the milking shed. The dogs didn't come to greet him and they weren't among the cows. Maybe they were in the dairy.

Cows mooed occasionally but as he approached the building, there was very little other noise. He frowned. Kit always listened to music when she milked.

Was something wrong?

If only he had his gun. He peered into the shed. The lights were on, the interior he could see was empty and the milking equipment shushed and chugged as it worked. The earthy scent of hay and cow wafted out.

Slowly he crept towards the milking section, peering around the corner. Kit worked alone in the milking bay. He stepped out, scanning the empty area. He breathed a sigh of relief. "No music today?"

She shrieked and spun around, fist raised. "Damn it, Lincoln, can't you make noise when you walk in?" Her face was pale.

He grimaced. "Sorry. When I heard no music, I was worried."

"So you decided to sneak up on me?"

"I was quiet in case you were in trouble."

She scowled and went back to work. "They'd be stupid to come around when I'm milking," she said. "They'd get caught."

"Or find you alone."

She paused mid reach, just for a split second but it was enough. She really was scared.

Guilt filled him as he trotted down the steps towards her. "You're right to be cautious, Kit. We don't know what Harry might do. He knows the drone may prove he shot Paul, so he's desperate. We've never been able to pin anything on him before."

"So it was Creepy Guy."

Damn, he hadn't meant to say that.

She moved on to the next cow. "How did things go with the detectives after I left?"

Shit. He didn't want to tell her now.

She turned to him, frowning. "Lincoln?"

He ran a hand through his hair. "They took me off the case."

Her eyes widened and she backed away. "What?"

He sighed. "Bosch asked me what our relationship was and I told her it was no longer platonic."

She stilled, her eyes glistening. "Have you lost your job?"

His breath caught in his throat. "No. It's just this case, but they'll keep my team in the loop. I'll continue to protect you, Kit."

Her face screwed up. "Damn it, Lincoln. I told you to stay away! I'm not worth losing your job over." She stormed away from him. "You should have listened to me, you should have left me."

"Never," he growled. He strode after her, took her hand, tugged her closer. "I won't leave you again."

She stiffened, but didn't move away, her eyes searching his, fear, hope and despair in them.

A car door slammed and Lincoln stepped in front of Kit, shielding her. Who was it? The dairy gave them nowhere to hide, but they could sneak out through the gates the cows came through. Footsteps came closer.

They needed to move.

"Kit, I've finished for the day."

Elijah.

Lincoln's muscles relaxed as Kit pushed past him with a curse.

"How did it go?" she asked.

"I should have it finished by tomorrow." He spotted Lincoln and waved. "Hi."

Lincoln nodded and continued with the cows as Kit and Elijah discussed their plans for the week. Elijah's arrival had shown him how vulnerable she was here alone. He had to find Smith.

By the time Kit returned, the last batch of cows were done. She hesitated. "I need to write my notes. Can you clean up?"

"Sure." This wasn't where he wanted to have a heart to heart.

She nodded her thanks and jogged up the steps.

When he was done, he stopped by her office. Empty. His heart jumped. "Kit?"

No answer.

Hurrying out of the shed, he scanned the yards in the fading light. The ute was still parked outside, and her motorbike was in the shed. A dog barked and he turned towards the house to see Montoya and Roberts in the backyard. Kit had to be there.

He switched off the lights in the dairy and shut the door. He was almost certain she'd be fine, but he strode quickly over to the house nevertheless. The lights were on inside. "Kit," he called out as he entered.

"In my office."

The tension left his shoulders. She sat behind the desk, her laptop on, her hair damp and she'd changed clothes. She was safe and she'd already showered, which meant she was still mad at him. She glanced up. "Everything go all right?"

He nodded and then hesitated. It would be better to talk at dinner. Then she couldn't use work as an excuse not to talk to him. "Do you mind if I have a shower before I make dinner?"

"Suit yourself."

"Thanks." He grabbed his bag and had a quick shower before heading for the kitchen. Kit was still working in her office. He took the ingredients out of the fridge and began to chop. He had to prove his job wasn't in danger *and* that she was worth far more to him than it was.

The dogs snuffled around the kitchen as he prepared the sauce, set the table and then put the pasta on to boil. When he turned around, Kit was leaning against the doorway.

Her long brown hair fell messily past her shoulders and her blue T-shirt stretched nicely over her breasts, accentuating them. As his gaze dipped, he noticed her loose black shorts showed off her deliciously long legs. Damn, she looked good. He shifted to hide his reaction. "Are you finished?"

She nodded.

He stirred the sauce and then poured a glass of red wine, handing it to her. "Take a seat and I'll dish up."

She looked at him for a long moment and then sat at the table.

Yep, he had a lot to make up for.

He dished up the pasta, drizzled the sauce over the top and carried the two bowls to the table. He fetched his own glass of wine and then sat down. "*Buon appetito.*"

"Thanks, Lincoln. It smells good."

She was talking to him. Progress. "Hopefully it tastes as good." He ate a mouthful. It wasn't half bad. "Is Elijah working out well?"

She nodded, but scowled at him.

Maybe some simple conversation would soften her up. "He hasn't forgotten what he learned at the ag school while he was in Europe?"

Her fork clattered against her plate. "What are you doing, Lincoln?"

He blinked. "I'm making conversation."

Her eyebrows raised. "You want conversation? How about you tell me what happened with the detectives?"

The anger in her tone made him flinch. "There's not much to tell. They asked about our relationship, I told them the truth and they took me off the case."

"So what happens now?"

He shrugged. "My boss will probably slap me over the wrist." He was almost certain that's what would happen.

Kit pushed back her chair, eyes flashing. "How can you pretend like everything's fine?"

"Everything is fine."

"No, it's not. You've been taken off the case." The concern

in her eyes was real. "You should have listened to me, should have stayed away."

"They'll catch Smith."

"That's not what I'm afraid of." She got up, paced away from the table.

He stayed where he was, not wanting to agitate her further. "What then?"

"Lincoln, being a police officer is your dream job. If you lose it, you'll end up hating me."

"That will never happen."

She threw her hands up in the air. "You don't know that. You need more than me in your life. You'll be miserable without your job."

"I've been more miserable without you."

She stopped pacing, pressed her lips together. "I'm not worth the risk, Lincoln."

He hated she thought that way. Slowly he stood. "You're worth everything to me, Kit." He kept his voice gentle. "I'll call my boss tomorrow. Sort everything out." He wanted to smooth out the worry furrows on her brow.

She shook her head. "Lincoln, I come with so much baggage. You don't deserve to be weighed down by it."

"I'm used to your moods, Kit."

She rolled her eyes and slid back into her chair. "I wasn't talking about that, but thanks for pointing out another flaw."

The humour was a good sign. "What then?"

"I'm superstitious."

"I promise not to open any umbrellas inside."

"That's not what I mean." She squeezed her eyes closed, let out a breath and then straightened. She looked right at him. "Everything good in my life has come at a price."

Lincoln's heart squeezed at the anguish in her eyes. "What do you mean?"

She pushed the pasta around her plate. "When I was little, I really wanted a brother or sister. I got Brody, but Mum stopped paying me attention." She glanced up at him. "I wanted the farm and I lost my family, I wanted Jamie to come home and he lost his job and got dumped." Kit's eyes were full of misery. "One of us will lose something if we stay together."

He could understand her point of view, even if she was wrong. He stood, pulled her into his arms. "No, we won't. We gain everything by being together."

Her arms slipped around his waist and she rested her forehead on his shoulder. She felt so right there.

"I'm scared, Lincoln," she whispered. "I've wanted you for so long that all of this still feels like a dream I'm going to wake up from. I keep waiting for something bad to happen."

"Whatever life throws at us, we'll get through it." He kissed the top of her head.

"Yesterday I thought the price would be Creepy Guy killing me."

His heart froze. "No. That's *not* going to happen."

She pulled away from him. "You can't promise that. We don't know where he is and he's killed before."

He hated that she was right. "I'll do everything in my power to make sure it doesn't happen."

Her smile was small. "I know."

Lincoln kissed her gently. "Any other issues I need to know about?"

Kit slid back into her chair. "Isn't that enough?" She ate a mouthful of pasta. "You know Elijah's been really great. He's working long hours this week to get the crop sown before it rains."

And just like that she was back to being the Kit he was used to. He'd play along, but he wouldn't dismiss her concerns. He'd talk to his boss tomorrow. "That's great. How's his shoulder?"

"He should be resting, but he won't. He doesn't want to leave me here alone."

Lincoln's estimation of the man increased tenfold.

"Hopefully he'll be out of the sling by next week." She drank the last of her wine and stood, gathering their empty bowls. "I'll wash."

He grinned. She'd always hated to dry the dishes. He picked up the wine glasses and followed her into the kitchen. As she ran the water, he found the play-list he wanted on his phone and pressed play.

As the first song began, Kit's eyes widened. "You don't still have the cleaning play-list?"

"Of course I do." He hadn't been able to delete it, but he hadn't played it since he'd moved out. It held too many memories of better times when they would clean the house together and Kit would dance around singing at the top of her lungs.

She gave a small smile and switched off the tap. "Do you still know the words?"

He waited a beat for the song's chorus to start and then began to sing.

Kit winced.

He grinned. She probably regretted asking him.

Because one thing that hadn't changed was his terrible singing.

Lincoln was killing her.

Not only was his singing slightly off pitch making her cringe, but the fact he still had her play-list was a stab straight to her heart. She hadn't been able to listen to it since he'd left.

She half-heartedly tried to plug the holes in her argument to stay away from him, but she was running out of fingers and inclination. She wanted this to work, wanted to believe there'd be no consequences.

He twirled the tea towel into a thin roll and whipped it at her. "Come on, Kit Kat. Get to work."

She leaped back. "Steady on."

His grin melted her. She bit her lip and stuck her hands into the hot, soapy water. As she placed the first bowl in the drying rack, her voice joined his, unable to resist the lure of the tune and she moved her hips in time to the beat.

Eight years — give or take — since they'd stood side by side like this, cleaning up, singing together. She'd never thought they would again.

She pulled the plug out of the sink and watched the water flush away. What now?

She wanted him to stay. It would hardly matter to his job.

But still part of her worried.

She turned to him as he hung the damp tea towel over the oven handle. He was so damned handsome. His dark hair was tousled, still a little damp from the shower and his T-shirt clung to his broad chest. Perhaps she should stop being pessimistic.

Maybe she should embrace what they had while it lasted.

In her mind she could still visualise Harry pointing his gun at her.

The future wasn't guaranteed.

His brown eyes met hers.

She ran her tongue over her lips. Yes, she should definitely enjoy herself. She stepped closer to him. "I've always had this fantasy of you doing me on the kitchen bench."

His eyebrows raised. "Really?" He glanced at the bench then back at her.

She lifted herself up onto it and beckoned him towards her.

He hesitated for only a second before he fit himself between her legs. He was so warm. She wrapped her arms around his neck. "Want to make a girl's dream come true?" Her lips were only millimetres from his.

"I want to make *all* your dreams come true."

His words were like lightning, bright and electric, kick-starting her heart. She pressed her mouth to his.

She kissed him hard, and he drew her closer, his firm chest pressing against her breasts.

He tasted divine; red wine, pasta sauce and Lincoln, the man she'd loved forever. Her tongue met his as her hands reached for the bottom of his shirt, tugging it up so she could touch his skin.

He groaned against her mouth and power surged through her.

She leaned back, stripping off her own top, glad she hadn't bothered with a bra. His mouth found her breast and he licked and sucked, sending heat straight to her groin. She wanted him now, hard and fast, before any thoughts got in the way.

She dipped her hand in the front of his pants, found his cock, hard and ready.

Oh, yes, this would be good.

She stroked him slowly, once, twice and he swore under his breath. "Kit, you're killing me."

She loved her name on his lips.

Lifting herself up, she pushed her shorts down her legs and he grabbed them and threw them to the floor. Then he moved between her thighs again, his hardness pressing against her groin.

It had to be now.

She guided him in, sighing as he filled her and then she

wrapped her legs around his waist, pulling him closer. "Fuck me, Lincoln."

He thrust into her fast and she urged him on, squeezing him with her legs as the rhythm increased. She closed her eyes as sensation after sensation filled her.

It couldn't get any better than this. This was Lincoln.

He bit her neck, his teeth sliding along her skin sending a shock through her. "More," she moaned.

He bit her again, his tongue softening the pain as he licked and sucked while he thrust into her. She was going to explode. She wanted more and more and she rocked with him as her orgasm built.

"Look at me, Kit."

The order had her eyes shooting open and she met his gaze. The intensity in them stole her breath.

As the orgasm swept over her, he said, "I love you."

And then he came.

Her heart thumped in her chest, her breath coming in gasps. Lincoln held her tightly as he found his release. She couldn't help holding on to him but she wanted to run away, pretend he'd said nothing.

No way was she trusting anything that came out of a man's mouth as he was coming. That was the euphoria talking.

She desperately wanted it to be true, even when the idea terrified her.

He sighed and released his hold, his chuckle tickling her heart strings. "If I'd let myself fantasise about having sex with you, the kitchen bench definitely would have been on my list."

She was trapped until he moved and he didn't look like he was inclined to. She smiled. "Pretty good, huh?" Montoya trotted into the kitchen and she sighed in relief. "But now I want to cover up before I scar my dog for life." She nodded towards him.

Lincoln grinned. "We can't have that." He handed her her shorts and she slid off the bench and quickly dressed.

"How about we watch some Netflix?" Lincoln asked as he stepped back. "There's a great series I just started about King Arthur."

She knew the one he was talking about. It was on her to-watch list, but it reminded her of the movies she'd liked as a child, and of the ceremony the musketeers had held to make Lincoln their knight protector. Lancelot to her Guinevere — it was doomed from the start.

He waited for her, expectantly. She couldn't refuse him. "Sure. Why don't you set it up and I'll make a cuppa?"

He frowned. "Is everything all right?"

Her smile felt forced. "Of course. We just had great sex." She filled the kettle, waiting for him to leave.

He didn't move.

"Kit, I get the feeling I've done something wrong."

Why couldn't he be like most guys and be satisfied with sex? Normally by this time they were out the door. "Nothing's wrong with your moves." She switched the kettle on, turned to get mugs out of the cupboard and bumped right into him.

"How can I fix it, if I don't know what I've done?"

What could she say to get him to go away?

"Tell me the truth, Kit." He searched her eyes, and she looked away. He inhaled. "It's because I told you I love you." He placed a hand under her chin and gently turned her head to face him again.

"We all say things in the throes of passion."

He nodded. "And I meant every word. I do love you, and in time I hope you will believe me." His kiss was soft, then he walked out of the room.

She exhaled, her legs shaky. When he looked at her like that, with an expression so earnest, she wanted to believe him.

More than anything.

But the cliff she stood on had vicious jagged rocks at the bottom that would split her open if he didn't catch her.

She couldn't bring herself to leap.

Chapter 16

Kit took her time making the tea, not quite ready to face Lincoln. Her home phone rang in the living room. The only people to call that line were her family. Everyone else used her mobile.

When was the last time she spoke to her father? Probably a month ago.

She wandered into the living room and picked it up. "Hello?"

"Hey, Sis. How's things?"

Kit frowned. Brody almost never called her. "Everything's the same as always. How's uni?" She turned her back on Lincoln and his raised eyebrows. She didn't need to worry her family about Paul's murder or the shootings. There was nothing they could do about it.

"Not bad. I've got a couple of assignments due." He paused. "Are you sure nothing's wrong?"

"I had the musketeers over for dinner last night, which was fun." She walked back into the kitchen to finish the tea. When she turned around, Lincoln stood in the doorway. She handed him a mug.

"Hang on, Dad wants to talk to you."

Kit winced as she heard her brother say, "She says everything is fine," and then her father came on the line.

"How's my Sunshine?"

Hearing her nickname was bittersweet. It reminded her of the days when she was a kid, before Brody was old enough to join them, and she would hang out with her dad on the farm. He'd been her hero, and she'd thought he'd never leave her. "I'm fine, Dad. How are you and Mum?" She picked up her own mug and followed Lincoln back into the living room.

"We're fine. What's this I hear about Paul dying?"

"Who told you?"

"Rosa called Monica."

Damn Mrs Z. "He died last week, Dad. I've already replaced him, so the farm is fine."

"I don't care about the farm. How are you coping? Rosa said it was made to look like suicide?" He whispered the last word.

She squeezed her eyes shut. "Yeah, but it wasn't."

He swore. "Is there a psycho on the loose? Are you safe?"

Kit blinked. Her father was never this animated. "The police are investigating and I'm being careful. Don't stress."

"I should come down. You shouldn't be alone out there."

"No! I'm busy on the farm and you'll get in the way." She glanced at Lincoln. Maybe he could convince her father. "Lincoln's on the case, Dad. He'll have it solved in no time."

"Can he stay with you? I should call him, tell him to watch out for you."

It hadn't taken him long to switch from coming down to dumping her on Lincoln again. She shouldn't be hurt by it. "I'll ask him." Her face heated and she averted her gaze from Lincoln.

"Make sure you do." He sighed. "I worry about you down there all by yourself. The farm's a lot of work."

"I manage, Dad. And I have the musketeers to support me."

"You're doing a better job than I ever did."

Kit sat on the couch. It was the first time her father had ever acknowledged her work on the farm. "Thanks, Dad."

"I don't tell you enough how proud I am of you."

She couldn't speak. She leaned into Lincoln, needing his touch. "I'll talk to you later." She hung up and sighed.

Lincoln squeezed her. "You didn't tell them about Paul?"

She shrugged. "What's the point? There's nothing they can do."

"They could support you."

"I've got the musketeers for that." She shifted away, sipped her tea. "If Dad came down, he'd be someone else Harry could target."

"You're right. Should I call him tomorrow? Tell him I'm watching out for you?"

She shook her head. "No. He'll have forgotten it by then. He only called because your mum rang Monica." He'd felt obligated. She reached for the remote. "Shall we watch the show?"

Lincoln nodded, but from his expression she knew the conversation wasn't necessarily over.

That was fine. As long as she could delay it a bit longer.

She hit play.

The next morning Lincoln woke before Kit's alarm went off. His eyes were gritty and he'd tossed and turned most of the night, unable to stop thinking.

She hadn't believed him when he'd said he loved her.

Though it hurt, it made sense. She'd been rejected by a lot of people who were supposed to love her unconditionally.

So now he needed to figure out how to make her trust him.

He definitely shouldn't have told her he loved her while they were having sex. It was straight up foolish, but he hadn't been able to keep down the words. He wanted to tell her every day, every hour that she was the woman for him. He wanted to spend the rest of his life with her.

He snuggled into her, needing to be closer.

From what he'd heard from her phone call with her father, their relationship wasn't great. When he'd lived with Kit, Mr van Ross had called every week to check on her. She'd moaned about him keeping tabs on her, but she'd seemed pleased he'd trusted her with the farm. She'd always said she was happy they were enjoying Perth so much.

But perhaps it had all been an act.

Maybe she'd been pretending to be fine for that long.

Kit's alarm squawked and she slapped it off, but instead of leaping out of bed, she snuggled back down into his arms. "Morning." She smiled and hope illuminated his day.

He kissed her cheek. "Good morning. What can I make you for breakfast?"

She sighed. "You keep cooking for me and I'm going to get

fat."

"Never gonna happen. How about an omelette?"

"That would be great." She stretched, her breasts pushed forward, and he resisted the urge to kiss them. "Let me take a quick shower."

She walked naked across the room and down the hall. When the bathroom door closed behind her, he grinned so wide it hurt his mouth.

She wasn't pushing him away.

He went into the kitchen, prepared the ingredients for breakfast, fed the dogs and made them both a coffee. When the shower switched off, he heated the frypan.

Kit walked in as he plated up, picked up her coffee and took a deep sip. "You always made better coffee than I did."

Lincoln smiled. "It always tastes better when someone else makes it." Maybe the way into Kit's heart was to remind her of all the good times they'd had together. He checked the time. "I'd better go. I need to stop by my place on the way to work, but I'll check the sheds before I go."

"All right."

He hesitated. "Can I come back tonight?"

Her smile was cautious. "I'd like that."

So would he.

Kit glanced up at the cloudy sky. They weren't rain clouds yet, but they were definitely condensing. Hopefully Elijah was right about finishing the seeding today. In the meantime she needed to check the pregnant cows, bring them to the paddock closest to the house so she could watch them. They'd begin calving soon and the whole process would begin again. Then she'd need to separate the current milking herd and dry some of them off so they could get pregnant.

And so the cycle continued.

The young bulls from last year were fattening up nicely, ready to be sold off for their meat. She didn't like doing it, but she had little use for the males.

She chuckled. Of any species.

Lincoln was an exception. She was getting used to waking up

in his arms.

Her phone beeped and her pulse skipped as she saw the message.

Can't wait to see you tonight.

Her whole body smiled as she typed her response. *Me too.*

She shook her head. Now wasn't the time to stare dreamy-eyed over the paddock. She needed to get those pregnant cows moved. Whistling to her dogs, she got on her motorbike.

As she rounded the cows up, one young heifer stood by herself. Her udders were bigger than normal and she shifted away from the herd as Kit tried to guide them towards the new paddock.

Damn. It looked as if she would calve early.

Kit left her where she was and focused on getting the rest moved, relying on her dogs to round up those who broke away from the group.

When they were settled with a bit of fresh hay to sweeten the deal, she headed back to the lone cow. This was her first pregnancy and Kit didn't want to stress her unnecessarily, so she parked the bike and moved forward on foot.

The cow had her tail raised and she kept a wary eye as Kit approached. She was one of the smallest of the herd, and if she went into labour, there might be problems. "Come on, girl. We need to move you closer to the sheds."

The cow shuffled a few feet away.

She wasn't going to go easily. Just what Kit needed. She circled behind her and with the dogs either side, she waved her hands and made noises. Bit by bit, the cow headed in the right direction.

Kit pulled out her mobile and called the vet. "Oscar, I've got a young heifer who looks like she's going into early labour."

"How early?"

"About three weeks. This is her first and she's showing all the signs. I'm moving her closer to the sheds now."

"Think she'll have trouble?"

"Not sure. She's one of the smaller ones. I'll monitor her, but wanted to give you the heads up."

"Noted. Give me a call if I'm needed."

"Thanks."

She hung up. Now the cow was moving, she appeared eager

to be reunited with the herd. Kit opened the gate for her and the heifer hurried through, going to stand at a distance from the rest.

The cow lay down and then got up again with a groan, moved a few paces and lay down again.

Yeah, definitely getting ready to give birth, but it could be a couple of hours yet. Kit would monitor her throughout the afternoon.

Whistling to her dogs, she fetched her bike and then headed for the dairy.

Lincoln arrived as Kit went to check the cow for the second time. He drove up, a light dust following his car, and she tried to control the pleasure in her chest from seeing him. She waved as he climbed out still in his police uniform and turned her attention back to the cow. She was lying down again and dilated. Not too long now.

Moving back towards the dairy, Kit climbed through the fence and met up with Lincoln.

"Hey, how was your day?" He pulled her into his arms and kissed her.

Her heart squeezed. So natural. So comfortable. So right. Focus. "I've got a cow going into early labour."

"Is that bad?"

She shrugged. "It's her first and I'm monitoring her in between the milking." She gestured for him to follow her. "So, how was your day?"

He scowled. "Frustrating. Bosch won't tell me if any forensics have come back."

Her chest tightened. "Did you speak to your supervisor?" She held her breath.

"Yeah."

She waited for him to say more. "And?"

"I'll get a note on my file." He grimaced. "I have to talk to the psych about why I did what I did and I need to go to a couple of training seminars about ethics and such."

It didn't sound too bad. "Your job is safe?"

He smiled. "My job is safe."

The tightness in her chest eased. "Good." It was enough for today. Tomorrow she'd worry whether there'd be some other price to pay.

They entered the dairy. "Let me help, then I'll make dinner."

She hadn't eaten this well in a long time. Usually she made a bulk batch of something and then ate it for the rest of the week. "Thanks."

They worked side by side and then as Lincoln began cleaning, she radioed Elijah.

"You nearly finished?"

"One more row to go," he replied.

She smiled. Great news. "I'll see you when you get back."

She helped Lincoln clean and on the way out she grabbed some long gloves.

"What are they for?" Lincoln asked.

"In case mama cow needs some help."

He grimaced as they headed back to the cow in labour.

The animal's contractions had started, her whole belly convulsing as she pushed. A hoof stuck out and the cow mooed.

"Holy shit!" Lincoln said.

Kit grinned. "Have you never seen a cow being born, Slinky?"

He shook his head, his eyes wide.

Rookie. "Well stick around. It won't be too much longer now." The second hoof popped out and the tension in Kit's shoulders released. The calf looked to be the right way around.

"Do you need to do anything?"

"No. Mama's got it all sorted." With the next contractions, the calf's nose and then the head popped out. The cow groaned, shifting a little. Kit checked the herd, but they weren't paying her any attention.

"Wow." Lincoln stared at the baby, half in, half out of the cow.

Kit laughed, wrapped her arm around his waist, happy to share one of the joys of her work with him. "Not something you see every day."

"No."

She'd been six when she'd first witnessed a birth and her father had stood next to her and explained what was happening. She'd thought him a hero when he'd pulled the calf out. She'd called it Sunshine.

Another contraction and the baby slithered out with a plop.

Kit pulled Lincoln back a couple of steps as mama cow clambered to her feet and licked the calf.

It was a girl, and her eyes fluttered open.

Alive.

Kit let out the breath she held.

"That was incredible," Lincoln said, squeezing her. "What happens now?"

"The calf will get to its feet soon and have a feed. At some stage over the next few hours, the afterbirth will come out as well." As they watched, the calf shook its head and after a little prodding from mama, scrambled to its feet, wobbling a little.

She would be fine.

Lincoln shook his head. "I can't believe this is the first time I've seen a birth. And you were so calm."

She laughed. "All the cows in this paddock will give birth in the next month or so," she said. "I'm used to it."

He scanned the paddock. "You're incredible."

"I'm not doing any of the work."

"But you know what to do if something goes wrong. You've got those gloves…" He whistled low. "It's impressive. I couldn't do it."

His praise washed over her, lifting her spirits. "I'm not Super Girl. I have the vet on speed dial." Which reminded her. She called Oscar. "We're all good. Calf looks healthy."

"Great. I'll come out in the morning if you want."

"No, it's fine." She hung up and glanced at Lincoln. "Have you seen enough yet?"

"Yeah. How about I make you dinner?"

She smiled. "Sure." As they moved towards the house, Elijah arrived back in the tractor.

"I'll get started." Lincoln kissed her briefly, waved to Elijah and walked off.

The casual kiss, no reluctance of a public display of affection made her heart ache. Pushing it aside, she jogged over to where Elijah had parked outside the machinery shed. "How did it go?"

Elijah shook his head. "Nah, uh. You don't get to kiss the sexy policeman and pretend like it didn't happen. Are you two a thing?"

She glanced over at Lincoln. "I'm not sure what we are yet."

His expression immediately changed to worry. "Everything will be fine, honey."

She nodded though she wasn't as certain.

"The seeding is done."

"That's great. Thanks so much." One less item on her job list.

"My pleasure. What's next on the program?"

"We need to do some paddock rotation and we got our first new calf today."

"Is that early?"

"Yeah, the rest are due next month." She'd review her records before she finished for the night. "Are you coming to the motocross on Sunday?"

"I might stop by. I don't have a bike to ride."

"You can borrow one of mine," she said.

"Thanks." He grinned. "I'll think about it."

She waved him goodbye and then trotted back to the office in the dairy to record the first baby of the season.

Night had fallen by the time she finished. She switched the lights off and was plunged into darkness. The only light was from the house in the distance. She shut the door and headed for Lincoln.

Something squeaked in the machinery shed across from her.

Her heart pounded. Bracing herself, she peered into the darkness where the noise had come from. It was probably a door open, swinging in the wind.

Except there wasn't any wind.

Goosebumps leaped to her skin. She wasn't stupid enough to explore further, not with Harry around, and the only light the torch on her phone. She fumbled it on and strode for the safety of the porch light, wishing the ute wasn't already over at the house. Her phone rang and she jumped. Lincoln. "I'm almost back," she said as she answered it. "Just leaving the shed now."

"Good." He came outside, stood on the verandah and peered towards the sheds.

"I can see you." Though she was still a hundred metres away.

"I'll feel better when I can see you," he said. "What took so long?"

"I wanted to record the calf details." Having his voice in her ear calmed her. She didn't dare look behind her though her shoulder blades itched. She was being paranoid. There were often noises around the shed, metal contracting in the cool air, wind blowing things about —this wasn't anything different. "Is dinner ready?"

"Just about."

Montoya and Roberts ran to greet her and having them close gave her a sense of security. She passed the hen house and then entered her yard. She hung up and trotted up the back steps. "Thanks." She kissed Lincoln and took her boots off. "Shall we get inside? I'm starving."

He frowned at her. "Is everything OK?"

She wasn't telling him about the noise. He'd want to investigate and he'd be at a distinct disadvantage in the dark. Plus Creepy Guy had a gun and Lincoln wasn't armed. "Yeah. I'm ready to get off my feet."

Before she could blink, he swept her up in his arms. She shrieked.

"Let me help you with that." His grin pierced her defences, hit straight in the centre of her heart.

But tonight she wouldn't fight it.

Tonight she was happy he was here.

Chapter 17

Kit's damned alarm screeched Lincoln awake at five-thirty. He groaned as she slapped it off. He might have the day off, but a farmer never did. He would have to get used to it. Pushing himself up on his elbow, he watched a beautifully naked Kit take some clothes out of her dresser. "Want a hand?"

"No, go back to sleep. You don't need to get up."

"What if I want to?" He got out of bed and pulled her into his arms. Her body fit so perfectly against his.

She rolled her eyes. "Sex at this time of the morning is not my thing."

He brushed her lips with his. "Good, because you weren't getting any. I want your company, not your body." He let her go and dressed.

She stared at him and he swallowed his smile. He liked being able to surprise her.

"Suit yourself. I'd still be buried under the blankets if I had a choice."

"I'd rather spend time with you."

She gave him a small, but genuine smile as she slipped past him and headed for the kitchen.

He grinned. Slowly he was getting through to her. He followed her, filling up the kettle as she fetched the cereal out of the pantry. "Got much on today?"

"I want to clean the seeding machine and the tractor," she

said.

The first drops of rain hit the tin roof, loud and irregular at first and then coming down faster like automatic machine gun fire and so loud it was almost deafening. He peered out of the kitchen window and in the dawn light saw the dark clouds and rain. "You should park it outside."

She grinned. "Good idea."

That was better. She was relaxing.

"So what are you doing on your day off?" she asked.

"Hanging out with you."

"Don't you have anything better to do?"

"There's nothing else I want to do." He'd wasted enough time not being with her.

"If I'm your best option, you need to get a life." She laughed as she said it.

Lincoln's gut twisted at her easy dismissal of herself. "I couldn't have a better option."

She glanced down at her bowl, bit her lip, but her lips tilted upwards in a slight smile.

He ate his breakfast as she fed the dogs and then took her Driza-Bone off the hook. "Have you got a rain jacket?"

"No." He'd deal with a bit of rain.

She took a blue rain jacket off the hook. "This might fit you."

It was a bit of a squeeze, but better than nothing. Together they ran out to the ute. A thin line of light shone on the horizon, but the clouds obscured most of it. As he climbed in, he brushed off the rain. "How long until you get your car back?"

"I'm waiting for the insurance payout to come through. I'll need to buy a new one."

He'd read the report of the incident and she was lucky to be alive. If Harry had hit her harder, if the tree had been closer to the road…

He shuddered. He had to catch Harry fast.

Kit pulled up outside the dairy. "You get started inside and I'll move the tractor out."

Lincoln scanned the sheds. It was still dark and anyone could be hiding in there. "How about I come with you? Make sure you don't hit anything."

"OK."

He blinked at her quick agreement. Maybe she wasn't as unconcerned as she appeared. They ran over to the machinery shed and Kit drove the big tractor out from under the roof line. The seeder was still attached and the rain was heavy enough to wash the surface layer of dirt off at least.

By the time they raced inside the dairy, his jeans were drenched and his shoes squelched. Kit squeezed out her ponytail and stripped off her long jacket, hanging it on a hook by the door. Her clothes were dry. "If you hang around, we'll have to get you one of these."

If.

He had a long way to go. He simply smiled. "Shall we get started?"

She flicked the switches while he opened the gates to let the first pass of cows in. It was simple work and he sang along to the tunes playing on Kit's stereo as he prepped and milked the cows. This was something Kit did every day, twice a day. He didn't understand the appeal, but she'd always been a farm girl. His earliest memory was her playing in their backyard with Jamie, telling him he had to train his dog to herd cows. She'd ridden her little peewee fifty motorbike over with her father and she couldn't have been more than five.

Her step-mother had tried to clothe her in dresses and ribbons, but it had been pants and boots for Kit. He remembered Monica complaining to his mother about Kit's wild ways.

Kit had known who she was from a young age.

He'd admired her for that.

He hadn't a clue what he wanted to be until the silly ceremony when the musketeers had knighted him the protector of their group. He'd been about sixteen and had agreed to it because Kit had been pig-headed even at ten years old and he'd had a sweet spot for all the musketeers.

But when they'd placed the banksia crown on his head and proclaimed him their protector it had felt so incredibly right. He wanted to protect people, to help them feel secure. The next day he'd explored what he needed to do to join the police force.

He'd never told the musketeers.

The rain had settled in by the time they finished. The sky was grey and water fell in an endless stream. Kit put her Driza-Bone jacket back on. "Why don't you sit this one out, Slinky?"

He wasn't letting a bit of water stop him. "I'll be fine. Show me what you need to do."

She showed him the parts of the seeder that needed cleaning and handed him a brush while she wielded a high-pressure hose. "You take that side."

Several hours later he was completely drenched, but the seeder and tractor were sparkling clean. Kit reversed them back into their bay and then they trudged over to the house to dry.

"Anything else you need to do today?" Lincoln asked as he stripped off his soaked jumper and shirt in the laundry.

"Just prepare the bikes for the race meet tomorrow."

"Me too."

She glanced at him. "We could head into Blackbridge for lunch," she said. "You could pick up your bike then."

His heart leaped. She wanted to spend more time together and in public. "Sounds perfect." His phone rang and when he saw the number he bit back a curse. "Give me a second."

"Nicole Wellard is asking to speak with you," Bosch said.

Lincoln blinked. He'd arrested Nicole last month when she'd tried to kill Fleur. The woman had been disposing of chemical waste for the drug ring Smith was involved with. She hadn't been willing to tell them much about who had hired her. "Isn't she at the women's prison in Perth?"

"Yes. We can set up a Skype session this afternoon."

They wanted whatever information Nicole could give him. So did he. He glanced at Kit. "I can be at the Blackbridge station at two."

"We can set it up at Albany."

No. He wasn't playing their game. "I have plans today and can't get to Albany, so it's Blackbridge or nothing."

"We'll meet you there at two." She hung up.

Lincoln placed his phone on the table.

"Who was that?" Kit looked back at him, head tilted as she dried her hair with a towel. So very beautiful.

"Lincoln?"

He shook his head. "Detective Bosch. Nicole wants to talk to me."

Her eyebrows raised. "Think she'll tell you more about who she was working for?"

"I hope so." He took the towel she handed him. "Do you mind hanging around in town for a little longer while I do this? You could see if the musketeers are free for a coffee?"

"Not at all." She smiled. "If Nicole can give you a lead, I'm all for it. I'll call Fleur now."

When she finished, she glanced at him. "I need a hot shower to warm up. Want to join me?"

His heart cheered. "Always."

The grassed river foreshore was deserted but Kit still had difficulty finding parking at midday. Lincoln pointed out a bay about a hundred metres away from the cafe entrance. They would get drenched again.

"Maybe we should have lunch at your place," Kit said.

Lincoln smiled. "A little rain won't hurt." And he wanted to be seen in public with Kit, wanted everyone to see they were now a couple.

"If you say so." She didn't look convinced.

"On the count of three," he said. "One, two—" They both opened their doors and sprinted across the road to where the shops' overhang gave them cover.

Kit laughed, her eyes alight with mischief, water dripping down her face as she attempted to brush off the drops. Gorgeous. He swept her into his arms, kissed her hard. She tasted like raindrops and she clung to him, kissing him back just as passionately.

A wolf whistle pierced his brain and Lincoln reluctantly pulled back. Jeremy grinned at them both. "Get a room, you two."

Kit gave him the finger, her face tinged slightly red. "You're jealous."

"Sure am." He laughed. "See you tomorrow."

Lincoln couldn't remember the last time he'd seen Kit blush. It was sweet. He slipped his hand into Kit's and they walked down to the cafe.

A few people stopped and stared as they found a table at the back.

"We seem to be the centre of attention," Kit murmured.

"They'll get bored when they see us together all the time."

She smiled, and then focused on the menu.

He grinned. Soon everyone would know he and Kit were dating.

After lunch, Kit drove Lincoln to his place. It had been a long time since she had been in his home, and a shimmer of nerves swept over him as he unlocked his front door.

"Make yourself at home." He headed for his bedroom to change into his uniform. "Where are you meeting the musketeers?" he called.

"We're going to Hannah and Ryan's," she said, coming to the bedroom door. "I'll drop you at the station first and after you're finished, we can come back here and load your bike on the back of the ute."

"Thanks." He kissed her and then tucked in his shirt.

She watched him, a predatory look in her eyes. "I do love you in uniform."

Her gaze had him hardening. Minx. He pulled her closer to him. "I'm glad to hear it." She clung to him, wrapping one leg around him to tug him closer and running her fingers through his hair.

The urge to strip her naked and bury himself inside her was strong. The woman made him wild. When she tugged at his shirt and her hands touched his skin, it took every bit of resistance he had to pull back. Duty called. "I have to get to the station."

Her eyelids were heavy, her expression full of desire.

He swallowed, took two steps back into his room. "You can help me out of it when we get back."

She grinned. "Consider it done."

He let out a deep breath and re-tucked his shirt. Focus. He had to go to an interview. "Let's go."

Kit dropped him at the station and he dashed inside and fired up his computer. A tap at the front door told him the detectives had arrived. He let them in, both of them slightly damp and then logged into Skype. "What do you know about Nicole's request?"

"We received notification Mrs Wellard is ready to talk, but she only wants to speak to you. Her lawyer is hoping to get her a lesser sentence if she can give us information that will lead to the arrest of whoever is in charge of the drug ring."

"What did we agree to?"

"Depends on what information she has."

They weren't being very forthcoming, but maybe they hadn't promised anything. He logged into Skype and waited for Nicole to come on the line.

Her black hair was tied back in a severe ponytail and her eyes were sunken. The fluorescent light in the room gave her skin a washed out, sallow tone, further ageing her, and the loose purple shirt of the prison uniform did nothing for her figure. She'd always been someone who cared about her appearance. He might have felt sorry for her if she hadn't tried to kill Fleur three times.

"How have you been, Nicole?"

"I'm in prison." She scowled. "How do you think I am?"

He ignored her tone. "How can I help you?"

She lowered her voice. "I need to get out, Lincoln. I don't deserve to be here. I made a couple of bad decisions. I was desperate."

A couple? She was fooling herself. "What can you tell me about who hired you?"

"I was going through the details with my lawyer and remembered something Gordon told me," she said. "He got his mate Paul involved in selling drugs. Paul Maddock."

Lincoln made a note. If he told her Paul was dead, she might stop talking. "All right. What else have you got?"

"Harry Smith met with me the first time, told me what to do."

"Where did you meet?"

"It was out towards Albany, past the cheese factory."

He didn't flinch. "Towards the van Ross dairy?"

She nodded. "There's a road which kind of leads nowhere between two farms. I met him there."

She had to be talking about the road between Kit's and Foley's place. "Could you point the road out on a map?"

"Yeah."

"Did you see anyone else at the time?"

"A guy rode a motorbike on one of the farms."

"Which one?"

She shrugged. "The one on that side." She pointed to the

right.

It didn't help. "Was it the dairy or the sheep farm?"

"Must have been the sheep farm. That's the one that had the shed fire, wasn't it? I'd picked up some waste from there about a week before the fire."

Foley's farm. They'd investigated him at the time of the fire, but he'd sworn he hadn't known anything about the bulk chemicals that had been stored in his old shed. They hadn't had enough evidence to charge him with anything. "Did you see anyone when you picked up the waste?"

"No."

"Did Gordon tell you about anyone else who was involved?"

She shook her head.

In other words her information was useless. "Is there anything else you can remember? Background sounds you heard when talking to Harry, any addresses, any regularity with your pickups?"

Nicole frowned. "I always figured he was on a farm. I'd occasionally hear a dog or a sheep in the background."

Could Ian be hiding Harry Smith?

He grimaced. Ian couldn't hide him without Foley's knowledge. But Foley was a well-respected member of the community. He helped Kit whenever she needed it, was a volunteer fire-fighter, was always the first to lend a hand, even after his wife had left him and he was struggling himself.

Bells went off in his head. Foley's wife had taken everything, and yet Foley had bought the motocross club a brand new water tank to replace the one Nicole had destroyed. He'd said it was from insurance money, but initially they weren't going to pay out. He made a note. "Thanks Nicole." He glanced at the detectives who sat out of view of the camera. They shook their heads. No questions from them. "If you think of anything else, let me know."

"Lincoln, I've helped, haven't I? They'll reduce my sentence, won't they?"

"It's not my decision, Nicole. I'll tell them you were cooperative."

She slumped in her seat. "Thanks."

A guard switched off the camera. Lincoln disconnected and said, "We need to investigate Greg Foley further. His property is next to Kit's, he had a fire caused by drug chemicals a couple of months back and he's been struggling financially since his wife left him." He tapped his pen on the desk. "Foley claims the insurance company finally paid out on the shed fire, but initially they weren't going to because it was an unoccupied structure." He pulled up the incident report, read out the insurance company name, which Khan wrote down. "Can we cross check what we know of Smith's background with Foley? They might know each other from the past."

"How much do you know about Foley?" Bosch asked.

"Not much," he said. "We should check if he has a criminal record."

"Will do."

"Foley should be at the motocross meeting tomorrow," Lincoln continued, his mind racing. "I'll see who he speaks to."

Khan pursed his lips. "We might have been too hasty taking you off the case."

Lincoln hesitated. He wanted to be back on, but he had to be honest. "I won't stop seeing Kit."

Bosch exchanged glances with Khan. "Your knowledge of the community is an asset to the case," she said. "We'll keep you involved, but any leads you get, we'll chase up."

It was the best he was going to get. "Thank you."

He walked them to the door and then switched off his computer and locked up. As much as he wanted to call Kit immediately, he also wanted to give her some time with her friends. She was still hesitant and if anyone could convince her to trust him, it was the musketeers.

The rain had eased and he could dash from shop to shop without getting too wet. He'd buy a coffee before he called her.

As he strolled down the main street, he spotted a long oilskin jacket in a shop window. He grinned. It was time to buy himself a Driza-Bone.

Show Kit he planned to stick around.

The gentle chimes of bells broke through Kit's consciousness and she woke. What was that noise? She tried to clear the sleep from her mind. A glance at her clock told her it was five- twenty-eight.

Lincoln pulled her closer, nuzzled into the back of her neck. "Isn't that a nicer way to wake up?"

It was his phone. "You may have a point." She stretched. "Why don't you stay in bed? We'll see each other all day at the motocross."

He inhaled deeply as if thinking about it and then said, "Nope. It sounds like I'll get to test my Driza-Bone this morning."

The rain hadn't let up overnight and still fell steadily against the roof. Her chest squeezed. She hadn't believed it when she'd picked him up yesterday to discover he'd bought himself a three hundred dollar oilskin jacket. She hadn't thought he'd paid any attention to her throwaway comment.

It seemed he was listening to her now.

Turning over, she slapped off her alarm before it could squawk and got up. "All right then, if you're going to be my farmhand, you'd better get your gorgeous butt out of bed."

He grinned. "With pleasure." He threw back the bed covers and exposed all of his gloriously muscled chest. His boxer briefs fitted him to perfection and as he stood, his butt was a perfect peach.

She looked her fill as she dressed and then headed for the kitchen. No time to fool around this morning, not if she was going to get to the motocross in time to sign on.

Lincoln made coffee while she fed the dogs and got the cereal. Could she dare to hope this was truly an everyday possibility?

Outside the rain had stopped, but the dark clouds threatened it wouldn't be for long.

She and Lincoln settled into a rhythm at the dairy. She wasn't used to having so much help, but it was nice having him next to her, even if they didn't talk. They shared glances as they sang the chorus of a song off-key and occasionally bumped into each other.

When they finished, she checked the ute and trailer with the bikes and the sidecar to confirm they had everything they needed.

"Ready to go?" she asked.

"Absolutely."

By the time they drove into the track, most people had already staked their claim in the pits so Kit pulled the ute up just outside. "We'll sign on first and then unload."

Lincoln followed her over to the clubhouse. A line of riders and their bikes waited to be scrutineered and she waved to a few friends.

"How's the dairy, Kit?" the race secretary, Barbara, asked.

"It's doing fine." Kit smiled. "I've got a new farmhand. Do you remember Elijah Johnson?"

Barbara frowned. "Kind of scrawny kid?"

Kit nodded. "He's back in town, but not so scrawny anymore."

"I'm glad you found someone after what happened with Paul."

Kit hummed in agreement as she handed over her money and signed the necessary paperwork.

"Are you being careful?" Barbara asked.

Kit winced. "Always."

"You're not scared some lunatic might be out there?"

She glanced at Lincoln. "No."

"How are you, Barbara?" Lincoln distracted the woman by giving her some money.

"Oh, you know, same old, same old." She pursed her lips. "It was a dreadful business with Paul. Have you got any leads?"

"I can't discuss the case," he said.

"Well, is Kit in any danger?"

Her heart softened at the concern in the older woman's voice.

"I'm keeping a close eye on her." Lincoln slipped his arm around Kit's waist and kissed her cheek.

Barbara's eyes widened. "Oh, well. I didn't realise." She smiled at Kit. "You're in safe hands."

Kit resisted the instinctual urge to step away and declare her independence. She didn't need anyone to take care of her — she'd managed fine on her own for years — but having him by her side was… nice.

Barbara handed Lincoln his change. "Have fun, you two."

As they walked out, Kit murmured, "You've started the gossip mill running on full speed."

"It was going to happen sooner or later." Lincoln slipped his hand into hers and damn if it didn't feel right. She would deal with any fallout when it came. She could always go into Albany rather than Blackbridge until the gossip died down.

Mai and Hannah had already unloaded their own bikes and Fleur was ready to help with the sidecar.

"You riding today?" Kit asked.

"Absolutely. I've got my mojo back and I'm ready to go. Looks like we've got five sidecars today."

"Awesome." She couldn't wait to get back out there with Fleur. They had ridden together for so long they understood each other and the bike. Some people thought it took a particular level of stupidity to swing on a sidecar — she loved the thrill of it.

"Kit, I wasn't sure you'd make it."

She smiled at Foley's voice. "Wouldn't miss it. How's things with you? You had a break-in the same day as I did, didn't you?" She should have called him, but after Harry had rammed her, it had slipped her mind.

He nodded. "They mostly made a mess. It wasn't a big deal."

"That's good." Foley had been through enough of late, what with his wife leaving him last year and the shed fire early this year. She'd wanted to help him, but he'd said he didn't need it.

"Any news on who killed Paul?" Foley asked Lincoln.

Lincoln shook his head. "Albany has taken over the case."

"What does that mean? They don't tell you what's happening?" Foley asked.

"Can we not talk about that today?" Fleur said. "Let's focus on the good things. It looks like the track is going to be nice and muddy."

"The sidecars will clear most of it," Foley said.

"We'll have to make sure we're not at the back." Kit grinned.

He raised an eyebrow. "You'll get some mud being behind me."

Trash talk. "Like that will ever happen."

He laughed and shifted to the side to make room for Ian.

"You telling the girls how much we'll beat them by?" Ian asked, his helmet dangling from his hand.

The black skull caught her attention and she stiffened. The same helmet as the guy in the footage with Paul and Gordon. Was Ian involved too?

"Kit?" Lincoln nudged her and she blinked. Ian was obviously waiting for her response.

"Sorry, I zoned out." She forced a smile. "I figured he was just protesting his manhood." She winked at Ian.

Ian laughed. "You'll keep. I'll see you out there." He and Foley walked away.

Someone called out to Fleur and she sighed. "Duty calls."

When she was out of earshot, Lincoln said, "What was that about?"

Kit hesitated. What if she was wrong?

"Kit, talk to me."

"Ian's helmet." She didn't need to say anything else.

"Yeah."

She glanced at him. "You already spotted it."

He nodded. "Be careful, but it might not be Ian. I've seen another two guys with the same helmet."

She scanned the members chatting or tinkering with their motorbikes. Could one of them really be involved?

"Have you seen Ian much since Paul died?" Lincoln asked.

Her skin crawled. "I found him in the machinery shed. He said he needed to borrow my fencing clamps." And still hadn't returned them. Could he have been searching for the drone?

"You didn't think to mention it?"

She scowled. "I didn't suspect my neighbour. We often borrow things from each other."

"Sorry." His gentle smile soothed her a little.

An announcement called for the riders' brief in five minutes. She should get her head into the game. She needed to pretend everything was fine.

And hope Ian wasn't involved.

Chapter 18

Lincoln drifted towards the entrance gates to ensure he was far enough away from everyone not to be overheard when he called Albany station. His gut tingled with the surety that Ian was their mystery guy. It was a good fit, but it also increased the likelihood Foley was involved too and that would devastate Kit.

As Lincoln made the call, he scanned the grounds and found Foley watching him.

Interesting.

At least the news they'd found the murder footage hadn't been leaked. No one knew what information they had or how close they were. Even Foley's casual question about Paul wasn't particularly suspicious because Barbara had asked the same thing. The whole town wanted to know when they would catch the murderer.

But no one really thought it could be one of their own.

Detective Bosch finally answered. "What have you got?"

"I think I've identified the fourth rider in the drone footage," Lincoln said.

"Who?"

"Ian Demidenko."

"What proof have you got?"

"He's got the same helmet, body type and has access to the bike we saw. He works for Foley and was good friends with Paul and Gordon."

"Could he be the ring leader?"

"No. Ian's not smart enough to pull it all together. We should call him in for questioning though."

"All right, but I don't want to tip Foley off if he is responsible. We'll wait until tomorrow for confirmation about the insurance claim and to get hold of his financials." She paused. "We ran Foley through the system and he had a stint in jail in his early twenties for breaking and entering. Smith was in the same jail at the same time."

His body tensed. Had Harry approached Foley looking for a new drug base? They couldn't bring him in for questioning without further proof. "When will you get the financials?"

"It's our priority tomorrow."

"All right." He hung up as the final call for the riders' brief went out over the PA. He joined the group gathered around the steward and club captain and stood next to Kit. There was no reason for Foley or Ian to attack her — but he wasn't taking any chances.

After the briefing, he joined the musketeers and his brother under one of the pit bays. "Ryan not coming today?" he asked Hannah.

"He's bringing Felix in later," she said. "There's no point in them coming until the racing starts, and he's giving Nicholas a lift out too."

With Ryan there, they'd both be able to keep an eye on Foley. And Nicholas could take care of Ryan's son if necessary. Lincoln glanced at Fleur. "Will not coming?"

She shook her head. "Noisy, smelly bikes aren't his favourite thing," she said. "He and Elijah were going out for breakfast."

"He could still turn up," Kit said. "Elijah said he might drop by."

Bikes around Lincoln roared and spluttered to life, the air filling with the grumble and pop of different engines and the sharp smell of two-stroke oil.

"Are you going out in the first practice?" Kit asked.

Foley kick-started his bike. "Yeah. You?"

She nodded.

They got ready and headed for the start line, Lincoln lining up away from Foley. No point making him nervous.

He had to pretend this was like any other race day.

When the starter gave leave for them to begin, Lincoln stayed at the back, happy to follow the other bikes. It was just practice and today he wouldn't ride hard. He couldn't afford to get hurt, didn't want to be distracted and let anything slip.

When they finished their three laps, Fleur and Kit got the sidecar ready for practice as did Foley and Ian.

Over in the spectator area, Ryan arrived with Felix and Mai's partner, Nicholas. Lincoln strolled over to greet them.

"Hi, Lincoln! Have you raced yet?" Felix's exuberant greeting made him smile.

"Just been out on the practice lap," he said. "The racing will start after this round."

"Which one is Kit and Fleur?" Felix asked, scanning the sidecars out on the track.

"The ones in red and blue."

Ryan and Nicholas were already moving towards the pits. "Ryan, can I have a word?"

Ryan nodded. "Felix, why don't you go with Nicholas? And remember, no running around the pit area."

"Sure, Dad." The boy grasped Nicholas's hand and dragged him over to where Hannah and Mai chatted to a couple of other riders.

"What's up?" Ryan asked.

"I think Sue was right about our mystery biker."

Ryan's eyes widened. "Ian's got the helmet?"

Lincoln nodded. "Same physique too. I've called Bosch and she's been looking into Foley." He explained everything that had happened over the weekend.

Ryan whistled. "What do we do now?"

"Bosch is still waiting for information. In the meantime we need to keep an eye on Ian and Foley. I'm worried Kit might have given herself away when she recognised Ian's helmet. Foley's been watching me." Maybe he was being paranoid.

"And if he believes we're on to him, he might react badly."

"Exactly."

"I'll watch him."

"Thanks." Lincoln breathed a little easier knowing he wasn't the only one on alert.

The PA announced the first race as the sidecars came in. "I'm up."

He wandered over to where Kit prepared her solo bike.

"Everything all right?" she asked.

He nodded. He couldn't tell her his suspicions about Foley now, not until they'd been confirmed. She wouldn't react well if her friend and mentor was involved in Paul's death and he wouldn't cause her unnecessary pain.

He'd tell her as soon as he had confirmation.

And stick by her to keep her safe in the meantime.

Kit finished her first race at the back half of the pack, having no urge to race. Her mind looped back to finding Paul and the idea Ian might be involved. But Ian couldn't be the person who had seen Harry pull the trigger. Surely he would have stopped him, or at least told someone. Unless he was scared.

The urge to take Ian aside and demand he tell her the truth was so strong, but she had to resist, had to pretend everything was fine. As she switched off her bike, Mai walked over. "Isn't the bike running well?"

"It's fine." Kit placed the stand under it.

"Then why aren't you racing?"

If Mai had noticed, others would have too. Kit had to get her shit together. "Just warming her up. Wait until the next race." Kit moved over to the sidecar. She cleaned the mud from her goggles and the familiar routine focused her. Nerves and excitement hummed along her skin as she stepped onto the sidecar platform, her grip loose on the bar she would hang from, and nodded to Fleur to let her know she was ready. They pulled up at the line next to Foley and Ian.

Damn She wanted to keep her distance from Ian, didn't want to give anything away. She should have told Fleur what she suspected.

Ian gestured to her and stepped off into the mud.

She tensed, glad her helmet hid her expression. Relax. He couldn't know she'd seen the footage. She shook her arms, stretching them ready for the race as she joined him, leaning her head close to his so she could hear what he said over the growl of both the engines.

"We'll let Dean out first and then give the spectators a show." He gestured towards a couple of people leaning up against the spectator fence.

Dean was the slowest sidecar rider. He was new and his bike wasn't particularly fast. "Keep him up front for the first two laps?"

Ian grinned. "Yeah, then all bets are off."

She nodded. People loved to watch the sidecars race and with the slowest chair out front, the others could tussle at the back for position until the last lap. It made for exciting viewing and they didn't race for points. Plus it was then more of a challenge to get past the sidecars in front. It would be fun — if a little muddy.

The other three sidecars pulled up to the line and Ian told them what they were going to do. The sidecar teams had a good camaraderie, bonded by their love of the three-wheeled machines and by the fact everyone else thought they were nuts.

"What's happening?" Fleur asked.

"Dean's going out first."

Fleur grinned.

As the starter waited for their acknowledgement they were ready, Kit gripped the bar tighter and perched side-saddle on the bike behind Fleur. Excitement swept through her as she waited. The five second board flashed up and then the start lackey flicked away.

Dean accelerated with a roar and a spray of mud and Fleur wasn't far behind. The chase was on.

Kit stood on the platform, her eyes on the two chairs in front as they came into the sweeping left-hand corner at the end of the straight.

She hung off the chair, her butt almost touching the dirt as they went around, ducking her head to avoid the mud being thrown up. She used the momentum of the corner to pull herself up to standing as they rode up the steep hill and over a small jump before leaning out left again as they went around the next corner.

The track was so familiar she could have raced it in her sleep. She glanced behind to locate Foley and the other sidecar. Ian waved at her as they slid around a right-hand corner, both of them behind their respective riders.

Cheeky bastard.

She focused on the next corner, letting her muscle memory take over as she changed positions depending on the direction of the corner. As they came to the end of the first lap, all the sidecars were still bunched up together and even more spectators lined up against the fence.

She grinned.

They put on a show.

The next lap Foley and the other sidecar jostled, trying to get past. Fleur held her line, but drifted out to prevent them from passing.

As they came down the hill before the final lap, Fleur yelled, "Are you ready?"

"Yep!" Kit gripped the bar a little tighter and readied herself for the acceleration. The others were close behind.

No way were they passing.

Fleur crossed the line right behind the two sidecars in front and she accelerated hard. There wasn't much distance before the first corner but she tore around the outside of Dean's chair and Kit hung out as they hit the corner and passed him. She grinned as they sped up the hill with only one sidecar ahead.

The next corners were tight S-bends that didn't have much room to pass but the long back straight would be perfect. She checked behind her and found Foley right there, his expression intense.

She glanced forward and swore, moving late into position for the next corner. Fleur looked sideways and Kit nodded to tell her she was fine.

They sped down the back straight, the roar of Foley's bike close now. Fleur drifted right to stop him passing and then prepped for the next left-handed corner. Kit hung out again, and discovered the front mud-guard of Foley's bike only inches away from her back. Was he going to let off?

She met his focused gaze.

His wheel hit her back and she jerked out of the way. The sidecar lurched and veered to the right without her weight on the left-hand side. Fleur struggled to turn and left the track, crashing through the bush. The chair bounced and bumped on the uneven ground and Kit lost her grip on the bar. She flew sideways, directly towards a tree. Shit.

Hands out in front of her, she hit the tree hard. Sharp pain swept through her left arm, and then her head hit the trunk and she landed on the ground with a thud.

She gasped, head spinning, pain ricocheting through her. Where was Fleur? Her vision blurred, she found Fleur running towards her, yelling.

Relief filled Kit. Fleur was fine. Kit flopped back and waved her good arm to show she was alive and closed her eyes, fighting the dizziness. The darkness drew her in.

Fleur knelt down next to her, touched her good arm.

Kit forced her eyes open.

"Are you hurt?" Fleur fumbled with the straps of her own helmet and removed it.

"My arm's broken." She swore as Fleur prodded it and Foley ran up.

"Shit, I'm sorry, Kit. The throttle stuck for a second."

The expression on his face hadn't been one of panic. She glared at him. "Bullshit." His desire to get past was going to make her life a bitch for the next couple of months.

Foley opened his mouth to say something, but Dean joined them and asked, "Do we need the ambulance?"

"No," Kit said at the same time as Fleur said, "Yes."

"I'm fine," she told her friend, and tried to sit up.

Fleur held her down. "You're not moving until I tell you." The fear in her eyes was real.

She squeezed Fleur's arm. "I can feel my legs, Fleur." This wasn't like last year when an accident Fleur was involved in had paralysed one of their members.

"Dean, get the track ambulance, and the rest of you can go back to the pits," Fleur said. "Have you got any dizziness, blurred vision?"

"I hit my head pretty hard."

"Kit!" Lincoln sounded frantic.

Kit frowned. He didn't ride sidecars. Where was he? She waved her hand as he ran over and dropped to his knees beside her.

"Are you hurt?"

"I broke my arm."

"What happened?" he asked.

"Foley crashed into me."

"What?" Fleur asked.

"I swung out at the corner and he tried to cut under us. His front wheel hit me and I had to stand or get squashed, which forced the bike off the track."

Lincoln swore. "Was it an accident?"

"He said his throttle stuck," Fleur said.

Kit glanced at Lincoln. "He wanted to win."

Lincoln gripped her right hand, his expression fierce as he scanned her body, obviously searching for injury.

"I don't want to move her yet," Fleur said. "Are you certain you can feel your legs?"

"Yeah and every damned atom in my body."

"Good."

Kit scowled. Trust the nurse to think it was a good thing.

The track ambulance wasn't more than an old van with a stretcher and first aid kit in the back. Mai, Hannah and Jeremy jumped out as it arrived. "This vehicle is getting too good a work-out of late," Jeremy complained.

"I'm fine." Kit flinched as pain pierced her arm, but at least she wasn't seeing two of everything now.

Fleur examined her, splinted her left forearm and then finally gave her leave to move.

Lincoln helped her sit and his arms around her soothed some of her pain.

"Hop in the ambo," Jeremy said. "We'll drive you back."

Mai said, "I'll help Fleur with the sidecar."

It was deep in the bush where Fleur had left it, not far from where a protective fence was set up around some orchids Will had found last month.

Kit got into the van with Lincoln by her side.

"So what happened?" Jeremy asked.

She wouldn't be a tattle tale. "Foley's throttle stuck," she said. "Hit me on the way through."

"Damn. Glad it wasn't worse."

Worse than having a broken bone? Yeah, it could have been worse, but for her, this would be bad enough. She needed to be physically able to work.

When they got back to the clubhouse, people flocked around her. The race steward wanted details for his race report.

Lincoln interrupted everyone. "Fleur can tell you what happened. I need to get Kit to the hospital."

No one argued.

As they drove out of the track, Lincoln asked, "So what really happened?"

She shrugged. "I think the red mist descended," she said. "He was determined to get past, whether or not he hit me."

Worry crossed his face. "Lucky it wasn't more serious."

"It's bad enough. Between Elijah's injury and this, we've only got two healthy arms." She would have to hire some temporary help.

He swore. "I'll do as much as I can."

She shook her head. "You've got your own work."

"I'd rather take care of you."

Her heart softened and then a bump in the road jolted her arm and she swore at the pain.

For once her heart was the only thing that didn't hurt.

And that was kind of nice.

Chapter 19

Lincoln had only been at work an hour on Monday when his phone rang. He grinned. Kit. "How are you feeling this morning?" She'd stayed the night in the hospital.

"Like I need to break out of this place. Can you pick me up?" She sounded like her normal self.

"The doctors have cleared you?"

"Yeah. Fleur wouldn't have let me call if they hadn't."

"I'll be there shortly." He got up and called to Adam. "I'm going out for an hour. I need to pick up Kit from the hospital."

Adam frowned. "What happened?"

"An accident at the motocross yesterday. She broke her arm and had a concussion. She had to stay overnight for observation."

"Tell her I hope she feels better."

Lincoln nodded and strode out the door to his car. When the track had fallen silent yesterday and he'd realised something had happened, his heart had stopped. He'd vaulted the fence and run over, only to see Kit on the ground, unmoving. His heart hadn't resumed pumping until he'd heard her voice.

She'd bitched about the order to stay overnight, but Fleur had backed the doctor up.

Lincoln walked into Kit's room and found her dressed, sitting on the bed, waiting for him.

"Took your time," she grumbled, but her smile was sweet. Her broken arm had been plastered and put in a sling and she was dressed casually in jeans and T-shirt.

He kissed her, careful not to touch her arm. "I'll get you home soon enough."

"Good," she said. "I've got too much work to do."

"I'll help and so will the musketeers. Elijah's got the milking under control."

She sighed. "I don't like being injured."

He picked up the overnight bag he'd packed for her and slipped his arm around her waist. "We'll get through this."

On the drive out to the farm she said, "Thank you for picking me up. You must have work to do."

"I wanted to. Besides, Albany's still following up a few leads and I'm owed some time."

She shifted, wincing a little.

"Did they give you any painkillers?"

"Yeah, but they make me woozy. I'll take one tonight."

He frowned. "I don't like seeing you in pain."

"And I don't like being in pain. But I need to have my wits about me, at least until Elijah and I figure out how to split the work over the next month."

Speaking of which. "Elijah had a doctor's appointment this morning," he told her. "But he did the milking before he left and I asked him to feed the dogs."

"Thanks. I hope the doctor gives him the all clear."

It was tough for her, but he'd never really thought about how tough. A broken arm would really hinder what she could do. As soon as Foley and Smith were behind bars, he'd take some time off. Help her on the farm.

They drove into the property and Kit sat up straighter. "Why are my chickens loose?" Half a dozen chickens were in the nearby paddock, pecking at the ground.

He slowed the car, scanned the area. A red and white motorbike leaned up against the hen house. "Get down, Kit." He opened the clasp of his gun holster. Kit hadn't moved. "I mean it. Slide down in your seat," he ordered as he drove closer, past the house. He couldn't afford to let her out without knowing exactly where the trespasser was.

For once she did as he said.

He hit the button to automatically wind down his window and

then drew his gun. The scent of fresh hay wafted through the windows and a couple of chickens clucked. The dogs trotted towards them from the direction of the sheds. Had they not heard the intruder, or had he been here long enough for the dogs to lose interest?

Lincoln stepped out, keeping the open door between himself and the hen house. Both the pen door and the door to the perches were open. He continued scanning. No movement in the garden around the farmhouse.

"Lincoln," Kit whispered.

"Stay down. No one's coming out." He pressed his radio, called it in.

"I'll be right there, Sarge," Adam said.

A movement in the hen house and Lincoln focused. Smith peered through the entrance. Lincoln grinned. He had him. "Come out with your hands up, Smith," he called.

No response.

"Back-up's on its way."

The gun shot echoed through the air and Lincoln ducked as the bullet slammed into the car door in front of him.

"Lincoln, get in the car!" Kit yelled.

"Keep down, Kit, it's fine." His heart beat rapidly. Smith couldn't stay holed up there forever, and while Lincoln would have preferred Kit to be a long way away from the danger, he wasn't letting Smith get away.

"What are you planning to do?" he yelled. "You've got limited bullets and all you're doing is adding to the list of charges you'll face — resisting arrest, assaulting a police officer." He peered around the door. Smith was still in the little building, gun in his hand. "Drop the weapon."

"Shoot out his tyres," Kit said. "He can't get away on flat tyres."

Lincoln grinned, his focus never leaving Smith. Trust her to think of solutions, not cower away. He didn't want to engage in a fire fight with Smith. Too much risk of a stray bullet hitting Kit, and he wasn't wearing his bullet-proof vest.

Suddenly Smith fired and Lincoln ducked behind the door again. The bullets came in rapid succession, each thunk hitting the door. Lincoln waited for a gap, his muscles tight.

The roar of an engine.

Damn. He was on the bike. Lincoln peered out. Smith fired wildly behind him as he rode away. Lincoln sighted the tyre, his arm steady, and fired.

The bike bucked, Smith dropped his gun as he fought for control, but he was too slow. The bike fell on to its side and Smith was thrown clear.

Lincoln kept his gun trained on Smith as he stepped out from behind the car door and advanced, scanning for more weapons.

Smith groaned, tried to get up.

"Stay down. Hands behind your head," Lincoln called. Smith's gun wasn't within his reach but he might have something else on him. "Lie down on the ground. Move slowly." Lincoln's heart thumped, his focus fully on the man in front of him, the man who'd murdered Paul, shot Elijah and threatened Kit.

Smith scowled, but slowly placed his hands on his head.

"On your stomach."

Smith did as he was told and Lincoln quickly closed the distance between them, kneeling on Smith's back as he handcuffed him and then checked him for other weapons. "You're under arrest for the murder of Paul Maddock."

Smith swore as Lincoln read him his rights and then radioed Adam. "I've got Harry Smith in cuffs. Where are you?"

"Five ks out," Adam said.

Lincoln helped Smith to his feet, led him over to the car where Kit waited.

She glared at Smith. "Bastard."

Lincoln smothered his smile and turned his attention to Smith. "Are you here alone?"

Smith scowled.

"You're going to prison for a very long time. You might as well tell us who else is involved."

Smith scowled. "You've got nothing."

Lincoln didn't respond. Let him stew, wonder what they had.

Adam arrived in the police car.

Smith was silent the whole time.

"Adam, can you bag Smith's gun? It's over near the bike."

Adam hurried to do as he was told as Lincoln helped Smith into the back of the police car. "We'll take him straight to

Albany," he told Adam.

Adam nodded.

Lincoln turned and Kit flung her good arm around him, squeezing him tightly. She stepped back, let out a deep breath, and her hands shook. "I can't believe you've caught him.

He hugged her, inhaling her cinnamon scent. She was unhurt. Gently he moved her away. "I need to check your house and the sheds.'

"You think there might be others?"

"Let's not take the risk." He turned to Adam. "Stay with Smith.'

It didn't take him long to search the house, which had been locked, and then he headed over to the sheds.

Clear.

Unease settled over him. Why had Smith been here now? If Ian or Foley were involved, they would have told him Kit had been injured and was in hospital. Why hadn't he searched overnight?

Perhaps he was wrong about Foley and Ian.

He phoned Elijah. "What time will you be back?"

"Is everything all right?"

He didn't want news of Smith's arrest to get out yet. Kit was talking to Adam, her good arm wrapped around her. She was smiling and relaxed. "Yeah, but you know Kit. She'll attempt things herself and I don't want her to injure herself further." And he'd feel so much better with another set of eyes on the farm.

"You're right. I'll be about forty minutes. I need to pick up a couple of things before I head back."

"Great. Thanks."

He hung up as he reached Kit. She should be fine alone for that long. "How's the arm?"

She grimaced. "Fine. A little pain never stopped me from doing anything."

"Elijah won't be long. Why don't you take some painkillers and have a cuppa until he gets back?"

She gestured to the paddock. "I'm too wired and I've got chickens to round up."

She was stubborn. No point arguing with her and she shouldn't injure herself herding chickens. Plus she'd be out in the open, so she'd see anyone coming.

"Sarge, we've had Albany on the radio. They want to know where we are," Adam said.

Lincoln sighed. He had to get Smith behind bars, had to question him to find out who else was involved. "All right." He kissed Kit's cheek. "Take care of yourself and don't touch his bike. I'll be back as soon as I can."

She nodded. "Be careful."

"I will." He climbed into the driver's side, checked Smith was still properly restrained.

It was time to end this.

The police car drove away and Kit rubbed her goosebumps.

Did this mean it was over? Would Harry tell them who else was involved? Could this all be finished by tonight?

She hoped so.

Her phone rang and the sharp noise in the still air made her jump. "Hi, Mrs Z."

"Kit, I'm glad I caught you. How are you?"

"I'm fine. I just got home."

"Good. I hate to be the bearer of bad news but I'm on my way into town and noticed one of your fences has fallen over. The paddock has a lot of cows in it."

Kit swore. Not what she needed right now. "Thanks, Mrs Z." She hung up. At least she didn't have time to dwell on what had happened. She might be able to set up some kind of barrier until Elijah returned and she could get the equipment ready. The chickens seemed perfectly happy in the cow paddock. The fence had to be her priority.

She walked towards her ute and then swore. Ian still had the fencing clamps. She dialled Foley's number.

"How's the arm, Kit?" Foley asked as he answered.

"Broken," she said. "But I'm out of hospital and I need my fencing clamps. Can I come and pick them up?"

He swore. "Didn't Ian return them? I told him to. I can drop them off at lunch if you want."

"No, I need them now. Mrs Zanetti told me I have a fence down on the highway. I'll be over shortly." After she'd picked up the clamps, she'd load the ute with the rest of the equipment and drive out to examine the damage. Elijah might even be back by then.

As she drove, the muscles along her shoulders relaxed. Harry had been caught. Paul's murder was solved and things would go back to normal, she wouldn't have to worry about noises around the shed, or creaks on the verandah.

She didn't stop at Foley's farmhouse, instead driving straight towards the shearing shed. Ian was drenching sheep in the pens. She went inside and found Foley working at the bench that ran along one side. Piles of rusted equipment lined the walls above the bench and the scent of lanolin hung heavy in the air from shearing in days gone by. His shed was a lot grimier than hers and the floor was covered in grease and dirt.

He smiled, handing her the clamps. "Here. You need a hand fixing something?"

Foley had his hands full drenching the sheep. She shook her head. "Elijah will be back soon."

"I'm really sorry about your arm," he said. "You've had a lot of shit to deal with over the past couple of weeks, what with Paul dying and Elijah being shot. I'm worried about you out there alone."

She hesitated. "Lincoln's staying with me."

Foley raised his eyebrows. "You two seemed cosy at the motocross yesterday."

Heat rushed to her cheeks. This wasn't the type of thing she normally talked to Foley about. She shifted her feet, not sure what to say.

"Is it serious?"

She shrugged. "Maybe. We'll see how it goes now the murderer's been caught."

Foley's eyes widened. "They caught someone?"

Shit. She shouldn't have said that. "You can't tell *anyone*," she said. "Not until it's been announced. Lincoln's literally driving the guy to the station as we speak. He caught him at the farm when he brought me home."

Foley's face paled. "Who?"

"It's the same guy wanted over the drug stuff that happened with Mai a couple of months ago." She should go. She'd call

Lincoln and tell him her slip up on the drive home.

Foley wandered towards his workbench. "What's the guy's name?"

Kit frowned. Odd question. Her gaze caught on something hanging on the board behind Foley's head. Fencing clamps. Rusted, but not broken. Ian had lied about why he'd been in her shed. She had to leave.

"Kit?"

She answered automatically. "Harry Smith."

He sighed, picked something up from the bench and turned around. "I was hoping you wouldn't say that."

She froze, eyes glued on the gun pointing straight at her.

"Drop the clamps," Foley ordered.

Kit blinked, the words and what she was seeing not really computing. "What are you doing? Put the gun down." She stepped forward and he took the safety off.

Shit. Every hair on her body stood up and her fingers let go of the clamps. They clunked on the ground at her feet. "Foley?" This was her mentor, her friend. Why was he pointing a gun at her?

"Call Lincoln. Tell him to bring Harry here."

"Why?"

"Tell him if he doesn't, I'll shoot you."

What was he talking about? Why would Foley care about Harry? Unless Harry knew something...

"You're behind this." Horror and betrayal slammed into her and robbed her of breath. The chemicals, Gordon's death, Nicole's arrest, Paul's murder — was Foley responsible for it all? Had he been the man in the footage, the one who'd seen Paul get shot, who'd done nothing to stop it?

Foley didn't answer. "Call Lincoln."

"No." She wasn't letting Harry escape.

His eyes narrowed. "I'm not playing, Kit." He straightened his arm.

She'd never seen such coldness in his eyes. Slowly she slid the phone out of her pocket, her hand shaking. Get a grip, girl. She braced herself and dialled.

"Put it on speaker," Foley demanded.

"Hi, Kit Kat. What's up?"

Her shoulders relaxed and she breathed out. "Ah, I've got a bit of a problem." She glanced at the gun. "Foley wants you to bring Harry to his farm."

"What? Where are you?"

She winced. "At his farm. I needed to get the fencing clamps he borrowed."

Foley stepped closer. "You've got ten minutes to bring Harry here, Lincoln," he said. "I'll swap Kit for him, but if you call in back-up, she's dead."

"Kit, are you OK?" Lincoln's tone was authoritative, with a hint of fear.

"Aside from having a gun pointed at me, I'm fine," she said. What else could she say to him? She didn't want him to come, didn't want to put him in danger.

"If you're late, she won't be," Foley said. "For every minute, she'll get a bullet."

Kit stared at him. The dead, determined tone of his voice was like nothing she'd ever heard from him. "Foley, please."

He grinned, fired the gun in the air and then ripped the phone from her hand and disconnected before throwing it back at her. "That should get him here fast."

Anger pushed past the shock and she embraced it, welcoming its comforting familiarity. "You're a psycho."

Footsteps pounded and Ian ran up, gasping. "I heard a gunshot." He looked between Kit and Foley. "What's going on?"

"We've got a bit of a problem. Harry's been arrested."

Ian took a step back. "Shit. What do we do?"

"We negotiate. Lincoln is bringing him here because we've got Kit."

Kit shook her head. "Lincoln's not going to turn Harry over to you. The man murdered Paul." She studied Foley. She needed to get through to him, needed to make him worry.

"It was self-defence." Ian stepped forward. "Paul drew a gun on Harry, he wanted more of a cut, and Harry accidentally shot him in the tussle."

Kit raised her eyebrows. She didn't know if it was true, but Ian might not either. She had to make him doubt Foley, get him on her side. "That's what you were told?" she asked. "What did they tell you about Gordon's death?"

"Shane killed him."

Kit laughed. "You're not the sharpest tool in the shed, are you?" But it explained why Ian still worked for Foley rather than going to the police.

"Shut up," Foley said. "Why do the police believe Harry murdered Paul?"

She said nothing. Smiled at him. He could sweat. All her friends had been in danger because of him. He didn't deserve to be told. Arsehole.

Foley swore. "You found the drone."

"Drone?" She tried for her best innocent expression.

He pointed the gun directly at her, his eyes narrowed, his arm straight. "Tell me what they know."

Her insides went cold. He wasn't messing around. She'd trusted him, relied on him to be there for her and she'd been fooled again. She swallowed hard. "They found it a few days ago, on top of the hen house, in plain view." She couldn't help taunting him. He'd lied to her. "The footage shows Paul being shot." Her stomach turned to lead as she replayed it in her mind. "You were under the trees." It was a guess.

"He threatened to turn me in. I'm not going back to jail."

Back? She had no idea he'd been in jail. "I don't get it, Foley. Why do this? Why drugs?" Keep him talking. If he'd killed Paul to keep the secret, then her life expectancy was rapidly decreasing.

"Not all of us can make our farms a success like you," he said.

Appeal to their shared history. "Didn't you have a bumper crop last year?"

His laugh was brittle. "A bumper crop of meth," he said. "What's the point of working my arse off when Collette still left me? The bitch gets half of my money."

But his drug money was off the books. "So meth was your way to financial freedom?"

He nodded. "I wasn't the only one in town doing it rough. I wanted to help others too."

Gordon had lost his job, Nicole's husband had been unable to work and Paul... "Why did Paul get involved?"

Foley scowled. "Gordon brought him on. Said he wanted money to buy his drones, but the little shit was recording everything we did. He had the gall to threaten Harry, wanted to take him in." Foley shook his head. "Stupid kid had a hero complex."

So that's what happened. "And now they're all either dead or in jail."

"Harry's motto was 'dead men can't snitch'."

The words and the determination in Foley's eyes sent terror through Kit. He believed it, which meant he wouldn't leave her alive. "Foley, we can sort this out without any more killing."

He shook his head, his expression sad. "We really can't. I'm going to the airport, getting out of here." He sighed. "I've admired you for so long. I really don't want to kill you, Kit."

Ian gasped, his eyes wide. He'd just realised the seriousness of what was going on.

She barked out a laugh. "That's my preference too." The rumble of an engine reached her. It had to be Lincoln. She couldn't let Foley shoot him. Couldn't bear to see him die. Foley's attention was focused outside the shed, but he was between her and the bench with equipment on it. She shifted and he pointed the gun back at her.

"Don't do anything stupid, Kit."

She didn't respond. What else could she do? Her foot hit the fencing clamps at her feet. They were nice and heavy but too far away. Foley wouldn't let her pick them up.

The police car pulled up outside the shed. Harry was in the back seat but Adam was missing. Lincoln slowly got out, and Kit focused on him. How could she send him the message to shoot Foley without getting himself shot in the process?

"Foley. Ian." Lincoln nodded a greeting. "Kit." His gaze scanned her and the lift of his eyebrow asked her if she was OK.

She shook her head. Nothing about this was OK.

"Get Harry out," Foley demanded.

"How about you put the gun down first?" Lincoln was friendly, seemed unconcerned to see Foley pointing a gun at Kit, but the tension in his shoulders and the intensity in his gaze showed Kit he was ready to respond.

"No." Foley straightened his arm, pointing at Kit's head. "The police know Harry killed Paul, don't they?"

"We do," Lincoln said.

She swallowed hard. She needed a distraction.

"Get him out," Foley repeated.

Lincoln uncuffed Harry and the man climbed out. "There's another cop here. Lincoln dropped him at the entrance gate. Told him he had to go alone."

"Thanks." Foley swung his arm around, pointed the gun at Harry and shot him twice in the chest.

Kit ducked, dropping to her knees as Harry fell to the ground dead. Lincoln reached for his own gun.

"Don't even think about it." Foley moved the gun to aim at Lincoln. "Take it out very slowly and throw it on the ground."

Ian swore. "What the fuck, man?"

Kit stared at the dead man, her heart lodged in her throat. Foley — the man who never hesitated to offer her help, had always been there for her — hadn't hesitated to pull the trigger.

None of them were getting out of this alive.

"Oh, Ian. You should have stayed with the sheep," Kit said.

Ian frowned. "What?"

"You seriously believe you'll walk out of here when he shot Harry because he knew too much?" She laughed. "I guess you were the brawn of the operation." She almost felt sorry for the dumb schmuck.

Ian stared at her. "You don't know what you're talking about."

Foley sighed. "Yes, she does." The bang was piercing and Kit flinched as Ian fell forward.

Two down. Two to go. Kit wanted to be sick. Nausea swirled around her stomach. "Why?"

Lincoln answered for him. "Because they were a liability. They could say how Foley was involved and if he'd let Harry run, it wouldn't have been long before we found him again — maybe before Foley could get away."

Foley nodded.

Where the hell was Adam? Shouldn't he have made his daring rescue by now? She'd watched way too many action films.

As if reading her thoughts, Foley said, "Now there's the little problem of the cop you left at the entrance. Was it Adam?"

Lincoln said nothing.

"It has to be." He raised his voice. "Adam, you can come out now. I know you're there."

Could she distract him, give Adam time to make it to the shed?

"Before you shoot us, could you give me a minute to say goodbye to Lincoln?" She widened her eyes.

Sadness flickered briefly in them. "I'm not stupid, Kit. You're staying right there." He glanced towards the entrance of the shed, the sunlight streaming in. "If you weren't so stubborn and had let Ian come and help you, he would have found the damned drone before the police. You wouldn't let him come even when Harry shot Elijah."

She rolled her eyes. "He is more of a hindrance than a help."

Foley nodded. "I thought that might be the case. That's why I hit you at the motocross yesterday." He kept his gaze on the entrance. "I was going to offer my help."

The hit had been on purpose. Her fingers brushed the metal of the fencing clamps right next to her knees and her heart lurched. She curled her hand around it and Lincoln shifted, catching Foley's attention.

Kit heaved the clamps upwards, hitting Foley's gun hand and following through so the metal hit him square in the face. He roared in pain and stumbled backwards, collapsing to the ground, the gun falling from his hand.

"Adam, cover him," Lincoln yelled, lunging forward to haul Kit to her feet, crushing her against his chest. "Are you hurt?"

She shook her head, not able to speak. Her heart raced as she clung to Lincoln. Adam stepped forward, his gun trained on Foley.

It was over. They were safe.

He kissed her hard. "You were amazing."

Her body shook and she sucked in deep breaths to calm her pulse.

"Foley, don't move!" Adam's voice rang out, slightly panicked. "Put your hands on your head."

Lincoln's eyes widened at something behind her. "Adam, shoot him!"

Kit recoiled as she twisted her head.

Foley lay on his back, raised his gun, his face screwed up in rage.

She was going to die.

Lincoln reached over her shoulder, shoving her behind him, putting himself between her and Foley.

"No!" she screamed.

The gun shot reverberated around the metal shed.

Lincoln stumbled backwards, hitting Kit and falling to the ground, taking her with him.

Two more shots rang out.

Kit scrambled to her knees, bent over Lincoln. His hands covered his chest, blood soaking his shirt. No, no, no. She pressed her hand against the wound. "Don't move."

He needed a hospital. A movement next to her and she whirled to find Adam bending over Foley, his eyes wide and face pale. "Adam, help me! Lincoln's been shot."

Lincoln's eyes fluttered and he groaned. "Kit." He fumbled for her hand and she gripped it. "Are you OK? You weren't hit?"

"I'm fine, but you're not."

"I love you. I wanted to marry you."

Her heart leaped. Why was he talking in the past tense? He wasn't going to die. "You still can." This wasn't going to be the price she paid.

His lips quirked upwards and his eyes closed.

"Lincoln! Stay with me." His pulse was light, thready.

Adam yelled into his radio for an ambulance. It would take too long. "Adam, get the ute."

He ran to the police car and returned with a first aid kit. "I put the ambulance on standby when I heard the first gunshot. It's not far. Back-up's on its way too."

"You legend." Kit fumbled with the latch on the first aid box, ripping off her sling that hampered her movement. She applied a pressure bandage, her hands wet and sticky with Lincoln's blood. Too much blood. "Hold on for me, Lincoln." Of all the stupid things for him to do. Foley had been aiming for her. She should have been shot.

Sirens reached her ears. "Go outside," Kit told Adam. "Make sure they can see where we are."

Adam raced outside.

"Wake up, Lincoln." She stroked his face. "I know it hurts, but I need you to talk to me, to tell me you're going to be fine." Her voice broke and she swallowed hard. She wouldn't lose him.

She checked his pulse again. Weak.

"Lincoln, please wake up. I love you." She blinked back the

tears burning her eyes. "I promise if you get through this, I will never doubt you again. I'll tell you every day that I love you. I'll marry you. Just please don't leave me."

The blood was already seeping through the bandage. She added another one, pulling it tighter.

Where was the damned ambulance?

The siren was louder now and then it cut off as the vehicle pulled to a stop outside the shed.

Finally.

"Please help him." She moved back as the paramedics ran over, checking Lincoln, lifting him onto the stretcher.

One of the paramedics glanced at the other bodies. "What about them?"

"They're all dead," Adam said.

Kit climbed into the ambulance. "Let's go."

Chapter 20

Kit paced the emergency room. Lincoln had been in surgery for over an hour.

Way too long.

Mr and Mrs Z and Jamie all sat waiting for news, but she couldn't sit still. What if he didn't make it? What would she do if she lost him?

The entrance door slid open and the musketeers rushed in with Ryan. "How is he?" Fleur asked.

"No news."

Fleur strode over to the triage desk and Hannah hugged Kit. "He'll pull through."

Mai squeezed her next. "What happened?"

She shook her head as her friends surrounded her in kindness. "He can't die," she whispered.

"He won't." Fleur said it with such conviction she almost believed her. But life didn't always serve happily ever afters. Especially not to her.

Seconds ticked by like minutes, minutes like hours.

Mrs Z finally coaxed her into a chair, clutching her hand. Kit squeezed her eyes closed. They were going through hell too.

Every time a door opened she stood, but it was never Lincoln, or a doctor reporting on his condition.

She got to her feet and paced. The waiting room wasn't big, but she refused to leave in case there was news.

Finally a doctor appeared at the door. "Are you all here for Lincoln Zanetti?"

"Yes." She strode over to Mr and Mrs Z.

The doctor smiled. "The surgery went well and he's in the recovery room. We'll wake him soon and then you can see him." He gazed around. "Though maybe just two at a time."

Her legs went weak and she gripped Mr Z to stop falling. "He's going to be fine?"

The doctor nodded. "Yeah. The bullet nicked an artery, but he's going to live."

Kit looked up at the ceiling and thanked every deity that ever existed

The musketeers hugged her. Lincoln was going to live.

She burst into tears.

By the time her crying jag ended, Kit was exhausted. She'd used the musketeers' combined stash of tissues and her head throbbed.

A nurse walked in. "Lincoln is awake and he's asking for Kit."

Her heart jumped and she stepped forward. "That's me." She dabbed at her eyes and glanced at his parents to see if they were coming with her.

"We'll give you a couple of minutes first." Mrs Z smiled at her.

Her heart swelled.

She strode after the nurse and into a cubicle where Lincoln lay, his face pale, a drip in his arm and wearing a hospital gown, but his beautiful brown eyes were open and they were the most gorgeous thing she'd ever seen.

"Hey, Slinky."

His smile lit up his face. "Kit. Were you shot?"

She sat down on the plastic chair next to him, clutched his hand, the warmth of it assuring her he was indeed alive. "No, you were."

"Elijah was right — getting shot does hurt like a mother-f'er." He smiled. "Everything's a bit hazy. I remember Adam arriving and you hitting Foley with those clamps." Lincoln smiled. "Nice hit by the way."

"Foley was going to kill us all."

"When I saw him lift the gun, point it at you..." He

shuddered.

The image of him pushing her behind him, stepping in front of her flashed into her mind and with it came anger. "You shouldn't have got in the way."

Lincoln shook his head. "I will protect you, always."

Frustration welled up in her. "Damn it, Lincoln. You could have died."

"Better me than you." He squeezed her hand. "Besides, I would have been a pretty shitty Knight Protector if I hadn't." He flashed her a grin.

His smile cut through her anger. "Whatever." He shouldn't have scared her.

His expression sobered. "I never told you that was the reason I became a police officer."

She frowned. "Huh?" Were the drugs making him a little loopy?

"When you knighted me the protector of the musketeers, it felt so right that I decided to become a cop."

She gaped at him. "Really?"

He nodded. "So thank you." He shifted, wincing a little.

"Great, so what you're telling me is, it's my fault you were shot?"

He chuckled. "No, that was definitely Foley's fault. What happened afterwards?"

"Adam killed Foley. He'd already called in back-up and an ambulance so it arrived not long afterwards and took you to the hospital."

He pursed his lips and his eyes twinkled. "I vaguely remember telling you I love you. Remember you promising me something…"

It took her a second to realise what he was talking about. Butterflies fluttered in her stomach and she brought his hand up to her lips, kissed it. "I love you, Lincoln. I'm sorry I didn't tell you sooner. I didn't trust myself, didn't think I was worth loving."

He brushed her hair off her face and she closed her eyes, revelling in his gentle touch. "You are worth loving. You're my everything. When Foley said he had you and he was going to shoot you… when I heard the gunshot and didn't know whether he'd hurt you… nothing else mattered except getting to you."

She blinked. "Would you really have let Harry go?"

He nodded. "If I had to, to save you."

How could a girl resist him? She certainly couldn't. She wanted him in her life forever. "Hey, Lincoln?" Her heart beat rapidly in her chest and her skin tightened.

"Yes, Kit?" He smiled.

She took a deep breath and leaped off the cliff. "Will you marry me?"

His grin lit up her world. "Absolutely. Just tell me when."

Love flooded her. She'd waited long enough. "How about now?"

Lincoln woke and it took him a second to remember where he was. In hospital. After being shot. Kit sat next to him, playing with her phone and she looked up at his movement and smiled.

"Hey, Sleepyhead. How are you feeling?"

His chest throbbed something fierce and his eyes were grainy. "Like I've been shot."

Worry crossed her face. "I'll get the nurse to give you some painkillers."

He grasped her hand. "In a minute. What time is it?"

"Almost five. You zonked out after everyone left and the detectives finished questioning you."

It had been pretty intense, but he smiled. "Then it's been too many hours since I told you I love you."

She flushed, but her smile was bright. "You're such a sweet-talker. It's lucky I love you too."

Someone cleared their throat at the door. Adam stood there, still in his uniform, but his shirt was untucked and his eyes were red. He looked exhausted.

"Come in." Detective Bosch had told Lincoln Adam had fired the two shots that had killed Foley.

"Take my seat." Kit stood. "I was about to grab a bite to eat." She stopped in front of Adam and flung her good arm around him. "Thank you for saving Lincoln."

Adam's arms hung by his side and he nodded as Kit left the room. She turned at the door and mouthed, *Talk to him.*

Lincoln smiled. That was the plan. He focused on his

constable as Adam sat. "Some day, huh?"

Adam didn't look him in the eye. "Will you be all right?"

"Yeah. Doctors say I'll be on restricted duties for a while, but I'll be fine."

Adam's breath whooshed out of him and tears welled in his eyes. "I'm so sorry."

Lincoln's heart went out to him. "You've got nothing to apologise for."

Adam shook his head. "I did everything wrong. It took me way too long to get to the shed. When I heard those gunshots, I thought I was too late."

It had to have been terrifying for him. He'd never had to deal with something as intense as this. "I kicked you out of the car," Lincoln said. "I could have dropped you closer."

"You expected me to come after you?"

Lincoln nodded. "You did exactly what you were supposed to do. You called for back-up, you reported the shots and ordered an ambulance and you made it to the shed in time to save Kit and me."

"No." He shook his head. "I froze. You almost died because I didn't take the shot when I could have."

Lincoln's chest squeezed as Adam continued.

"I had Foley in my sights before he grabbed the gun."

"So why didn't you shoot?"

"I couldn't. My finger wouldn't move. Foley was right there, but I'd never shot anyone before."

He wished the kid hadn't hesitated, but he couldn't blame him. "I hope you're never put in that situation again." He sighed. He didn't like to tell the story, but Adam needed to hear it. "The first time I drew my weapon on the job, I killed someone."

Adam's eyes widened. "What happened?"

Lincoln shifted, wincing a little. "I'd been on the job for six months, up in Perth and we responded to a domestic dispute. The woman was yelling for help, so we went in. The husband had a knife, and had her cornered." He swallowed. The memory still made him sick. "I shot him in the back."

"Fuck. What happened afterwards?"

He'd grieved. "There was an investigation, I got counselling, but the wife came into the station a few days later and thanked me. She'd been living in fear for years and could now sleep at night." It had made the death easier to deal with. "This job isn't easy," Lincoln said. "And you never stop learning, never stop being challenged."

"I keep closing my eyes and seeing you get shot. There was so much blood." He met Lincoln's eyes. "I'm so sorry I didn't shoot faster."

If he didn't say something now, Adam would continue to blame himself. He needed to ensure they didn't lose a good cop. Lincoln patted him on the shoulder. "It's not all bad. Kit finally admitted she loved me, and she proposed."

Adam gaped at him. "Seriously?"

Lincoln nodded. "Turns out we have to wait a month to get a marriage licence but then we'll be married. I don't know how long it would have taken me to wear her down, so thank you." He grinned. "After I'm discharged, I'll take you to the range and you can practise your shooting."

"Thanks, Lincoln." Adam got to his feet.

"Any time. Now go make an appointment with the counsellor."

"All right." He left the room.

Only a minute later Kit returned, a couple of sandwiches in her hand. "How is he?"

"Pretty shaken. I'll keep a close eye on him over the next few months, make sure he talks to someone about it."

She handed him a chicken and salad sandwich. "I checked with the nurse and she says it's fine for you to eat it. The food in here is supposed to be terrible."

Lincoln grinned. "Are you taking care of me, Kit Kat?"

"Of course. Got to look after my investment." She winked.

"I think I'm fairly solid," he said.

"Yeah." She smiled. "I've got nothing to lose."

Epilogue

Kit swore as she bumped her broken arm against the door of the kitchen in her rush to greet Lincoln. He swept his good arm around her and kissed her deeply. "Honey, I'm home."

She wouldn't ever get tired of hearing him say it. He'd moved in the day he'd been discharged from hospital. "How was your day?"

"Really great. I've got some news to share, so I've invited the musketeers for dinner."

"What news?"

He grinned at her. "You can wait. Is the milking done?"

"Elijah and Jamie are taking care of it. School holidays couldn't have come at a better time." Jamie had offered to help and he'd been invaluable as she figured out her limits with only one working arm.

Lincoln smiled. "I'm glad my little brother is being useful. I'll text them to come over when they're done." He drew his phone out and typed a quick text.

Kit got a beer out of the fridge and handed it to Lincoln. "So your leave starts today?"

"Yep. Albany don't need me for anything else. I thought we could plan the wedding."

Her heart fluttered and she ran her thumb over the gold band on her ring finger. "Think we can organise it in three weeks?"

"I know we can," he said. "I'm not waiting longer than I have to." He wrapped his arm around her waist and squeezed her.

She was so lucky. If the arm cast didn't remind her regularly, she would have pinched herself to confirm this was all real.

Outside, Montoya and Roberts barked a greeting so she went to see who it was. Hannah, Ryan, and Hannah's dog, Joe. Kit hugged Hannah. "Where's Felix?"

"Sleepover at Jacob's," she said. "He was asking me questions about the musketeers and he's planning on forming his own club."

"That's sweet."

Lincoln brushed past them to help Ryan get groceries out of the boot.

"Should you be carrying that?" Kit stopped him and took one of the bags. He was still recovering from being shot and had refused to take any sick leave until the reports had been done. Kit whistled for her dogs and they headed inside. As the others unpacked bags, Kit asked, "What can I do?"

"You can feed the dogs," Lincoln said.

She raised her eyebrows. "Are you well enough to cook?"

He flashed her a grin. "The others will be here soon."

The dogs were busy eating as Nicholas, Mai, Fleur and Will arrived and took over the kitchen.

"Ryan, you can set the table," Hannah called.

"Nicholas, we might need to bring the outdoor table inside," Mai said.

"Who wants a daiquiri?" Fleur asked.

Kit grinned. She loved that they made themselves at home.

Before long, everyone had drinks and the food was almost ready. "Will, can you head over to the dairy to see how much longer Jamie and Elijah are going to be?" Kit asked. She didn't want them to miss out on dinner.

"No need," Jamie called as he walked in. He inhaled deeply. "Something smells good."

"Wash up," Mai ordered, "and I'll start dishing up."

Kit felt a little useless as she carried a single bowl into the dining room where they'd set up an extra table. It would be another five weeks until her arm was healed. So frustrating.

"You deserve to be waited on," Lincoln murmured in her ear as he sat next to her.

She smiled. Having Lincoln by her side wouldn't get old anytime soon.

When they were all seated around the table, Nicholas raised his glass high. "Here's to an end to the drug ring."

"I'll second that," Mai said.

Kit clinked her glass against Lincoln's and then took a long sip of the strawberry daiquiri. Over the past week, she'd had an endless stream of phone calls from people wanting to know exactly what had happened. The town was in shock that one of their own had done this. She'd only told Ian's sister all of the details.

"I've got a bit of an update," Lincoln said. "Albany gave me permission to share since you've all been involved."

"Spit it out, Slinky," Fleur said.

Kit grinned as Lincoln rolled his eyes.

"We finally got access to Paul's full cloud account," he said. "He'd been putting together evidence which would have put Foley, Ian and Harry behind bars if they'd lived." He grimaced. "We found a letter explaining everything, as if he was worried he might die before he could take it to the police. He gave us names of other distributors and with that, and the information we found on Foley's computer, we'll be able to close down the whole network."

She hoped it might provide Paul's parents some measure of comfort.

"Why would he do that?" Mai asked.

"I spoke to his parents and they mentioned he was really close to a cousin who died of a drug overdose. He blamed himself for introducing his cousin to Gordon, for not being able to pull him away from the drugs."

"So what now?" Hannah asked.

"Now, hopefully things will go back to some semblance of normal," Ryan said.

"We've also got weddings to plan," Mai added.

"At this rate, there'll be babies next," Jamie said. "I bet I'd make a great uncle."

Elijah grinned at him. "I bet you will."

Kit smiled and squeezed Lincoln's hand. She could picture a bunch of little dark-haired Lincolns running around the farm.

She would always make sure they knew they were loved, would be there for them whenever they needed her.

"We could get started after everyone leaves," Lincoln murmured, running a hand over her thigh.

Her body heated and she grinned. "Sounds good to me."

Thank you for reading!

I hope you enjoyed the book. It would be super awesome if you could leave a review wherever you bought it, because I love to hear what you thought of the story. If you want to keep up-to-date with me and my books, make sure you join my reader group at https://www.claireboston.com/reader-group/

ACKNOWLEDGEMENTS

I have so many people to thank for this book. A huge thank you to everyone who provided me with information to make this book as accurate as possible: Matt Hartfield for all things policing, Ian Leggett for talking about gun shot wounds and hospital procedure, Libby Corson for information about the ag college, Jennifer Maughan for the dairy farming info, Tony Reichelt for chatting to me about harvesting and seeding and Fiona Palmer for more farming information.

I must also thank my husband, Luke for brainstorming all the ways I could make things worse for Kit and Lincoln, and for helping me to fix the ending.

And finally thank you to my production team: Lana Pecherczyk for the cover, Ann Harth for her structural edits and Teena Raffa-Mulligan for copy-editing.

Want more Blackbridge stories?

A whole new series is coming in 2019.

To find out when it's being released, join my New Release list. https://www.claireboston.com/new-release-signup/